I0563314

A Fatal

Reunion

An Arabella Stewart Historical
Mystery-Book 5

D.S. Lang

Copyright ©2022 by Debra Sue Lang

All rights reserved.

No portion of this book may be reproduced in any form without written permission from the publisher or author, except as permitted by U.S. copyright law.

Paperback ISBN: 9798986731827

Cover Designer: Karen Phillips

Copy Editor: Alyssa B. Colton

This book is a work of fiction. All characters, places, incidents, and events are products of the author's imagination or are used fictitiously. Any resemblance to any real place, incident, event or persons (living or dead) is purely coincidental.

Chapter One

♥

Ohio—June 1921

"Are you two Miss Stewart and Miss Byington?"

Arabella Stewart and her best friend, Ida Byington, turned toward the speaker. A wiry man of medium height and middle years stood on the deck of an impressive boat. Clad in a faded shirt of indeterminate color, gray trousers held up by ragged suspenders, and a battered cap, he wasn't apt to be the craft's owner. Uneasiness hit Bella. The man must be their escort to Winnabee Island, the site of their weekend reunion with college girlfriends. "Are you Mr. Eyelers?" she asked.

"I'm Eyelers. No mister needed," he replied. "Miss Florence sent me to pick up another two girls. You the ones? The rest is already at the house. They come this morning, but not together, so I've made three trips now." His tone clearly indicated the repeated forays were burdensome.

"Sorry," Ida replied, "but we couldn't get here any sooner."

"Come aboard," Eyelers said. "We need to get a move on. I've had a long day after a terrible night, and a nap is in order."

1

When the man made no move to help with their bags, Bella and Ida exchanged a glance before grabbing their portmanteaus and stepping on to the boat. Before they could say more, Eyelers pulled up the anchor and went to the wheel.

"So much for a warm welcome." Bella pointed to a bench along the railing. "Let's sit over there."

The women were barely settled when Eyelers headed the boat away from the dock and into Lake Erie. "The boatman who picked us up when we came a few years ago was much friendlier," Ida whispered.

"And he didn't look hung over," Bella replied as she again looked at Eyelers. Even from a few feet away, his red-rimmed and heavily shadowed eyes were easy to see, while gray stubble covered his lean cheeks. When the man had passed her, Bella caught a whiff of liquor.

"He said he had a dreadful night," Ida said.

"Maybe." Bella figured the man was hungover, but where had he gotten illegal booze? Prohibition made it difficult, but not impossible. She brushed back her concern and focused on their surroundings. The next few days were a respite, and she planned to enjoy them. As the boat moved away from the dock, it created ripples in the lake. Bella glanced over the side. "I wonder if the water is warm enough for swimming."

"Since we brought our suits, I plan to go in no matter what the temperature is." Ida closed her eyes and tilted her head back. "I love the feel of the sun on my face, even though I'm likely to have even more freckles by the time we leave."

Bella smiled as the light breeze ruffled her hair. "I'm looking forward to this weekend."

"I am, too. It's been a long time since we were all together. Early 1918, right before you and I left for the Signal Corps. Sometimes, it seems like much more than three years."

"It does." The melancholy tinge in her friend's tone echoed inside Bella. They'd both suffered heart-wrenching losses, but those days were behind them. Right now, they'd enjoy the reunion, focus on happy memories, and savor free time. "I've exchanged a few notes with Florence since she sent the invitations. Before that, Blanche and I were in touch at times. I know you've done the same."

"I have," Ida said. "I wrote to Lina when her mother died and again when her great aunt passed. She sent thank-you notes, but she didn't respond to other letters, so I stopped writing."

"I had the same experience," Bella agreed. "I suppose it's natural to grow apart, but we were all so close once." From the first week of their freshmen year, the six young women had banded together, mostly due to being lodged in the only three rooms on their college dormitory's top floor. They'd formed strong bonds. "It'll be good to see everyone. I think." Humor underlined the last statement.

A chuckle escaped Ida. "Florence is a sweetheart, and she only sees the good in everyone, but I'm still surprised she invited Sylvia."

"They roomed together for three years, for a year-and-a-half after you and I joined the Signal Corps. From what Florence said last week when we spoke, she and Syl not only got close during that time, they still see each other often."

"It was just the two of them left at school, so it's not surprising they'd stick together." Ida winked at Bella. "Of course, Sylvia never flirted with any of Florence's beaus like she did with others, including yours."

Heat climbed into Bella's cheeks. "We've discussed this already. More than once. Jax and I weren't courting in those days. He simply served as an escort since he was my brother's best friend, and we all grew up together.

3

Besides, Sylvia flirted with Matt first." As always, her heart twisted when she thought about her brother. How she missed him.

"It's interesting you said you weren't courting back then," Ida said with a smile. "The important thing is that you are now."

Bella moved her mind back to the present. "We aren't courting now, either." How could they when Jax had been gone for over two months?

"But you will when he finishes his current case."

"If he comes back home. He sends a brief note every couple of weeks, and he seems to like the new job a lot." Possibly too much.

Ida's brow furrowed. "Does he like it, or does he feel compelled to stay because they haven't arrested the man who killed his buddy's wife yet?"

For a moment, Bella considered Ida's observation. "Could be more the latter. Jax told Mick O'Donnelly that he'll stay with the Prohibition Bureau until the hitman is in jail, which could be never." In Bella's mind, as time passed, it seemed less and less likely that justice would be done, so Mick's wife could rest in peace. Bella had known Jax since she was four. When he made a promise, he kept it. And he'd made a solemn promise to Mick.

"I still say he'll be back in Moreley as soon as he can." Ida straightened her beads, but continued to hold Bella's gaze.

"Maybe so." Although uncertainty plagued her, Bella wouldn't let it cast a pall over their trip. She scanned the horizon. "This side of Winnabee Island looks the same as I remember." Four homes sat on a bluff facing south. Shrubs, trees, and rocks climbed from the narrow beach to the top of a shallow hill.

Ida followed Bella's gaze. "Everything looks lush and inviting. It's a shame, but Florence said only two places are occupied right now. Her family's home and the one closest to it."

"I remember that place. The Remingtons have a large house, but their neighbors have a mansion. The two aren't all that close together, as I recall."

"Maybe a half-mile apart over land. About the same by water."

As Eyelers took the craft around the west end of Winnabee, another building came into view, and the two women turned to take closer looks. "All the homes out here look spacious. I was surprised when we first came during college. Florence called them cottages, but that term doesn't do them justice."

Ida chuckled. "No, it doesn't."

For several minutes, the friends fell silent. When the boat rounded to the north side of the island and passed a cove, Bella shifted again. A large boat, with two men on deck, was moored at the dock. In the distance, the top floor of a mansion was visible. Between the home and water, a gazebo sat on the bluff and several other out-buildings were visible. "I don't recall seeing this property from the lake when we came before," Bella said.

"I think the old boatman took us around the east end of the island coming and going. It seemed like a shorter route."

"You're right. I wonder why Eyelers took the long way." Their boat slowed down, which seemed strange since they had a way to go—about a half-mile—as Ida had already said. Bella turned to glance at Eyelers before continuing in a whisper. "He's making some sort of signal to whoever's on the other craft."

Ida looked from the cove to Eyelers. "He is." She kept her voice low. "Not really a wave. More of a sign. I wonder why."

"I don't know, but he seems like a genuine character."

"I won't disagree with that."

The boat picked up speed after passing the cove. Within a few minutes, they were headed toward a long dock. Eyelers secured the craft. "I got other chores to do before I can rest. Just head up that path. And stay out of the boathouse. It's got rotten boards."

Bella and Ida picked up their bags and disembarked without help.

"What an odd thing to say," Ida said. "I don't know about you, but I had no plans to look in the boathouse."

"Me, either," Bella replied before starting up the narrow trail. As she did, she wondered about Eyelers' warning, his greeting to the men next door, and his source for liquor.

An hour later, after briefly greeting their hostess and cleaning up, Bella and Ida were putting the finishing touches on their evening ensembles.

"Are you ready to go downstairs? Dinner won't be for an hour, but Florence wants everyone to mingle first. We didn't do that since we arrived so late." Bella shifted from one foot to the other as she watched Ida slide a sparkling barrette into her auburn locks. Bella touched the narrow, glittering headband in her own dark hair. Like Ida, she'd worn it in a bob ever since they'd gotten the trendy cuts in a Paris salon during the war. The sliver of rhinestones was subtle, but more than enough glamor for Bella, who was accustomed to wearing sporty things around Ballantyne, the resort she co-owned with Mac MacLendon. He had insisted she take a few days off for this reunion. Bella hadn't been sure since the summer season was in full swing, but now, she was glad she'd come and excited, too.

"Almost." Ida smoothed down her auburn hair before picking up a pair of earbobs and securing them in her lobes.

Determined to enjoy the holiday, Bella picked up her beaded bag. "For the next few days, I'm not thinking about the past or the future. I'm focusing on renewing old friendships and having a good time. Let's go downstairs and join the fun."

"A fine idea." Her friend picked up her own fancy purse. "I'm glad Florence told us to bring party clothes. We have few chances to get decked out these days."

What Ida said was true. "I'm happy you're at Ballantyne this summer. Having your help has taken a load off me, and it's fun to be together even though we're working every day."

"It doesn't seem like work to me. In fact, it's a pleasant break from the constant activity during the school year," Ida said. "Besides, I love being at the resort. It's a special place."

Warmth spread through Bella. Ballantyne was her home and her heritage. When she'd gotten back from France in December 1919, she'd feared losing the place, which had been on the brink of closure. With hard work and good luck, she and Mac had brought the resort out of decline. Pride and gratitude filled her at their accomplishment before her thoughts returned to the present. "You're used to a different sort of life." Ida had more experience with fancy social occasions, since she'd grown up in a wealthy Cleveland family. While Bella's own upbringing had been happy and comfortable, the entire Stewart clan had worked hard to make and keep their resort one of the best in the state. Even after her brother had fallen in France and her parents had perished from Spanish flu, Ballantyne remained the cornerstone of Bella's world. A world where casual clothes fit better than glittering dresses. Bella was comfortable in that world but gussying up was a treat.

"That's all behind me now," Ida said, "and I'm fine. Moving away helped."

Bella laid one hand on her friend's shoulder. "I'm glad." Only a year earlier, Ida's father had lost most of his fortune, which was why she was teaching at a girls' boarding school near Ballantyne. Since summer vacation began, Ida had been working at the resort and stepping out with Griff Biggins, the golf professional. Life was on the upswing for her friend, and Bella was glad.

Ida patted Bella's fingers and smiled. "When Jax is back, he needs to take you dancing in that dress."

As her friend spoke, Bella glanced into the mirror. After Ida had insisted they needed new frocks, Bella chose a straight-line dress of pale gold chiffon over darker gold satin. The drop-waist was in style, as was the skirt's high-calf fringed hemline. With a satin scarf and shoes matching the underdress, Bella felt stylish but not too flamboyant. As usual, Ida—who kept up on all the latest fashions—wore a slightly fancier gown of silver satin with pewter lace trim. "Griff should take you out on the town in your ensemble."

Pink rose in Ida's cheeks before she shrugged. "We'll have to go beyond Moreley."

Laughter left Bella. Her small hometown offered few opportunities to get dressed up. "I agree. Now, we should join the others."

The two friends made their way to a large parlor, where three of the young women had already gathered. As Bella paused in the doorway, she scanned the group, all of whom smiled and waved. A few years earlier, they'd seen each other every day. Too much time had passed since they'd all been together.

Florence Remington, their hostess, crossed to Ida and Bella before hugging them. "We've been chatting. Can I get you two something to drink?" A giggle left her and her pale hazel eyes shone with amusement. "Non-alcoholic, of course. My parents had Eyelers get rid of their entire supply of liquor when Ohio went dry. Now, we have lemonade, limeade, and grape juice." She gestured to the bar behind them.

"Lemonade sounds good." Relief spread through Bella at Florence's words. Since Jax had left his job as their town constable to become a Prohibition agent, Bella was increasingly aware of the evils associated with bootlegging, and she was glad her old friend wasn't contributing to the illegal trade. But she wondered about Eyelers. Had he held back some of the alcohol for personal use?

"Lemonade for me, too," Ida said.

After serving drinks to Ida and Bella, Florence ushered them to the other side of the spacious room. Two long couches, one vacant, flanked the fireplace. Florence perched on the loveseat facing it. "Make yourselves comfortable. I had our butler, Stricket, start a fire because it can get cool in the evening."

"Very nice," Bella said.

As the two friends seated themselves on the empty couch, the others greeted them.

"Bella, Ida, it's wonderful to see you again," Lina Hartley, a petite blonde with bright blue eyes, said. Her smile reinforced the sentiment.

"Yes, it's been too long," Blanche Carriger agreed. Tall and shapely, she was a stunning woman with nearly black hair and pale green eyes.

As the group exchanged greetings, Bella glanced around. All but one guest was present, and each of the girls was clad in a trendy dress with a dropped waist and no sleeves. Colors and materials varied, as did skirt lengths, although none fell below mid-calf. Once again, Bella was glad Ida had helped her shop. Although she was a modern young woman in most ways, Bella wouldn't have chosen her current attire if Ida hadn't assured her it was perfectly appropriate.

Conversation flowed easily, mostly about personal news. Blanche was married, while Florence happily shared her betrothal and proudly showed her ring. "That's one reason I wanted us to get together. After the wedding, I'll be living in San Francisco, and I won't get back to Ohio often."

That evoked comments and questions from the others. After Florence gave details about her fiancé, a lawyer with aspirations to become a judge, Blanche scanned the group. "What about the rest of you? Anyone else headed to the altar?"

"And miss the fun of being out and about? Not me." Sylvia Sawyer entered the room and crossed to sit next to Florence. "Good evening, girls." She slipped a hip flask from her satin bag and took a long swallow.

Every head turned toward the newcomer. Bella immediately noted that, while similar to the dresses of the other five, Sylvia's frock was shorter with a lower neckline. The material, a silky satin, shone in the firelight, as did the crystal drop earbobs and matching beads. Bella noticed Sylvia's shoes, as well. Patent leather t-straps with high heels. The entire package—clothing and flask—evoked a question in Bella's mind: did her former classmate frequent speakeasies? Bella wouldn't be surprised. Sylvia had been fast during their college years, and she evidently hadn't slowed down.

Several of the group laughed at Syl's comment. When the giggling ebbed, Blanche turned her attention to Bella. "What is Jax Hastings doing? He escorted you to events at school, and I always thought the two of you were sweet on one another." Her tone indicated genuine interest, not catty nosiness. "I remember when Sylvia tried to put her claws into him." Although the words were pointed, she offered them with a smile. "But she began with your brother, Matt, if I recall correctly."

Bella started to reply but was cut off.

Sylvia waved one hand in the air. "Forgive me, Bella, but both were rather stodgy. Although I hate to speak ill of the dead."

Gasps preceded murmurs of sympathy directed at Bella. "Thank you. I miss my brother." She acknowledged her friends, all except Syl, but kept her attention on the glass of lemonade. Sylvia hadn't been so gauche or abrasive when they'd first met as freshmen, but the girl had gotten increasingly impulsive over the following two-and-a-half years. Evidently, she was continuing on the same path. And who knew how much she'd already had to drink? Liquor lessened a person's self-control, and Sylvia had never possessed that trait.

"You didn't say how Jax is doing." Sylvia studied Bella as if she would be fascinated by the answer.

Bella shifted uneasily. She didn't want to discuss Jax or their relationship, which was unsettled, at best. While Bella pondered a reply, Florence spoke. "Did he go back to being a golf pro after the war?"

Before she got interrupted again, Bella hurried to answer. "He was wounded twice and has lingering problems, so golf isn't an option right now. Jax might have surgery, but there's no guarantee it will make a major difference. His father was our constable years ago. Right before Jax got home, the constable turned in his resignation, and the town council offered the job to Jax."

"You must see him often," Florence said.

Bella's tension increased. While she hadn't planned to reveal Jax's current job, how could she avoid it? None of the women lived in Philadelphia, where he was working, which meant they probably wouldn't know about Jocelyn O'Donnelly's murder. Or plague her for details about it. "Actually, Jax took a temporary position with the Prohibition Bureau." She hoped it was short-lived. Because Mick had saved his life during the war, Jax felt obligated to help the other man pursue justice. But how long would it take? The question remained in the back of her mind.

"Jax is a prohi?" Shock widened Sylvia's silvery blue eyes and derision was in her voice.

The derogatory term for Prohibition agents irritated Bella. "He's a federal agent enforcing a federal law."

A throaty laugh escaped Sylvia. "Like I said, he was always a dull stick. Easy on the eyes, though."

"All men appeal to you," Lina said, her tone tart. Her earlier good humor was gone as she stared at Sylvia.

"You sound jealous," Syl replied, "and that's not appealing."

Anger flashed in Lina's gaze. "Seeing you drunk and breaking the law isn't appealing, either. I suppose you brought an entire supply of bootlegged booze with you."

Syl rolled her eyes. "You're still such an innocent. Putting glass bottles in my luggage wouldn't have been wise. Hired help is so clumsy. No sense in wasting good liquor when the bottles broke. Of course, I've been out here before and know where to get more." She giggled and winked.

"Florence, you said only one other house is occupied right now," Lina said. "How could anyone get liquor?"

Their hostess scowled at Syl before schooling her features. "Syl is kidding, and it's not funny."

Another burst of laughter left Syl. "Florence, shame on you. It's a sin to tell a lie."

Following the assertion, an uncomfortable silence descended. Syl's revelation deeply disturbed Bella, as did Florence's reaction. The exchange between Lina and

Syl was also cause for discomfort. Exactly what had happened after she and Ida left school? Bella had only a vague idea. Probably something to do with Lina's beau ending up engaged to Syl. But he'd perished in the trenches almost three years ago. Why were they at odds now?

"Liquor is still easy to get, especially around here," Syl said, before taking another tipple.

Their hostess once again looked furious. Bella wasn't sure what to say or do, but Blanche stepped into the breach.

"I'm afraid illegal alcohol is easy to get most places," she said. "Both my father and my husband have treated patients who drank bad booze. A couple of cases resulted in death."

"How awful," Ida said.

"It's only what they deserve. Buying alcohol from bootleggers is foolish and criminal." Lina sent Syl a killing glare.

"Practically everyone does it," Syl said, seemingly oblivious to disapproval.

"That doesn't make it right," Lina insisted. "Not that you ever cared about doing the right thing."

Before more angry words ensued, Bella spoke. "No, it doesn't, but it's awful to think people died from drinking. I'm proud of Jax for wanting to protect the public." She didn't look at Syl, who likely disagreed.

Once again, Blanche moved to calm troubled waters. "Heroic and handsome, as I recall."

"You recall correctly," Ida put in, "and he's kind and reliable, which is even more important."

A chortle left Sylvia. "If you like that type, and I guess you do, since Alan Brewster was a dead bore."

Gasps followed the statement. For long moments, silence filled the room. Like Bella's brother, Ida's betrothed had died in France.

"Sylvia." The single word was a harsh reprimand from Blanche.

"Oh, piffle. Ida knows I meant nothing by it. She was engaged to Alan, so she knew him well." Sylvia lifted her flask toward Ida and Bella. "How about the two of you? Want a splash in your lemonade?"

"Why don't you mind your own business, Syl?" Lina asked. "No one else wants any."

"I don't," Ida replied.

"No, thank you," Bella said. With great effort, she kept her voice well-modulated. Sylvia was grating on her nerves in a big way. But Lina seemed even more disgusted.

At that moment, Stricket, the butler, interrupted. "Dinner is ready, Miss Florence." The man shared a similar build with Eyelers, but any similarity ended there. Stricket, nearing eighty, was impeccably groomed and dressed.

After the announcement, Bella felt relieved, and Florence looked it. Within moments, the group was seated at the massive dining room table, which could have held twenty people. Ida and Bella hurriedly found chairs far from Sylvia and her annoying chatter.

Unfortunately, Bella wasn't as lucky after dinner. Since the weather was clear, the group headed to the expansive terrace overlooking the lake. Sylvia immediately sat next to her on one of the wrought-iron loveseats. Wondering how she could gracefully find another seat, Bella took a sip of lemonade and scanned the horizon. Maybe ignoring Sylvia was the best strategy.

"Come on and have a little nip." Sylvia held up the silver hip flask. She'd been imbibing throughout dinner and was sloshed. "A bit won't hurt you, and Jax will never know."

Sylvia's silver-blue eyes, slightly unfocused, narrowed on Bella, who turned down the offer again. "I don't care for any."

"Oh, come on, Bella. Don't be a stick in the mud like your brother and Jax. A dash will loosen you up." Syl took another drink.

"I don't want it." Bella didn't even try to keep the impatience out of her voice. A sudden urge to knock the flask from Sylvia's hand hit Bella hard. Maintaining her usual composure proved to be difficult. She and Syl hadn't been especially close at school, but they'd been part of a group—this group. As Bella looked at the others, she wondered how they'd navigate the rest of the weekend. Florence barely acknowledged Syl during dinner, and Lina had been staring daggers at her all evening.

A harrumph left the other woman. "You were always a goody two-shoes, but we're grown up now. Come into the 1920s, girl." The words were slurred, but her voice was shrill.

Bella's annoyance escalated. "I'm not a goody two-shoes. I simply don't want a drink."

Syl's heavily plucked eyebrows rose. "Really? I know you live in the back of beyond. In the city, there are plenty of places selling booze every day and every night. I knew we'd be stuck out on this island far away from nightlife, so I brought two filled hip flasks. Of course, no matter that Florence tried to deny it, I can get more here." When Bella didn't reply, Sylvia continued. "Are you afraid to break that ridiculous law? Don't want Jax to arrest you?" A chortle left her before she took another long swallow.

Fresh irritation filled Bella. Months before the Volstead Act went into effect, Ohio had gone dry. Neither event had created powerful feelings on her part. After hearing about Mrs. O'Donnelly's murder, that changed. Knowing Jax was putting his life on the line as an agent only hardened her opinion. Anyone who bought illegal booze was making his job harder and supporting bootleggers, many of whom were gangsters. Gangsters who had hitman to eliminate their adversaries. If innocent civilians got in the way, the criminals didn't care. Disgusted with her old friend, Bella rose, but the other woman grabbed her arm. "Let go of me." Despite being drunk, Sylvia had a relentless grip.

Sylvia scowled. "I heard you've been playing detective in some murder cases. Didn't know you were also an amateur prohi. They're even starchier than you, so Jax must fit right in." Another humorless guffaw escaped the woman, followed by a hiccup.

As anger coursed through Bella, she pivoted toward Sylvia. How dare she insult people like Jax? How dare she insult *him* repeatedly? Bella jumped to his defense. "Prohibition agents are brave men and women who risk their lives to keep the peace."

Sylvia pursed her lips. "All they're doing is putting people in jail for something that was perfectly legal two years ago and is still legal most every place else in the world. A lot of darn foolishness, and a waste of time and money to pay them."

Bella wrenched her arm free, put her hands on her hips, and stared down at the other woman. "Gangsters distribute and sell alcohol, and they don't care who gets in their way. They only care about money. When you buy bootlegged booze, you support shootings in the streets. You support crooks who kill average people and lawmen."

Sylvia lifted the flask to her lips and took another long swallow. "Good thing you live in Moreley. You'd never survive in a big city like Chicago. Almost everyone looks the other way. And a lot of the coppers get paid to ignore speakeasies and blind pigs. If those prohis are smart, they do, too. Not your precious Jax, of course. He'd never do anything wrong."

Disgusted, Bella spun on her heel. As she did, she noted a figure in the bushes alongside the terrace. Bella paused for a moment, but the man—someone of wiry build and medium height—stepped back and out of sight. Since she'd only seen a silhouette, Bella wasn't sure if it was the butler or the handyman. Both had the same body type and, although Stricket was decades older than Eyelers, either might be listening. But why?

Bella brushed off her errant thoughts and continued to an empty chair near Ida. For the rest of the evening, she steered clear of Sylvia, but her anger didn't ebb. Neither did her concern. If Sylvia got liquor on the island, who sold it to her? And who had been skulking in the bushes?

When Bella and Ida returned to their room, they got into their pajamas and climbed into the side-by-side beds.

"I hope Sylvia won't stay drunk for four days," Ida commented after Bella shut off the lights.

"So do I." Bella fluffed up her pillow and laid down. "I'm sorry she criticized Alan." And she was still aggravated about the woman finding fault with Jax. More than angry. Bella was furious. The depth of emotion surprised her, since she and Jax weren't actually courting. But they'd been friends for years, and her loyalty to him was strong. No matter what happened in the future, it always would be.

"I'm sorry she did the same with Matt and Jax. The odd thing is, she made eyes at both of them in college. She's making excuses now because they weren't interested. Alan and I were already betrothed when she met him, but any guy who didn't fawn over her was worthless in her eyes."

"You're right. She loved being the center of attention, and I'm sure she is at speakeasies."

"I agree. Her attire tonight was a perfect flapper outfit. Short flashy dress, lots of beads, high heels, sterling silver hip flask. The heavy makeup and crimped bob added to the overall effect."

"Florence's bob is crimped, too. In fact, she looked like a copy of Syl."

"She's trying for the same style, but Syl has a superb figure and her pale blonde hair is striking. Florence is pretty in her own way, of course."

"She is." But lithe and lean, Syl had the perfect shape for the current styles. Florence, with her light brown hair and hazel eyes, had never turned as many male heads. Plus, she was shorter and curvier, assets not enhanced by the straight-line, dropped waist dresses that were all the rage. Was Florence imitating Syl? If so, Bella hoped it was only in appearance, not in habits.

Although Ida was simply a silhouette in the dark, Bella turned to look at her friend. "Have you been to any speakeasies? You know a lot about what's worn in them."

"No. Of course not. But I saw similar outfits at a couple of parties I attended over Christmas. I'm pretty sure booze was served on the sly." Ida's low sigh was barely audible. "Jax has a very hard job with so many people flouting the law."

"He does." Bella knew he could handle the difficulty, but what about the danger? Often, violence erupted quickly—as it had when Jocelyn O'Donnelly died in a hail of gunfire. With determination, Bella pushed her anxiety away. Worrying wouldn't help. "My intention to simply enjoy the weekend was tested by Sylvia." And by her suspicions about bootlegging.

"She should be sober in the morning, although she may not stay that way," Ida said. "The exchange about her buying liquor on the island stunned me, and I wasn't sure what to make of Florence's reaction. She didn't seem surprised, just angry at Syl."

The observations resonated with Bella. "I felt the same way. Besides, there's no reason for Syl to lie about getting liquor out here."

"You're right. Florence was angry when Syl revealed that, though."

"She certainly was." Bella thought back to earlier in the evening. "But how would she get more booze? There are only ten houses and right now, only two are occupied."

"Since Florence's parents got rid of their booze, I wonder the same thing."

"Eyelers was charged with removing it. I'm wondering if he kept it to drink himself or to sell." Bella wondered if he was the figure she'd seen near the terrace. To her way of thinking, that seemed more likely than Stricket being there.

For several moments, silence ensued before Ida spoke. "Something about him bothers me."

"His bloodshot eyes? His scruffy beard? His dirty clothes?" Bella chuckled. "I didn't believe his story about a hard night. More like a night of hard drinking."

"You could be right about him keeping some of the Remingtons' liquor for himself."

"It isn't actually illegal to drink, just to make, distribute, or sell liquor. Florence's parents could've chosen to keep theirs. Many people did."

"Her dad is a lawyer, so that might've affected their decision."

"Maybe. As far as Eyelers, he looked hung over, and I caught a slight scent of liquor on him." Bella chewed on her lower lip as she considered the situation. "What bothers me now is Sylvia getting booze on the island.

19

Few people are out here, so she might have dealt with Eyelers. She came across the lake very early as the only passenger on that trip, which means they had time alone to make a transaction."

"You've given this some thought."

"It's built up in the back of my mind over the past few hours."

"Since you've become an amateur detective, that's hardly surprising," Ida said with a chuckle. "And I'm sure Jax is always on your mind, too."

"I wouldn't say always," Bella said.

Ida laughed again. "Would you say often?"

Bella chuckled along with her friend. "Yes." After making the admission, she thought back to her previous visit to the island. "The Remingtons had a very well-stocked bar when we visited years ago."

"You're right. They did. My parents kept liquor for entertaining, but they didn't have half as much as the Remingtons had here." Ida paused for a moment. "When my mother and father knew Ohio was going dry, they gave a lot away. They handled it themselves, though. Letting someone like Eyelers dispose of liquor seems imprudent."

Bella frowned. "While we were on the terrace, I saw a figure in the bushes near the back entrance. Maybe someone was only getting air, but maybe the person was eavesdropping. It was a man, so it could've been Eyelers or Stricket. When I stopped to look more closely, the person stepped back and out of sight."

"Why would either of them do that?"

"Just before we came inside, Syl walked into the garden." Bella hadn't really registered it at the time. She'd just been glad Syl hadn't continued haranguing her with criticisms of Jax. Now, she wondered what her old friend had been doing. "Maybe the man waited for her there. I don't know. I might be letting my imagination run away with me."

A chuckle left Ida. "You've always had a good imagination and working on homicide cases has likely enhanced it."

"Probably so." Bella offered a rueful smile.

Ida's expression became serious. "I'd say it was Eyelers in the garden. Stricket is elderly. Close to eighty. I can't see him lurking out there or meeting with Syl, although I suppose it's possible."

"Good points."

"Do you think a lot of money could be made from Remingtons' supply before it ran out?" Ida asked.

"Some, but Eyelers could be bootlegging. He could dilute the liquor and make it go further. He could work with others, too."

"Rumrunners?"

"Maybe. I can't shake the idea that this island is a perfect place to conduct such an operation. Since it's private, there's no constable out here. Some liquor comes down from Canada, which is a few hundred miles away. Canadians aren't breaking any of their laws by transporting the stuff. They could sell it to someone here, which seems more likely than bootlegging themselves. They get paid and don't run as much risk of arrest. I wouldn't think Eyelers is going to Canada himself and bringing liquor down. But he may have partners who do."

"Interesting," Ida murmured. "This island is rather remote, so you may be right. But would it really be worthwhile for him? Could he make a lot of money?"

"It depends on the operation. If he works with others, probably so. Plus, he may be creating more booze by adulterating it. Stuff coming from Canada is legally produced there, so it's perfectly safe but not cheap. The same with leftover liquor like the Remingtons had. Diluting the good alcohol would give them more product to sell. That might go on right here."

"Blanche mentioned how deadly it can be, and I read a couple of newspaper stories about it, too."

"It can," Bella agreed, "but bootleggers don't care. They just want to make money."

"You think someone here—probably Eyelers—could add ingredients to liquor and take it to the shore?"

"Maybe. He has constant access to the Remingtons' boat. Or maybe I'm being fanciful because..." Bella let her voice trail off as she realized what she'd been about to admit.

A giggle left Ida. "It's only natural that your beau and his job influence your thinking, and having Sylvia get sloshed on bootlegged booze had to bring those thoughts to the forefront."

Warmth invaded Bella's cheeks, and she was glad for the darkness hiding her reaction. Jax wasn't exactly her beau, but she withheld the comment since Ida would disagree. Besides, he might be soon. "I suppose so, but drinking illegal liquor isn't uncommon."

"From what we learned in March, neither is bootlegging in this area."

"No, it isn't. Policing activity on the lake and islands is a tricky job. Eyelers would be my top suspect in that, but you never know. He certainly has means and opportunity. The others might realize what's happening. Again, I could be wrong." Was she getting so suspicious that anyone seemed like a potential rumrunner?

"When you write to Jax again, you could mention the situation here."

Briefly, Bella considered the idea. "He's busy with the O'Donnelly investigation. When it's over, he's supposed to come home for good. He could alert his boss, though." Would Jax simply tell Amos Derringer about the possibility of bootlegging on the island, or would he get involved? The latter seemed possible, which left Bella even more apprehensive. Any additional investigation would keep him away from Moreley longer.

"That's the best idea. We can't do much ourselves and, with no constable on Winnabee, we don't have a place to issue an alert," Ida pointed out.

"You're right, but it's unsettling."

A yawn escaped Ida. "Sorry, I'm very sleepy."

"We can talk more tomorrow."

"Good night, Bella, and sweet dreams."

Bella bid her friend a pleasant evening but, as for sweet dreams, she had none. Instead, images of rumrunners battling Prohibition agents filled her mind.

Chapter Two

♥

Since all six friends had stayed up late, they didn't assemble in the dining room until ten o'clock the following morning. No more brittle exchanges occurred, which helped Bella relax. Maybe the worst was over. She hoped so.

After breakfast, they all went to the dock. When they arrived, Eyelers was arranging a group of chairs. The wiry man glanced up when the young women approached.

"Thank you for seeing to the chairs and such, Mr. Eyelers," Florence said.

"G'morning." As he bobbed his dark head, a lock of oily hair fell in his face.

The man's gruff voice didn't surprise Bella, since he'd sounded the same yesterday afternoon. His appearance wasn't surprising, either. He was still disheveled. Was he only drinking, or was he rumrunning at night? Bella wished she knew.

"Do you need help, Mr. Eyelers?" Bella asked.

He spun to face her, a hard look on his weathered face. "No, and mind you, stay away from the boathouse. There's rotten boards in the floor, and I don't need no trouble from girlies falling through."

Since the man had already told them as much, although maybe not the others, Bella looked at Ida and shrugged. Her friend responded in kind before both of them chose chaise lounges at the end of the row. Everyone sat down except Lina, who lingered on the edge of the dock near Eyelers.

"Eyelers looks even worse than he did yesterday," Ida murmured.

"He's at least as hung over as he was then," Bella agreed, keeping her voice to a whisper, too.

A giggle left Ida. "He had a hard night, remember?"

Bella rolled her eyes in reply.

"Mind if I sit beside you?" Blanche asked.

"Of course not," Bella said.

As Florence took a chair at the opposite end of the group, Sylvia surveyed her friends. "Some of you are stuck in the pre-war era." As her bloodshot eyes moved to Bella, Sylvia grinned. "You and Jax have a lot in common. Very stodgy. That bathing suit is antiquated."

"Ignore her," Ida whispered. "She has to have a doozy of a hangover."

Both Bella and Blanche nodded in response to Ida's words.

"After last evening's cool weather, I'm surprised it's humid already," Blanche observed as she stretched out on a chair.

Sylvia moved her attention away from Bella. "If you weren't wearing stockings, you'd be cooler, Blanche."

"Stockings still come with most suits," Blanche pointed out in a bland tone, "and they're required at many public beaches and pools."

A harrumph left Sylvia. "Rules are made to be broken."

"Of course, you'd think so." Lina, her lips pursed, crossed to where the others were getting comfortable.

During the exchange, Bella studied Sylvia, whose suit definitely defied the typical guidelines for swimwear.

The skirt hit Syl's slender upper thighs while the sleeveless, v-neck top left little to the imagination. Bella glanced down at her own recently purchased water attire. When she and Ida had gone on their shopping spree, they'd both bought new suits, suits with full skirts skimming the knee and blousy tops covering the chest. Of course, they also wore the requisite stockings. To smooth over the situation, Bella spoke to Lina, "Take a seat with us."

"Thanks, Bella." Lina sat down next to Ida and turned toward the lake.

As her friends chatted, Bella laid back and closed her eyes. For a time, she soaked up the sun, listened to the ripples of water against the dock, and let her mind drift. Her friends chatted, but Bella didn't focus on the words, and the voices became background sound as she dozed off.

Eventually, the hum of a boat interrupted, and she blinked in surprise when the craft pulled to a stop next to the dock. The Remingtons had a spacious boat, but it was nothing like the one now being secured by two young men and an older one. The craft's mahogany trim, a striking contrast to the fresh white paint on the rest of the craft, gleamed in the sunshine while the overall size was as impressive. A dozen passengers would be comfortable above deck, and the side portholes indicated space below-deck, as well.

After the trio secured the lines, the older fellow headed to the wheelhouse while the younger ones jumped off. Both were tall and lean, but one had coal black hair and silver eyes, while the other was blonde with blue eyes. They were nattily dressed in ivory flannel pants, suspenders, and light blue shirts. Not exactly what Bella considered boating attire. At least it wasn't in Moreley. But there was no watercraft like this one in or around her hometown.

The man with the dark hair spoke first. "How nice to see people out here, especially a bevy of lovely ladies."

"Hello, Bart." Sylvia smoothed her hair back from her face.

"Syl, how nice to see you again," the dark-haired man replied. He moved to sit on the dock but put his arm next to where Sylvia's legs laid on the chaise. His gaze moved on. "You, too, Flo. Who are the rest of your friends?"

Florence didn't smile, but she made the introductions and finished by providing a name. "This is Barton Lauger. Bart." She gestured toward the man perching next to Sylvia's chair. "His grandparents own the house closest to ours, although they seldom make it out here anymore."

"They won't this summer, either. Grandfather isn't well," Bart put in. His gaze again swept over the group. "I've been here for a couple of months, and it's been lonely—except for the party in May." He winked at Sylvia. "My boatman spoke with Eyelers, who mentioned you having company for a few days, Flo. Glad to see it." He pointed to the other man. "This is my business partner, Parker Darre."

The other man nodded. "Good to meet all of you."

"How nice that you're able to spend time on the island," Lina said.

"We have able employees," Darre said with a grin.

Bella watched as Barton's fingers extended until he was touching Sylvia's leg. Clearly, they knew one another well, since Syl didn't object or pull away. If anything, she looked happy.

"Sit down, Parker, and make yourself at home. I'm sure Flo won't mind if we join the party," Bart said.

Florence stiffened but nodded. "There are two more chairs in the boathouse."

"Unnecessary. I'll perch on the end of yours," Darre said. Before Florence could answer, the man dropped next to her. She quickly pulled her knees up to her chin. He smirked but didn't move closer. Or away.

Bella and Ida exchanged a glance. How well did Florence know this man? And what about the rotten boards in the boathouse? Or were only *girlies*, a term Bella hated, not allowed inside?

After a few moments of small talk among the group, Barton Lauger addressed Sylvia. "How about a brief ride out on the lake, Syl?" He looked at the others. "The rest of you are welcome, too. Plenty of room on the boat. If Syl and I want some private time, we'll go below deck." His fingers clasped her slender ankle as he spoke.

The man's words, tone, and gesture made Bella's skin crawl. He was no gentleman, but Syl didn't seem to mind.

"Let's go." Sylvia readily agreed, but none of the other women indicated any interest.

"You two go ahead," Darre said. "I'd like to chat with Flo." He shifted closer to her. Although Florence stiffened, she still didn't object to his proximity.

Bella turned her thoughts to Florence's behavior. Why didn't she ask him to move away? After all, she was engaged. Last evening, Florence had seemed somewhat different from when they were all in college. Not as sweet and shy, but Bella would have never expected her to let a man other than her betrothed get so familiar.

Barton Lauger winked at his buddy before glancing back at Syl. "Let's go, my sweet." He stood and pulled Sylvia to her feet.

She leaned against him. "I can't wait."

Both men were far too forward for Bella's taste, and she could see similar feelings etched on the faces of Ida, Blanche, and Lina. Bella glanced back at the boat. Lauger and Sylvia boarded the craft and disappeared below deck before his boatman even got away from the dock.

"That was interesting," Blanche murmured.

"Very," Ida agreed in a barely audible voice that didn't carry beyond their foursome. "Evidently, Syl and Florence know the two men well."

Evidently was an understatement. "Barton mentioned a party last month. It sounded like Florence and Syl were there," Bella said.

"It certainly did," Lina added. "Syl going is no surprise, but I thought Florence had better sense. I wonder what her betrothed would think."

Bella wondered, too. The quartet kept their voices low, so Darre and their hostess—seated fifteen feet away—couldn't hear. But the pair appeared to be in deep conversation. Only when a period of silence ensued did their words travel easily to Bella's ears.

"I said I'd take care of the problem, and I will." Florence's voice was strained. "I have a small inheritance from my grandmother that pays a quarterly dividend. Just wait until July first."

Darre moved his hand closer to the bare space between stocking and swimsuit. "You could pay me back in other ways than money. Bart is planning another party for next weekend. You and Syl should come and spend the night."

Stunned by the exchange, Bella turned to look at the two. When Florence noticed, she bowed her head and spoke more quietly. Whatever she and Darre said after that was inaudible.

"I don't know about the rest of you," Blanche said, looking from Bella to Ida to Lina, "but I'm going to swim out to the raft."

"Great idea," Ida replied.

"I agree," Lina said.

As the four women stood and headed to the edge of the dock, Bella addressed their hostess. "We're going to cool off." With that, they plunged into the lake.

The next two hours passed peacefully. From the raft, Bella noted Darre had moved to a chaise lounge but had pulled it close to Florence's chair. With determination, she put all doubt and dismay away. This weekend was supposed to be a fun time with friends, so she planned to enjoy it as best she could. As Ida had suggested, Bella could write to Jax about a possible bootlegging operation. As far as Florence, her problems were her own.

Sometime later, Lauger's craft returned, Blanche sat up and followed its progress toward the dock. "Both guys are smarmy, but we can't stay on this raft all afternoon."

The other three agreed, so the women swam back to the dock. They were almost there when Syl's voice, tart with anger, reached Bella.

"We can't wait much longer, Bart. You need to make good on your promise soon."

His words were hushed, and his tone was placating. "You need to see a doctor to be sure, my sweet. Right now, you're guessing."

"I don't need to see a doctor. I'm sure. Very sure." Syl's voice rose a fraction.

Lina, Ida, and Blanche pulled themselves to the dock's surface. The sound of their splashing washed over the conversation. Had they overheard what Bella had? They were farther away from the boat, so maybe not. When several seconds of silence passed, Bella knew nothing more would be discussed now, and she exited the lake but glanced over her shoulder.

Lauger, hand on Syl's elbow, moved forward. While his expression seemed calm, anger glittered in his eyes. Syl spoke, but he shushed her. "Be quiet. We'll talk later."

"How? I can't leave this little reunion tonight without creating suspicion." Syl's tone was urgent and beseeching.

"Invite Darre and me to dinner. You and I can take a walk in the moonlight afterward." Lauger's voice held a note of command.

"All right," Syl replied, "but be prepared to settle matters." Bart made no response.

With that, the pair moved along. Bella did her best not to keep looking at them, but she was relieved when the group broke up thirty minutes later. As they did, Sylvia extended the invitation suggested by Lauger.

"Come to dinner. I'm sure we'd all enjoy some male company." Syl clung to the man's arm as she spoke.

"We'd love to come," Lauger said, his gaze on his friend instead of on Syl. "Wouldn't we, Darre?"

"I certainly would. It would be kind of you to have us, Flo." Darre beamed at her.

Florence looked like she wanted to object. Instead, she offered an excuse. "I doubt you gentlemen would enjoy listening to our college reminiscences."

Bella hoped their future conversations would be mostly about their school days, just as she hoped the two men would stay away. The weekend might still be salvaged.

Darre let his hand trail down Florence's bare arm. "Reciprocating hospitality is important, and you owe both of us."

A chortle escaped Sylvia. "She owes me, too, since she borrowed a large sum the last time we were out on the town in Chicago. Winning at the tables is fun. Losing isn't."

Lauger and Darre guffawed along with Sylvia. "You're in deep, aren't you, Flo?" Darre made it a statement, not a question. "Like I said, there's more than one way to dig yourself out. With me, anyhow."

Bella watched the scene with growing trepidation. Florence must have gambling debts. Big ones. She wouldn't ask, but Lina had no such compunction.

"You told us about going to speakeasies with Syl. That was bad enough. Were you wagering money, too?" Shock and disapproval rang in Lina's voice.

A bright flush rose in Florence's face. "Why would you ask such a thing, Lina?"

Sylvia laughed again. "Because it's true."

Florence turned to Sylvia. "Don't tell tales, Syl." Her voice was sharp with rebuke, and her eyes snapped with anger.

A snort escaped Syl, but Bart was the one who spoke. "Come to the party next weekend. Maybe you can work your way out of the hole." He winked at Florence. "And Darre is right about returning hospitality. With that in mind, I assume you're extending a dinner invitation for this evening."

His sly tone and mocking grin further alerted Bella to things going on beneath the surface. Exactly what, she didn't know. The two men gave her the willies, and she hoped Florence withheld the offer. That proved to be a futile wish.

"Of course. Dinner will be served at eight o'clock," their hostess said with a tight smile.

"We'll be over around six-thirty for cocktails." Darre snickered and winked.

"My parents cleared out their bar over two years ago," Florence replied. Wariness clouded her gaze.

"They certainly did," Lauger agreed, his smile still in place. "But we'll manage." He gave a slight bow to the group, and his partner followed suit before the pair boarded the sleek craft waiting for them.

After the boat pulled away, Florence gathered her things and hurried toward the path leading to the house. "I want to bathe and nap before supper. Perhaps, the rest of you will do the same." Without a backward glance, she dashed away from her guests.

Ida, Blanche, Lina, and Bella looked at each other before getting their gear together. "That sounds like a good idea to me. I may have gotten too much sun, so getting inside is a good idea," Lina said before following Florence back to the house.

The others did the same, leaving Sylvia to bring up the rear.

"That was an interesting afternoon," Ida said after she and Bella got back to their room.

"Very interesting in a few ways." Bella put her gear on the floor and sat on the edge of her bed.

Ida took a seat, too. "We had a little chance to enjoy the sunshine and water and then...I don't know what to think about everything said and done after Syl and Lauger came back. They must be involved in more than a casual courtship."

"I'd say so."

Ida wiggled her eyebrows, and when Bella laughed, she did, too. "The flapper crowd is fast, but Syl surprised me by going out on the boat with him for such a long time. At least, she wasn't drunk again."

"Did you hear what she and Lauger said when they first came back?" Bella asked.

"A little, but you were closer." Ida folded her hands together. "It sounded like she might be with child, but maybe I misunderstood. I hope so."

"You didn't. That's exactly how it sounded. It also sounded like he once said he'd marry her if that was the case, but he tried to put her off today. He wanted a dinner invitation, so they can discuss it this evening."

Various emotions battered Bella as she considered Syl's situation. A dire one for an unmarried girl.

Ida's eyes widened. "What is there to discuss? He'll either marry her or he won't. I don't mean to sound unsympathetic, but I wouldn't rely on him to do the right thing."

A resigned sigh left Bella. "I wouldn't, either. They stopped talking when Blanche splashed around while getting out of the lake, so perhaps they'll come to some sort of agreement tonight. For Syl's sake, I hope so."

"I'm sorry I missed some of their exchange, but I agree. I hope he'll do the right thing. What about Florence and Darre? I was shocked at how close he sat to her. She looked uncomfortable, and it was worse when he talked about her owing him. She got snippy, which isn't at all how I remember her. Of course, I don't remember her letting any man get so familiar. Until last night, I'd never seen her be anything but sweet to everyone. She was never the type to go to bars, let alone illegal ones, or allow a man other than her fiancé to touch her."

"She seems different, and it sounded like she owes all of them, which means she's been doing a lot of gambling." Bella drummed her fingers on the bed.

Ida clasped her hands and put them to her chin. "Do you think Lauger and Darre saw Syl and Florence in Chicago? Or only on the island? How would she owe the two of them, if they only met out here?"

"Lauger has parties, and it sounded like he serves liquor. But how many people would come out here, even with booze available? It's a fifteen-minute trip across the lake. The four of them might've gone to Toledo or Cleveland from here. I'm sure some speakeasies in both cities offer cards and such for wagering. Lauger and Darre must have permanent homes somewhere else. Maybe Lauger lives in Chicago, like Syl."

"That's possible. But Florence is engaged. Is she stepping out with Darre, too?"

"It's hard to say. She'd have to buy a lot of booze to be heavily in debt, so she must be gambling." Jax had shared some information on speakeasies and bootlegging before taking his new job, but Bella had learned more by listening to resort guests. Although Ida had some of the information, she didn't have as many details, which made Bella offer more. "Gambling goes on in a lot of bars and in some homes. If Lauger has it at his parties, that's an extra incentive to come out to the island." She paused for a moment. "A couple of weeks ago, I overheard several of our guests at Ballantyne discussing a private party where illegal wagering took place and plenty of bootlegged liquor was served. I've gotten dribs and drabs of comments about speakeasies, too."

"I've heard a few remarks about similar activities, not at Ballantyne, but when I was home for a few days last month. Several old friends mentioned house parties with liquor and wagering. I didn't ask for more information, since I don't approve of such goings-on." Ida, now seated at the vanity table, swiveled to face her friend. "You could be right about Bart's gatherings. Liquor and gambling would draw a crowd."

"Since Winnabee is a private island, no one needs to worry about getting caught in a raid, which would be a big incentive, too."

"What do you think Lauger gets out of his parties? I wondered about functions in private homes when I first learned about them. What's in it for the host?"

Bella carefully considered the question. "I imagine he takes a cut from whatever gambling goes on. Players may have to pay to play and, if they lose, they pay more. At least that was part of the discussion I overheard. The guests chatted about whether they could gamble and drink in one of the cottages. It sounded like they were considering getting a bunch of other people to come and take part. I was in the butler's pantry off the dining room, so they didn't see me. When I returned to check on the table, one man asked if the cottages were booked all season. Luckily, they are. I don't want illegal activities going on at Ballantyne, and I'm sure Mac doesn't, either." At his age, seventy, he deserved peace of mind.

"I don't blame you. Did you tell Mac?"

Bella shook her head. "No, he doesn't need to worry about such things anymore. Besides, we don't have space this season. Before reservations drop off in the fall, I'll talk to Griff. You'll be back at school in September, but I want your perspective. I feel like we need a strategy to avoid potential problems."

"I'm glad to help." Ida beamed at Bella. "By fall, Jax is apt to be home, and he'll be more than happy to assist you."

Bella agreed before turning her thoughts back to the island and its goings-on. "I know he will. Right now, I'm worried about Syl and Florence. They've been visiting each other often and engaging in questionable behavior." She frowned. "I sound like the prude that Syl accused me of being."

"No, you don't," Ida hastened to assure her. "You behave appropriately. I do, too. Nothing wrong with that."

"You're right," Bella replied. "It bothers me that both Syl and Florence have been going to speakeasies. It seems out of character for Florence, but she's changed. She isn't as wild as Syl, though."

Ida shook her head. "Few girls are. The flapper crowd gets a lot of attention, but it's a small group. As far as Florence, she might indulge in parties and such before getting tied down with her marriage."

Bella considered her friend's observations. "That seems plausible, and going to Barton Lauger's parties is in line with the idea."

"Florence's parents are straightlaced. From what she mentioned about her fiancé, he is, too."

"Probably so, since he has hopes of becoming a judge," Bella said.

Ida rolled her eyes. "Florence won't want him to learn about her illegal activities."

"No, she won't. She'll want to keep her parents from knowing, too. That's most likely why she got so upset with Syl." Bella paused before continuing. "Remember Lauger saying Florence's luck might change at next weekend's party? I'd love to discover more about those events."

A worried frown blanketed Ida's face. "You're not thinking we need to investigate, are you?"

"No, of course not," Bella replied. "Besides, the party isn't until next weekend. We'll be gone by then."

Ida's gaze narrowed on her friend. "That eases my mind because I know you well, and I'm sure you'd want to go if it was this weekend."

Bella avoided a direct response because Ida was right. She'd love to see what went on at Lauger's parties and report to Jax. "I wish Sylvia hadn't said booze is available right here, and I wish Florence wasn't gambling. Not that we should stick our heads in the sand."

A long exhalation left Ida. "You can tell Jax about your suspicions. Write him a note after we get home. Let federal agents look into everything."

"Since we have no proof, that's not apt to happen." Even without a party, she might learn more by asking the right questions. Bella considered how she could proceed.

Ida put her hand on her hips. "Bella, you've said bootleggers can be violent. Surely, you don't want to run afoul of any while we're here. Or anywhere, for that matter. I don't like Syl and Florence possibly being involved, either, but we aren't equipped to investigate.

Even lawmen need significant clues. They don't look into vague hints or hunches."

Bella didn't classify their current knowledge as *vague*, but Ida was right. They had no hard evidence of wrong-doing, and no authority to curtail nefarious activities, either. "I'll do as you suggested and write to Jax when we get back to Ballantyne, but I'd like more information. I could ask Lauger or Darre about their business. That wouldn't be out of line. Seeing their reactions might reveal something."

"As long as you're not obvious or persistent."

"I won't be. I promise. I don't want to run afoul of bootleggers, either."

Relief smoothed Ida's furrowed brow. "Good. Now, let's rest before getting ready for dinner."

Bella agreed, but her mind remained on bootlegging, gambling, and Jax.

Chapter Three

♥

Bella and Ida dressed with less enthusiasm than they had the previous night, and they chose simpler outfits. By the time they entered the parlor, three of their friends and the two male guests were already seated near the empty hearth. Once again, Darre squeezed next to Florence on one couch while Lauger shared the loveseat with Sylvia. Blanche was on the other couch and patted it.

"Sit with me," she said.

After the two best friends did as bid, Bella asked about the other member of their group. "Where is Lina?"

"She got too much sun and asked for a tray to be sent to her room," Florence replied. Her posture, so stiff she might have been made of marble, matched her hard tone. When Darre moved closer, she tried to make space between them, but she was already trapped against the arm. Clearly, she wasn't happy about having the two men as guests.

Once again, Bella considered the mention of Florence's debts. Did she owe so much to Darre that she felt forced to accept his overtures? And what about Syl and Lauger? Both women seemed to be in dire straits. How could Bella learn more by asking a few subtle questions? *Subtle* being the key word. She'd witnessed plenty of interviews while working with Jax. Using that knowledge would be helpful, as long as she didn't sound accusatory. After all, she wasn't working on a criminal investigation. She was gathering information. At least, she planned to try. Although she was unsure if the Prohibition Bureau would look into bootlegging on Winnabee, in all good conscience, Bella couldn't ignore it.

Lauger slipped a hip flask to Syl, who smiled in return. "It's a bit more of what you enjoyed on the boat today."

She tucked the container into her bag. "Excellent."

Bella watched in dismay. Syl wasn't drunk, which was good, but she easily accepted the flask from Lauger. Bootlegged booze, Bella was sure.

An hour later, when the group adjourned to the dining room, Bella hoped eating would replace drinking. Syl had only sipped a little and, thankfully, remained sober. The men used their flasks sparingly, but the presence of illegal liquor made Bella uneasy.

Bella slipped into a chair, only to find Darre between her and Ida. Blanche and Sylvia sat across from them, and Florence took her place at the head of the table. Lauger seated himself opposite her and at a right angle from Syl. Little conversation occurred until after Stricket served asparagus soup.

"Thanks, Strick," Lauger said when the butler placed a bowl in front of him.

Stricket gave a slight nod of his head before disappearing from the room. The use of a nickname made Bella wonder if Lauger and Darre were frequent guests here. Or did they know the butler in some other capacity? Bella recalled Barton mentioning that his boatman had spoken with Eyelers about Florence having guests. How well did the groups know one another? And what were the associations? Bella's discomfort grew. Bootlegging could be what brought them all together.

"This is fabulous." Blanche lifted her soup spoon. "I noticed a vegetable garden in back."

Some of Bella's tension dissipated at her friend's casual remark. Blanche had a knack for introducing benign topics, and Bella was glad of it.

"The asparagus came from there," Florence said. "Mrs. Longley is an excellent cook, and she uses our vegetables often." She returned to eating without sparing a glance at anyone else.

Bella dipped a spoon into her bowl and tried to focus on the meal. Lauger, Blanche, and Florence discussed the meal, while Sylvia pecked at her food in silence. Periodically, she took a covert glance at Lauger. On the other side of Darre, Ida introduced a new topic.

"Mr. Darre, Mr. Lauger said the two of you are business partners. What type of business?"

Ida offered her sweetest smile, which made Bella smile, too. Her best friend was adept at being hospitable.

"Please call me Parker, Miss Byington."

"You must call me Ida."

"Thank you," Darre said before taking another swallow of soup.

When he failed to answer Ida's question, she tried again with the same grace. "What sort of business?"

Parker Darre smiled, too, but his grin was not as bright as Ida's was. "We dabble in a few ventures with like-minded people."

After he leaned forward to retrieve bread from the plate in the middle of the table, Ida shot Bella a frustrated frown over his back. Bella rolled her eyes. When Darre resumed his meal, she attempted to engage him. "Florence said Mr. Lauger spends much of the year on Winnabee. Do you, too?"

He dabbed at his mouth with the linen napkin before replying. "I come out periodically. Usually for a week before one of Bart's parties. Often, I linger afterward."

"How frequent are the parties?" Bella asked.

Darre lifted one hand, palm up. "There's no set schedule."

Of course, there wouldn't be if they were running illegal liquor and gambling operations, Bella thought. Establishing a pattern could put their businesses in jeopardy. While no local law enforcement policed the island, federal agents could come any time if they had solid reasons. "How many people attend? Very few are on the island now."

"It's close to Burnley Cove, and that's a popular tourist destination during the summer." Darre popped a bite of bread into his mouth.

The general observation provided little insight, which was undoubtedly what the man wanted. In the same vein, Bella tried a broad statement herself. "It's a short distance, but I'm not sure I'd want to make the trip after dark."

His lips moved into the semblance of a smile. "The Lauger house is quite large. With twelve bedrooms, it accommodates a fair number of guests, and there's a little cottage at the back of the property."

"So, party-goers often stay overnight," Bella said.

Darre gave a brief nod. "Many do. Some locals come in early afternoon and leave before sunset. A few guests have boats with berths below-deck."

"Those crafts must be fancy," Ida put in.

"It's a fine group of people who come," Darre told her.

Bella doubted they defined *fine* in the same way. Darre's revelations, concise as they were, only increased her interest and trepidation. Too many people ignored bootlegging laws. As she studied the man, Bella wondered about him and Lauger partnering with other businessmen. More information was needed before anyone at the Prohibition Bureau would take notice.

"Where is your home, sir?" Bella asked.

"Please, call me Parker, too," he replied.

"Thank you." Bella didn't suggest he use her first name as she waited for him to continue. When he didn't, she tried again. "Do you live nearby?"

A waxen expression descended on his handsome face, and his blue gaze looked chilly. "No, I don't. My home is in Detroit."

The response increased Bella's trepidation. Detroit was nearly one hundred miles away, but only a river separated it from Canada. Liquor could cross the narrow body of water. The two men had said they worked with other businessmen on their ventures. If they were running booze from Canada to more than one location on shore, Lauger and Darre might work with gangsters. And there were a lot of gangsters in the Detroit to Toledo corridor.

"What about Mr. Lauger?" Ida asked. "He's on the island often, but where is his regular home?"

Before responding, Darre took another bite of bread. "Bart is mostly with his grandparents for the rest of the year. They're in Toledo."

Mostly meant Lauger spent time in other places. Where? Since pressing Darre wasn't apt to help, and it might create suspicion, Bella let the byplay at the table follow a natural course while keeping more questions to herself. Later, she'd talk to Ida again and discuss other strategies. Writing to Jax about the situation was a must, but more details were crucial.

Florence seemed tense throughout the meal, but Blanche kept Lauger engaged in casual conversation. Occasionally, Syl joined in. When they all finished dessert, the men thanked their hostess, which finally lightened Florence's expression.

"I want to check on Lina, but why don't the rest of you sit on the terrace? It's cooler than the parlor, and the humidity has built up all day." Florence got to her feet.

"I'd like to see how she is, too." Blanche stood beside Florence, who nodded.

As the two men and other three women went outside, Lauger put one hand on the small of Sylvia's back. "Let's take a walk in the garden, my sweet."

"That sounds lovely." Syl looked and sounded tense, but she let Lauger escort her away from the others.

As the couple disappeared behind the row of boxwoods, Darre quickly commented. "How lucky I am to be with two beautiful young women."

When he extended an arm to each of them, Bella lightly put her hand in the crook of his elbow and noted that Ida did the same. She'd prefer not to touch him, but Bella didn't want to be rude. A little honey was better bait than vinegar.

Darre led the way outside. "Where would you ladies like to sit?"

"The grouping of chairs at the end is nice," Ida replied.

Within moments, the trio was seated. Just as Bella was about to ask Darre another question, she heard voices coming from the garden below the terrace. Raised voices. Deciphering the content was impossible, but the emotion was evident. The female voice, Sylvia's, was piercing, while the male one, Lauger's, was placating. Was he agreeing to marry her or still resisting the idea?

A low chuckle rumbled out of Darre. "The two of them are quite a pair."

The comment revealed nothing of substance, but it provided an opening. "How do you mean? Have they been courting?" Bella asked.

He laughed again. "I'm not sure that's the right term. They've spent time together since they met last summer. Syl would like to extend that time, but Bart isn't a one-woman man. Or even one at a time."

The observation couldn't be misconstrued, but Bella still asked for clarification. "He's been seeing other women? Does Syl know?"

A shrug lifted one of Darre's shoulders. "She may not want to know."

When Bella looked at Ida, she saw her friend looked troubled, too. Her heart raced with dread. What would Syl do if he refused to marry her? That seemed likelier than not. Sympathy filled Bella. Although annoying and indiscreet, Syl deserved better treatment—especially from the father of her child.

The voices came closer, and Sylvia got louder. Loud enough to carry to those on the terrace. "You swine. Of course, it's yours."

Whatever Lauger replied was much quieter. Then, slap! The sound of flesh against flesh was unmistakable. Syl dashed on to the terrace and into the house. A stunned Bella stared at the retreating figure until Lauger appeared. One tanned cheek held the outline of a palm print. Sylvia evidently packed quite a wallop. Although she didn't countenance violence, Bella felt no sympathy for the man.

"Let's get going, Parker." He glanced at Bella and Ida. "Please thank Florence for her hospitality."

Darre stood, bowed to the two young women, and said, "I hate to leave so abruptly. It was a pleasure to meet both of you. Enjoy the rest of your stay." He dashed off and disappeared into the garden.

"Even though Syl has been snotty, I feel sorry for her," Ida said.

"I do, too. Lauger is worse than a cad." Bella sighed.

"And poor Syl has no one to lean on."

"You're right. When her mother died during our first year of college, she still had her dad. But he remarried quickly, and we all know she didn't get along with her stepmother. She hardly ever returned home after their wedding."

"According to Florence, half of her father's estate was left to Syl when he died last year. She must use that money to go to speakeasies and such."

Bella thought back over Syl's behavior since they'd arrived on Winnabee. "That's probably why she took up with a man like Lauger."

"Him suggesting the baby isn't his...that's awful." Ida gave a little shudder. "This weekend certainly isn't turning out like I expected."

"I feel the same way," Bella agreed. Should they talk with Sylvia? Offer to help her? But how? A baby born out of wedlock was a scandal. Even with ample funds, both mother and child would be labeled pariahs. Perhaps, the group could provide moral support. Syl would need it.

Ten minutes later, Blanche joined Bella and Ida. After taking the chair vacated by Darre, she slumped back. "Lina got badly sunburned. Not surprising since she's so fair. She's resting with cold packs now."

"What about Florence?" Ida asked.

"She's tired and headed to her room." Blanche clasped her hands together and laid them in her lap. "I asked her about Syl, Lauger, and Darre saying she owed them money. She insisted they were teasing because she's prim and proper, not wild like Syl."

Bella mulled over the information. Nothing new, but they couldn't all be lying about being owed money. "Florence used to be sweet and prudish, but she admitted to going to speakeasies and Lauger's parties. It didn't sound like those are for the tame crowd."

"I know," Blanche said. "I didn't press her about gambling, but I asked about Lauger's and Darre's business. They have various ventures with some other men."

"That's pretty much what Darre said," Ida replied. "What bothers me most is both Florence and Syl have serious problems."

Blanche nodded. "They do. Syl's earlier exchange with Lauger was disturbing, even though I didn't catch all of it." She glanced around. "Are they still taking a walk?"

"No, they had another, even more volatile, conversation," Bella replied before revealing what had happened.

"That's much worse. I can't believe she and Florence have gotten themselves into such difficulties, although Syl has used poor judgment for a while." Blanche released a long breath. "I was surprised she and Kenton got engaged. When Florence wrote to me about it, I was already back east. I've never known exactly what broke him and Lina up."

"I don't know, either," Bella said. "Ida and I were in France by then. When we left school, I thought Kenton would propose to Lina."

"I did, too," Ida agreed. "I've never felt like I should ask Lina, though. We corresponded off-and-on for a while during and right after the war. She didn't mention Kenton at all. I only heard about him and Syl through Florence."

"That's how I found out, too," Blanche said. "If Lina ended things, it might not matter. But if it's the other way around. Who knows?"

"If Lina dropped him, Syl could have stepped in. She was pretty much alone then. Having a nice guy might've been a lure," Ida said. "And he was a very pleasant young man."

All three friends grew silent for a long moment. "But why would Lina be so cutting to Syl if she spurned Kenton?" Bella asked. "He must've ended their courting."

"That's a good point, but Lina may simply disapprove of Syl's goings on," Blanche suggested.

"It could be part of the problem," Ida agreed, "but I don't approve of Syl's actions, either, and I didn't get snotty over it."

"You've never been as judgmental as Lina. As far as Syl's behavior, she may feel even lonelier since Kenton died." Bella drummed her fingers on the chair arm. Was grief over losing her betrothed the reason for Syl's increasingly wild antics? "Syl wants someone who cares about her, and Barton Lauger is a charmer."

"A charming cad," Ida said.

Bella nodded. "Darre seems much the same."

Both Blanche and Ida agreed with the assessment.

"I want to talk with Syl and see if there's any way I can help," Blanche said.

"I had the same idea," Bella added.

"Me, too," Ida put in.

All three young women beamed. Bella felt glad that the others wanted to support Syl, despite her appalling behavior. They'd all been close once.

"Good," Blanche replied. "I don't like her drinking so much if she's expecting. My husband had several patients who worked in blind pigs and drank excessively. Two bore children with medical problems. Both my husband and my father believe the issues resulted from the mothers being inebriated regularly."

Ida pursed her lips. "I've heard the term *blind pig*, but I don't know how they're different from speakeasies."

"They're down a few steps. Definitely not posh. Blind pigs usually just serve booze. Most speakeasies have food and entertainment, along with liquor," Blanche replied. "Unfortunately, both serve adulterated alcohol.

The good stuff, distilled before Prohibition, is about gone."

"I hope Syl listens to you about drinking." Ida looked as grim as Bella felt. "She's taking a terrible risk by getting liquor from who knows where."

"At least Syl wasn't drunk today or this evening. But she was sipping off-and-on. Would that be bad for the baby?" Bella asked.

"It could be, but it could be bad for Syl, too. It doesn't take a lot of methanol to cause serious harm," Blanche replied. "That's what my husband's patients drank."

"I read about people going blind and even dying from it," Ida said. "One sizeable group in Connecticut died after a big party a few months ago. Afterward, authorities discovered the liquor was laced with methanol."

Fresh alarm hit Bella. "I've heard the same things. I know bootlegged alcohol can be dangerous. Now, I'm concerned about Syl getting some from Lauger and maybe Eyelers. She told us she could get booze on the island."

"Lauger handed her a flask," Ida said, "but we surmised Eyelers was hungover the first day."

"And probably this morning, too." Blanche yawned. "Sorry, the fresh air, water, and sun are making me sleepy."

"Me, too," Ida agreed.

"I'm for turning in early. Some rest will put everything in better perspective." Bella wished that would be the case.

"Good idea. I'll check on Syl before I go to my room," Blanche said. "A word of warning about illegal liquor might be in order."

"Since you're a nurse, she'd likely listen to you." As the group headed upstairs, Bella hoped Syl would take heed of Blanche's concerns.

Although she was weary, Bella found drifting off difficult. Normally, spending a day outside would bring deep sleep. Unfortunately, the emotional upheaval surrounding Sylvia and Florence plagued her. So did the cloying humidity, which had risen all day and into the night.

Questions swirled through her mind until, after much tossing and turning, she finally dozed off. But that reprieve didn't last long.

Sometime later, Bella woke to booming thunder, frequent lightning, and torrential rain. When she glanced around, she saw her friend sitting straight up. Ida reached for the lamp on the small table between the beds.

"It isn't working," Ida said after a moment.

A long exhalation escaped Bella. "I'm not surprised. In one of her notes, Florence said there's a private power system out here. I don't know how it works exactly, but she mentioned they lose electricity often."

"I remember her saying so, but it doesn't make being in the dark any easier." Her voice sounded shaky.

"With all the lightning, there's plenty of light right now. Off-and-on anyhow." Bella tried to inject a note of levity, since she knew Ida disliked storms. "Come over here and sit for a while."

Ida wasted no time in moving to perch on the edge of Bella's bed. "I wonder if the others are awake."

"Florence could sleep through anything in college. With a sunburn, Lina might be restless. As for Sylvia, who knows? Maybe she started drinking again." Bella wished she and Ida were sleeping through the storm. She'd barely dozed off when the thunder woke her up. As fearful as her best friend was, neither of them would get any rest until the bad weather moved out. While summer thunderstorms often came and went quickly, this one sounded especially violent.

"She wasn't sleeping an hour ago when I went to the bathroom. Sylvia's room is on the other side of it, and I heard her talking and giggling with someone. I couldn't determine who from the voices, but they sounded sober."

"Maybe it was Blanche, since she was going to check on Sylvia. She may have woken up and wanted to look in again."

"I suppose. Anyhow, Syl was in good spirits then, but not drunk. At least it sounded that way. There's something else..." Ida's voice trailed off.

Her friend's tone and hesitance put Bella on edge. "What?"

"When I was out of our room, I saw a man going down the back staircase, which isn't far from Syl's suite. I could only see that he was of medium height and wiry build.

Surprise briefly held Bella mute. "The description fits both Stricket and Eyelers."

"Yes," Ida agreed. "Why would one of them be up here at such a late hour?"

Bella's anxiety increased. "Not for any good purpose. Unless Mr. Stricket was checking on things. Did you hear the voices on your way to the lavatory and see the male figure on the way back?"

"That's right. I washed out a few items to wear them again, so I was in the lavatory for maybe fifteen minutes. I heard the voices when I left our room and saw the man when I was coming back."

"Could one voice have been male?"

Several seconds of silence ticked away before Ida responded. "I thought it was female, but I could've been wrong. I didn't dally." When more thunder rumbled overhead, Ida shivered.

"It's disturbing to think about how much Syl's changed since we first met her." Bella resolved to keep talking about their friends in order to distract Ida.

"That's certainly true. Our first term at college, Sylvia was quieter."

"Her mother's death and her father's remarriage only months later seemed to start the change."

"Probably, and she obviously hasn't changed back. In fact, she's a lot wilder."

Another crack of thunder made Ida jump. Bella laid a hand on her friend's shoulder. "It can't last much longer. The worst of it should move on soon." It could be one in a series of storms, but she wanted to offer reassurance.

"I hope so," Ida said, "but I wonder how long we'll be in the dark."

"That could be awhile. Since only one of the other houses is occupied, getting electricity restored won't be a priority, I'm afraid."

Ida brought her knees toward her chest and wrapped her arms around them. "That's creepy, too. I thought more people would be around. These are summer homes. It's still early in the season, but if the owners don't come now, when do they?"

"Around Independence Day maybe. That's when the six of us came before." Bella considered their last trip to the island. "When we were here prior to the war, the Remington family employed almost a dozen people. Now, there are only four."

When the door inched open to reveal a silhouette, Bella and Ida stopped talking. "Who is it?" Bella asked.

"Florence. We're all going downstairs. There are plenty of candles and gas lamps, so we can have light and not be alone. If you want to come, don't bother with dressing. Pajamas are fine."

Ida was quick to respond. "All right. We'll be right down."

Only two of the other four women were in the parlor when Ida and Bella arrived. While candles and oil lamps provided some light, shadows filled most of the room.

"Sit over here," Florence said, patting the couch where she sat.

After she and Ida took the seats, Bella glanced around the group. "Where are Lina and Syl?"

"Lina will be here shortly. I knocked on Sylvia's door when I went by. She said she'd rather stay in bed," Blanche said. "She didn't sound drunk, simply tired."

"Sylvia is used to being out late most evenings and sleeping until noon most days." Florence spoke in her usual sweet tone, but an edge was clear. "Going to speakeasies is common in the city."

"I live in the city, and I don't frequent speakeasies," Blanche said.

"You're married," Florence pointed out. "Sylvia lost her betrothed during the war." She turned to Ida. "You must know how difficult that was, Ida."

"Losing Alan was terrible, and I'm sure Sylvia was equally heartbroken by Kenton's death." Ida looked around at her friends before speaking again. "It's taken a long while, but I'm finally stepping out with someone."

Murmurs went around the group. Smiles followed.

"How wonderful," Florence said, although she still looked and sounded tense.

"Who is he? How did you meet him?" Blanche asked.

Ida grinned. "We met last summer when he came to play golf at Ballantyne. Bella and Jax crossed paths with him when they were investigating a suspicious death, and she invited Griff to play any time. We met then. This year, Mac retired from working full-time, and Griff was hired as the new golf professional."

"No wonder you're working there this summer." Blanche beamed at Ida.

"It works out well for me," Bella immediately said. "I can rely on Ida to pitch in whenever I need help, and Griff is doing a wonderful job. Plus, he's a really nice man. He gets along well with all of our staff and guests. He and Mac have gotten close, too." Years ago, all the girls had heard about Mac, her honorary grandfather and now, her business partner. A couple had met him.

Lina joined the group as Bella was speaking and took a seat on the ottoman. "That reminds me. You never said exactly what's going on with you and Jax now."

Immediately, Bella was sorry she'd spoken. Since she didn't know what was *going on* herself, explaining their relationship to others was impossible. When Jax left in April to join the Prohibition Bureau, they'd agreed to court once he got home. But when would that be? Because she didn't know, Bella searched her mind for a sensible reply.

Her best friend came to the rescue. "As Bella said last night, Jax has taken a temporary position as a Prohibition agent," Ida said. "They saw a lot of each other before he left, and I'm sure it will be the same when he returns."

Bella appreciated her friend's support.

"How wonderful," Lina said. "Perhaps both of you will be married soon."

"Jax and I are far from the altar," Bella said. "But it's different with Ida and Griff."

"Griff and I have only been stepping out for a few weeks, so it's far too early to think about a wedding," Ida replied. "What about you, Lina? Have you been courting with someone special?"

Even in the faint light, the other woman's expression was grim. "I've stepped out with several young men, but I've never completely gotten over Kenton. Maybe I never will." A slight catch in her voice made the reply ragged.

Did that mean Kenton had instigated their break-up? Evidently so, Bella thought with dismay. She wanted to ask for details but hesitated. Since she didn't like being questioned about Jax, she didn't want to put her friend on the spot.

Lina's words hung heavily in the room until only the high winds and slashing rain were audible. Finally, Florence broke the silence. "I hope you don't have hard feelings toward Sylvia."

Bella started in surprise. Florence had still been at school when Lina and Kenton ended their courtship. Now, it appeared the decision hadn't been mutual. Nor did it seem to be Lina's doing. Her heart ached for her friend. Being cast off had to hurt horribly, especially when another friend had taken her place. But was that Syl's fault? Kenton was surely as much to blame.

Lina's chin went up a fraction. "It hasn't been easy. I may never get over him."

Bella considered what to say, but Blanche offered advice first.

"I hope you'll stop carrying a torch for Kenton. You deserve to be happy, so don't rule out falling in love again," Blanche said.

"No, don't," Ida said. "It's hard to move on, but it can be good, too."

"I'll keep that in mind," Lina said, but her tone indicated otherwise. "Clearly, Syl has moved on."

That comment led to an uncomfortable silence. After several moments, Florence broke it. "Syl is in a difficult situation and could use our support."

Lina stared at Florence in apparent disbelief. "Why are you defending her? She wasn't worried about your feelings when she chided you about losing money. We all know that means you've been gambling and probably a lot."

Color surged into Florence's face. "Syl was only teasing."

A harrumph left Lina. "Was Mr. Darre teasing, too? I didn't catch all of your conversation but enough to know you owe him and Syl money. Mr. Lauger, too."

Dismay filled Bella. The look Florence sent Lina could only be called furious. Both women were in the grips of turmoil and tension, but she had no idea what to do for them or for Syl.

"You shouldn't listen to cruel mocking," Florence replied.

"Why would they mock you? It makes no sense," Lina said. "You admitted to going to speakeasies and to Mr. Lauger's parties. Gambling must go on since you owe both him and his partner money. In fact, Lauger suggested you might break even at his next event."

"I told you they were teasing me." Each of Florence's words fell like chunks of ice—hard and frigid. "I gambled a little, but they make a big deal out of it."

The admission didn't surprise Bella, but she wondered if *little* described Florence's gaming. She clearly hadn't wanted to ask Lauger and Darre to dinner, but she had. To pacify them due to her debts? Mentioning that fact wasn't likely to ease the situation, so Bella chose a benign comment. "Teasing isn't nice."

Florence nodded. "They can be pleasant a lot of the time, but not always. Let's talk about more agreeable things."

After that, four of the friends chatted casually while Lina sat in silence. She folded her arms over her abdomen and let her gaze move to some distant point in the room.

Off-and-on, thunder still rumbled and lightning flashed occasionally. The rain was more constant as it continued to pelt the windows. The sound lulled Bella into sleep.

When she woke again, Bella saw faint light streaming through the windows. Clouds still hung heavily in the sky, but the rain had dwindled to drizzle, and both thunder and lightning had moved on. Relief filled her. The worst was over although what was left in its wake remained to be seen. Bella swung her feet to the floor and stretched. As she did, she noticed Florence stirring. Soon, Ida was also awake.

The three friends, blankets around them, huddled together on one couch. "It's a lot cooler this morning," Ida whispered.

"It is," Blanche agreed with a shiver. "We won't be swimming today."

Bella moved to look out the windows. Ida and Blanche hurried to join her. The sight made all three gasp. "I don't know if we could get to the dock anyhow. Quite a few trees are down, and branches are everywhere." Several of the tall oaks had snapped off, while some of the smaller trees had been uprooted. Strong winds sent leaves and twigs swirling through the air. Bits of debris occasionally hit the windows.

"The storm sounded bad, but I had no idea there'd be so much damage," Ida said.

"It's awful, and look at the tree limbs swaying in the wind." Blanche wrapped her arms around her waist. "More could come down."

"Fiddle-faddle." Florence didn't bother to glance outside when she spoke from nearby. "Every summer, we get severe storms."

"With big trees toppling over?" Disbelief was in Ida's voice.

"Not necessarily, but Eyelers will get everything cleaned up," Florence replied.

"I'm going upstairs to dress," Lina said. "That will help me warm up."

"It's a good idea for all of us," Florence agreed.

"And we should check on Syl," Blanche added.

"She's most likely still sleeping since it's only nine-thirty." Florence pointed to the clock on the mantel. "She could doze until noon."

"All the same, I'll look in on her before I get dressed," Blanche said before heading upstairs.

The rest of the group followed her before going into their own rooms. Bella and Ida had just pulled on clean clothes when Blanche, pale-faced and wide-eyed, walked in. "Come with me to Syl's room."

"What's the matter?" Ida asked.

Blanche put one hand to her throat and shook her head.

Alarmed, Bella hurried to her side. "Are you ill?"

"No. It's not me. It's Syl. I think she's dead." Blanche, her voice thready and weak, trembled slightly. "I've seen dead people when nursing, but never a friend."

Shock held Bella mute for a long moment. Surely, she'd misunderstood. "Are you certain? Florence said Syl always sleeps late. Let's take a close look."

"I did," Blanche replied, her voice still thready. "The smell in her room hit me as soon as I opened the door, so I walked in. When I called to her, she didn't respond at all, so I went to the bedside." Blanche took a shuddering breath. "She was ashen and motionless. I checked her pulse right away. There was none." Tears filled Blanche's eyes, and she hastily wiped them away.

Ida's hand flew to her mouth. "Oh, no."

Bella wanted to believe Blanche was wrong, but her friend had been a nurse during the war. And Blanche's father and husband were both doctors, so she knew how to check for a pulse. What in the world had happened to Syl? Briefly, Bella recalled Ida hearing voices and seeing a male figure before the storm. Did that have something to do with the death? They needed to find out. "We'll go back to her room with you," Bella said, finally responding to Blanche's request.

The trio hurried down the hall and entered the chamber.

"What an awful smell," Ida murmured as she stopped dead in her tracks.

"There's vomit all over her and the bed. Some is on the floor, too," Blanche said.

Reluctantly, Bella moved forward. The stench got bad enough that she had to put one hand over her nose. Renewed sorrow hit her when she looked down at Syl. She didn't need to check for a heartbeat or breathing. Syl's lovely face looked like a waxy mask. Moisture filled Bella's eyes and splashed down her cheeks. "I can't believe she's gone." Her voice was husky with suppressed sorrow.

"I couldn't, either." Blanche stood next to Bella. "That's why I tried to find a pulse, despite how she looks. I didn't want to think she could be dead."

Ida went to the other side of the bed. "It's awful. How in the world did this happen?" Shock underscored each word.

"It looks like she died in her sleep." Blanche shoved her hands into her robe pockets.

"Could drinking too much have killed her?" Ida asked.

Blanche shrugged. "It's possible, but she didn't have much yesterday or last night. She was sober when I spoke to her last evening. After I warned her about excessive drinking being bad for unborn babies, she was upset. She didn't admit her condition, but she said she'd be more careful. I think she was sincere."

As Bella looked back at Syl's still form, she experienced another jolt of apprehension. "Was she still sipping on her flask?"

"It was by her bed," Blanche replied, "but she couldn't have consumed much since she was completely lucid."

Bella glanced around and pointed to the bedside table. "What about these bottles?"

All three women studied the nightstand. "Those are gin," Blanche said.

Ida nodded. "Very expensive gin. I'm guessing it originally came from the Remingtons' supply."

"Probably so," Blanche agreed as she stood at the end of the bed. "When we were here a few years ago, they only had top quality liquor, and that brand is at the very top."

"Syl said she didn't bring bottles, only the flasks, but she might've bought booze out here from someone." Bella chewed on her lower lip. While she wasn't ready to share her suspicions with all their friends, Bella found Blanche to be more circumspect than Florence or Lina. "Ida and I already talked about the possibility of bootlegging on this island. It's an ideal place, since booze could be brought down from Canada, diluted here, and transported to the lakeshore before being sent on to various places."

Blanche looked at Sylvia. "If she didn't drink enough to kill herself, which I doubt, she could have gotten bad booze. Depending on what was used to dilute it, and how much was put in, she wouldn't have needed to consume a lot."

"That's what worries me," Bella admitted. "Especially now that we've found the bottles. It seems all too likely the gin might have been adulterated to make more. One is half-empty, but the other is full. Jax told me that gin is the easiest for bootleggers to make." He'd shared the information in a letter.

"More booze. More profit." Blanche scowled. "It's awful, but not uncommon. Unfortunately, I nursed two young soldiers who bought cheap booze laced with methanol. Sometimes people call it wood alcohol. In any case, it's dangerous to consume. During the war, it wasn't so common to find bad stuff, but some folks took advantage of boys who were right off the farm and never had a drink, except hard cider."

"What happened to them?" Ida asked.

"They were lucky. Neither drank enough to go blind or die, but they were very ill. I hope it taught them an excellent lesson, and they aren't making the same mistake now." Blanche hesitated briefly. "If they got back from France."

An interlude of silence followed, and Bella knew all three women were thinking about how many lives had been lost in that awful war. After a bit, Bella spoke again. "If she only brought hip flasks with her, Sylvia must have drunk mostly booze she got here. When and where she got it is a puzzle."

Blanche looked at Bella. "I'm having trouble taking this all in. It's such a shock."

"I agree." Although Sylvia was clearly gone, Bella knew the reality hadn't completely registered with any of them. The sudden death of a healthy young woman was rare.

"I haven't told Florence yet," Blanche said. "Or Lina. Once I do, we need to contact the constable on Burnley Cove. He should have a doctor who can come over and...see to things."

"Of course," Bella said. "Ida and I will come along."

Florence was coming out of her room when the trio reached her. She glanced at them with a half-smile. "You aren't dressed yet, Blanche."

"I'm afraid there's bad news," Blanche murmured. Although still pale, her voice was stronger.

All traces of amusement left Florence's expression. "What kind of bad news?"

Blanche inhaled and exhaled before responding. "Syl is dead."

The stark statement made Bella bite hard on her lower lip to keep more tears at bay. As she watched Florence, she noted the same disbelief that the rest of them felt. But grim grief was nibbling away at the shock. As it did, memories of other losses arose. Keeping them at bay proved difficult, but Bella struggled to focus on the present.

Florence shook her head. "That's impossible. I told you. She often sleeps until noon, whether she's been out on the town or not. It's a habit."

"I checked her pulse. There was none." Blanche laid one hand on Florence's arm, as if to soften the shock.

"I don't believe you." Florence pushed past the others and hurried to Sylvia's room.

They followed and stopped inside the door. Florence was shaking Syl's shoulders. "Wake up. You need to wake up. You're scaring all of us, and it's not funny."

Bella went to Florence and slipped an arm around her. "She can't wake up. She's gone."

"No. That can't be." Florence's voice came out as a tremulous murmur. Finally, she seemed to take notice of the mess in and around their friend's dead body. A hand flew to her mouth. "She must have gotten ill with something. Influenza or another virus."

"I don't think so," Blanche said.

"What else would cause someone so young to be so sick and die?" Florence asked.

A beat of silence preceded Blanche's response. "Bad booze."

Florence swiveled to face her. "Bad booze? Do you mean too much booze?"

"Probably not. She drank little yesterday, and I talked to her last night about cutting back. She agreed," Blanche replied.

A tremor rippled through Florence. "Syl didn't drink rotgut. She bought only the best."

"She probably got some booze out here. Some must be in these, since only part of one has been consumed." Bella pointed to the two gin bottles.

Florence was quick to answer. "Syl probably got those from Bart."

"They look like bottles your parents had years ago." Blanche folded her arms over her chest.

"That's ridiculous. Bart's grandparents probably had the same brand, since all their liquor was top-notch," Florence insisted.

"How would Syl get two big bottles from Mr. Lauger?" Bella asked. "She might've had a little on his boat, but she didn't carry a big load off."

Florence's nostrils flared with a sharp intake of breath. "Why are all of you making it sound like she got booze here, at my home? I didn't give any to her. Bart might've met the boat when she arrived. Syl could've told him when she was coming. They've seen each other often in Chicago."

While the idea was possible, Bella didn't think it was likely. Florence was saying anything that would remove suspicion from herself and her family's employees like Eyelers. If bootlegging was going on, and Bella felt sure it was, Florence had to know about it.

"Mr. Eyelers picked Syl up early on Friday morning, didn't he?" Bella made the query.

"He did," Florence agreed. "He's our handyman and boatman. He picked all of you up."

Bella exchanged a glance with Ida before stating her supposition. "He looked and acted hungover."

Florence's eyes narrowed to slits. "Drinking isn't illegal. Eyelers, like many others, could've stockpiled liquor before Ohio went dry."

"If he has liquor, Syl could've gotten some from him." Bella made the comment in a calm, composed voice that placed no blame.

"No matter where Syl got liquor, an autopsy should be performed, so we need to call the nearest constable. There's probably a local doctor who does such tasks," Blanche said.

"An autopsy?" Florence echoed. "Is that really necessary?"

"Syl is twenty-five years old, which makes it unlikely she died of a heart attack or another such malady." Bella stared at Florence in dismay.

For several moments, Florence looked down at Sylvia.

"We need to contact the nearest constable. Florence, will you make the call?" Bella asked.

Finally, the other woman nodded. "Of course."

"I'll go down with you," Bella said before following their hostess out of the room and to the telephone alcove off the foyer.

Neither spoke as they made their way downstairs. When they got to the telephone, Florence picked up the earpiece and candlestick base. For what seemed like an eternity, nothing happened. Finally, Florence spoke. "Hello...hello." She started tapping the base. "Hello."

Tension knotted Bella's insides. Was the telephone out? That seemed quite possible, since the electricity was. "Can you hear the operator?"

Florence turned to Bella with a blank expression on her face. "Nothing yet."

"Here, let me try." If Florence kept poking on the telephone, she was more apt to disconnect than connect.

She seemed unwilling to let go, though. "Florence, we need to contact the authorities."

Before handing over the phone, Florence returned the earpiece to the base. Annoyance filled Bella, but she attempted a new call. After a short time, a voice came through, but so did crackling that nearly obliterated everything else. "Operator, I'm calling from Winnabee Island." When Bella made out the word *yes*, she hurried on. "I'm at the Remington house. We have an emergency. A woman died. We aren't sure how, and we need your constable and a doctor to come." Static again filled the line, so understanding the operator's reply proved difficult.

"We've had...storms over here..." The other voice was barely distinguishable.

The operator didn't seem to note their dire emergency. "We've had storms, too, but I need the constable," Bella said in a louder voice, although how that would overcome the static, she didn't know. But desperation drove her. "Please connect me."

"They're..." More inaudible words ensued. "Out...can I...message. I'll get...run...over there."

The woman must be asking if she could have someone take a message, so Bella quickly answered. "One woman died. We aren't sure what happened." She hesitated momentarily before voicing the concern in the back of her mind. "She might have consumed bad booze. We need the constable to come as soon as he can."

"Woman...died...bad booze?" The voice was barely audible.

The operator might have said more, but the line went dead. Bella tapped on the hook several times in vain attempts to reconnect. When her continued efforts failed, she returned the earpiece to the candlestick base and handed it back to Florence, who put it on the shelf.

"What did she say?"

Bella, sorrow and anxiety battling inside her, leaned against the door. "I only caught part of it, and I'm afraid she only got bits of what I said. Evidently, the storm did damage on the lakeshore because it sounded like she can't reach the constable's office. I think she'll send word to him about a death over here. It sounded that way at least."

A frown furrowed Florence's brow. "If the storm was as bad on the lakeshore as out here, he isn't apt to make it today. Besides, the lake is very choppy. He won't want to risk his life coming to check on a dead woman."

Florence's reference to her dear friend as a *dead woman* further unsettled Bella. So did the possibility that the constable wouldn't hurry to the island. "I'm sure he'll come as soon as possible." Wouldn't he? "In the meantime, I'll tell the others."

"All right. I want to speak with Mrs. Longley about breakfast. With no electricity, she'll have to rely on the old wood stove." Without waiting for a reply, Florence headed to the kitchen.

For a moment, Bella stared after her. Who could think about food when one of their friends was dead upstairs?

Chapter Four

♥

When Bella went back upstairs, she found Ida and Blanche in the open sitting area off the hallway, so she joined them.

"Is the constable coming?" Ida asked.

"Probably not soon." Bella sighed. "The connection was terrible. I could barely hear the operator, and she didn't seem to catch all of what I said, either. I told her twice someone died. Then, the line went out."

"Oh, no," Blanche murmured.

"From what I got, which wasn't much, the storm was severe at Burnley Cove, too. It's not surprising since it's nearby. The operator seemed to say she'd send word to the constable, but we're pretty much on our own for now." Bella glanced at Sylvia. "We shouldn't move her, since the constable will probably want to see her as she is, but I hate to leave her in that awful condition."

A shudder rippled through Ida. "I do, too. The bed is a mess, and so is she."

Uncertainty continued to plague Bella, as did shock and sorrow. "Maybe we should wait at least until the end of the day. The constable might make it over."

"That sounds like the best idea," Blanche agreed. "Now, I need to dress."

"Florence is checking with the housekeeper about breakfast. We'll finish getting ready and meet you in the dining room," Bella said.

"I'm sorry we only have fruit, leftover muffins, and coffee," Florence said when the group gathered at the dining room table. "Mrs. Longley is using the top of the stove, not the oven."

"I don't think any of us are starving." Bella looked at Lina, who was already eating. Her friend's calm countenance and apparent appetite were at odds with how Bella felt. Was Lina aware of Sylvia's death? She didn't ask because Stricket appeared in the archway between the dining room and foyer.

"Miss Florence, would you like me to start a fire in the parlor?" he asked. "You'd be more comfortable there after your meal. I'm afraid today's weather isn't conducive to outdoor activities."

"That would be wonderful," their hostess replied. "I'd like to speak with you after we eat, but the others can get settled."

"Of course, miss," the butler said before heading into the main hallway.

"Help yourselves." Florence gestured to the food on the table.

Florence's calm demeanor was as jarring as Lina's serenity. Bella, who still felt distraught over Sylvia's death, wondered how they could be so composed. She realized Blanche had similar thoughts when she spoke.

"Lina, you may not have heard the terrible news."

"About Syl? Florence told me." Lina lifted her cup with both hands. "A college boy back home drank himself to death last year with bad booze. If people only had sense enough to obey the law, they'd stay safe."

While what Lina said was true, she didn't sound sympathetic or sad. And what made her think Syl had consumed bad booze? Had Florence mentioned the possibility?

"We aren't sure Syl drank tainted alcohol," Florence said. "She could have fallen ill or simply had too much liquor."

"An autopsy will reveal a lot," Ida pointed out.

Florence shot her a sidelong glance. "I still don't think an autopsy is necessary. Besides, no one is apt to get out here for a couple of days, maybe longer." She carefully cut a muffin into four pieces and began eating.

Bella crumbled the muffin on her plate before pushing it away. She noted neither Blanche nor Ida was eating, either. Why weren't Lina and Florence more upset? It was perplexing.

"If you're done eating," Florence said, "go ahead to the parlor. I'll be in shortly."

"Good idea." As Bella pushed her chair back, Ida and Blanche did the same. Lina, whose plate was now empty, followed suit.

When the four made their way to the parlor, the butler had a cheerful blaze going.

"Thank you, Mr. Stricket," Ida said.

The man gave a curt nod before leaving.

"How are you doing?" Blanche said as she sat next to Lina.

Lina's gaze went from Blanche, to Ida, to Bella, and back. "I'm not relieved, if that's what you're thinking. I don't approve of Syl's behavior and haven't for some time. The rest of you didn't see her get her claws into Kenton, but I never wished her harm." She bit down on her trembling lower lip. "I thought he and I would get married. When he dropped me for Syl, I was crushed."

Lina's revelations explained a lot, but not everything. Bella proceeded carefully. "I hope you won't think I'm prying, but what happened? When Ida and I left, you and Kenton seemed smitten with one another."

Moisture shimmered in Lina's eyes. "We were."

When she said nothing more, Blanche spoke. "Syl was the reason you and Kenton ended your courtship." Blanche made it an observation, but it was clearly a question.

A scowl formed on Lina's face. "She was. My mother got influenza in the first wave, so I went home to care for her. When I got back to school, Syl and Kenton were stepping out. He said he was sorry, but he'd been in love with her for a while. *Love*. Ha." With one hand, she wiped at her eyes. "I was shocked and hurt."

"I'm so sorry," Blanche said. "I had no idea that it wasn't a mutual decision between you and him."

"It wasn't." Lina's voice was laced with venom. "Remember how Syl was. Flirting with every man who crossed her path. They were betrothed within a month, and he went off to war. My mother had a relapse and died shortly afterward."

"How difficult that must've been," Ida said. Her voice was soft with sympathy.

"Really awful," Bella added. Poor Lina. What a terrible situation for her.

"It was horrible. I couldn't sleep or concentrate. I got behind in my schoolwork and didn't finish the semester or go back. I just couldn't manage." She clasped her hands in her lap. "The doctor was afraid for my health and recommended a drink or two before bed. That helps."

"You're still having liquor at night?" Blanche asked.

Bella had also noticed Lina's use of present tense, so she listened carefully.

"I have a federal waiver for medicinal alcohol, so it's all legal." Lina clasped and unclasped her hands. "I'm not doing anything wrong. My doctor prescribes it for me. It's perfectly legitimate that way."

"It is," Bella agreed, but she knew the practice was a way for doctors and druggists to make extra money. For a few dollars, a person could get an order—written on a federal government prescription pad—from a physician and buy a pint of booze at a pharmacy. Often, people did so on a weekly basis. While some benefitted from the practice, others simply used it to circumvent the Volstead Act. She wasn't sure which category Lina fell into.

Lina's expression relaxed. "A swallow helps me relax and rest."

Again, Bella figured there was more to the story. If Lina had been drinking at bedtime for a few years, she probably consumed more than a gulp in order to sleep. "Are you working?"

"I took a secretarial job in my hometown after the war. I served with the Red Cross canteen between college and work. My great aunt was alone, and we shared her house until she passed a few months ago." Lina offered a small smile. "I appreciated hearing from all of you after I lost Mother and Auntie."

"Of course," Bella said.

"You know how it feels to be an orphan." Lina focused on Bella.

In her mid-twenties, Bella didn't think she fell into that category, but she withheld the comment. "I have Mac, who is like a grandfather to me."

"Still, I'm sure you've had your share of sleepless nights. It's hard to be all alone in the world. That's why the prescription is important to me," Lina said.

Silence resonated in the room. How important was liquor to Lina? Bella feared it was too important, but what did that mean in terms of Syl's death? Anything?

Before any of the others spoke, Lina said, "I'm glad Stricket started a fire. It's chilly in here."

The change in subject made it impossible for Bella to smoothly ask more about the length and depth of Lina's insomnia. But she stored the information in the back of her mind and did the same with the revelations about Syl and Kenton.

"Cold air followed the storms," Blanche said. "It's still rainy, though. And windy, too."

All four women looked out the wall of windows. Gusty winds sent rain splashing against them. "Even if the operator heard what I said, no one will come out in this weather. We can't see the lake now, but I'm sure the water is choppy. Florence thought so." As Bella spoke, wind howled down the chimney, making the flames dance wildly. The weather, Syl's death, and the possibility of bootlegging all combined to send shivers through her. Added to the mix were the reactions of Lina and Florence. Unsympathetic, almost callous.

"The weather is terrible." Blanche stared out the window as she spoke. "It's almost as dark as night despite only being mid-morning."

The sound of Stricket clearing his throat brought all attention back inside the room. "Excuse me, ladies, but I've brought more coffee. Mrs. Longley is making soup for later." Stricket placed a large tray on the table in front of the hearth. "Can I be of service in any other way?"

The group issued thanks before Bella asked a question. "Any idea of how much damage there is on the island?"

Stricket glanced at Bella. "I was outside for a bit. The dock is partially destroyed, and the boat was set adrift. A number of trees are down."

"Oh, my," Ida murmured. "The boat is gone?"

"How will we get back to the shore?" Lina asked, anxiety in her tone.

The butler shrugged. "We'll find a way. Have no fear."

"Would anyone from the mainland come out to check on the island when the weather improves?" Bella asked.

"Perhaps. That has happened in the past when we've gotten similar storms, but all ten houses were occupied. If telephone service is restored, Miss Florence can ask for help to come. We're only a few miles out," he said. "People on islands farther away fend for themselves. We have, too."

"So, we may be stuck here longer than planned," Lina said, in a grim voice.

He nodded. "Possibly. Now, if I can do nothing else, pardon me."

"Thank you again." Once Stricket left, Bella turned to the others. "Summer storms can be bad, but I hadn't considered what might happen if we had no telephone or electricity for days." She hadn't thought about anyone dying, either. Or about bootlegging on the island.

"I wish the boat was still here," Blanche added.

After pouring coffee for all four women and handing them cups, Ida settled back on the couch. "Bella, you thought the operator said she'd contact the nearest constable. Or send someone to do it. Certainly, he'll send help when he can."

"The connection was so bad that I can't be sure. I hope she heard me better than I heard her." Bella gripped her cup more tightly. The long weekend was supposed to be a pleasant reunion filled with fun. Now, it loomed as a dark abyss teeming with doubts and dismay. One friend was dead in an upstairs bed while their hostess was acting strangely in response. Her attention went to Lina, whose revelations and attitude were also disturbing. Then, there was Eyelers. Had he been too drunk to get the boat out before the storm? Or had he been engaged in some other endeavor? Rumrunning, for instance. What about Lauger and Darre? Questions tumbled around Bella's mind, but one remained at the forefront. Had someone meant to poison Sylvia? Lauger had a motive, but so did Lina. And Florence might, too. As for Eyelers, he could've been a go-between or an accidental poisoner. Syl's death was both troubling and suspicious. Bella couldn't change what had happened, but she planned to get answers as to why it had occurred.

Early on Saturday morning, Jax Hastings parked his Chevrolet Chummy in the Ballantyne lot, got out, and stretched. Every muscle in his body protested. Working eighteen-hour days to get time off had been exhausting, but so was driving all night. He ran one hand over his stubbled jaw and glanced around. The faint light of dawn illuminated the inn, and much of his tension ebbed. It was good to be back. The familiar structure had been a second home to Jax since boyhood. Built in the latter part of the last century as the home for an industrialist, it came to serve as the centerpiece of the Stewart family resort for over thirty years. For nearly twenty of those years, Jax had spent every free moment here. Much had changed since he and his best friend, Matt Stewart, had sailed for France in June 1918. But some things were returning to normal. Or soon would. At least, that was Jax's hope.

Despite fatigue and stiffness, he covered the distance between auto and building in long strides and took the porch steps two at a time. Bella was probably up, since she got breakfast going early. Usually, she was outside having a cup of coffee by this time. As he stared at the closed front door, Jax shifted from one foot to the other. No activity was apparent. Perhaps, she was in the kitchen. If so, he ought to go to the back door.

"Hastings. What are you doing here?"

Jax turned to see Griff Biggins heading his way. An automatic frown formed on Jax's face. He hadn't liked the golf pro when they'd met the previous summer, and he didn't like him now. Besides, what was the man doing up at dawn? Golfers wouldn't be out for at least an hour, probably longer. Was he making a habit of having morning coffee with Bella? Jax hoped not. With effort, he gathered his defenses. "I have some time off, and I wanted to spend it at home."

A grin lit the other man's face. "I hope you have at least three days. Otherwise, you're going to miss Bella. Even worse, she'll miss you."

For several moments, Jax tried to make sense of the words. How was he missing Bella? Why should she miss him? Lack of sleep slowed his mental processes, so he posed a question. "What do you mean?"

As Biggins scanned Jax's face, his amusement disappeared. "Bella and Ida went to a reunion of their college girlfriends. They left day before yesterday and won't be back until Monday evening. They're up at Winnabee Island. One of their friend's family owns a fancy summer home there."

"Florence Remington."

"That's the name," Biggins said. "You know her?"

"I probably know most of them, since Matt and I went to events at Bella's college a few times." More than a few, and Jax remembered each one because he'd been her escort. He smiled at the memories and at the hope of making more.

Biggins nodded. "Ida told me about you squiring Bella to some social occasions at their school."

The comment made Jax look more closely at the other man. He'd worried about Biggins being with Bella every day, but the other man didn't look or sound jealous. "Yep, I did."

Moments of silence ensued before Biggins spoke again. "I came over to make coffee. Mrs. Rogers will be out in a while since she's working more hours while Ida and Bella are away, but I promised to get the pot going." He opened the door. "Come on in."

The golf pro was much friendlier than usual, so Jax followed him inside. When they got to the kitchen, he sat down at the big table. Once both men had cups of coffee, Jax cleared his throat. "I'd like to talk with Bella. Does the Remington place have a telephone?"

Biggins grinned. "Ida said it did. If you call, Bella will most likely want to come right home."

The comment caught Jax off-guard. He held the cup with both hands and struggled to organize his thoughts. Finally, he asked, "Do you really think so?"

"I know so. Ida says Bella rereads your notes, few as they've been, repeatedly."

Jax's heart stutter-stepped. His missives were hardly fascinating enough for one reading, let alone multiple reviews. "I'm surprised Ida shares so many of Bella's thoughts with you." Jax was stunned that Biggins repeated them. What had gone on in his absence?

A shrug moved Biggins' shoulders. "Ida and I play golf most evenings, and we've stepped out a few times. Quite a few, actually. Occasionally, we convince Bella to come with us. Most often, she doesn't want to tagalong. Her assessment. Neither of us mind." He grinned again.

As Jax stared at the other man, he struggled to absorb the words. "You're courting Ida."

Low laughter rumbled out of Biggins. "I am. Does that surprise you? She's a beautiful woman, smart and funny, too. I'm a few years older, but not all that many."

"It's not that," Jax said.

The golf pro's amusement disappeared. "You knew her fiancé. Do you think she's still wearing the willow for him?"

Since the other man seemed anxious, Jax was honest. "She was heartbroken when Alan died, of course, but it's been almost three years. Although she may never forget him, she wouldn't step out with you if she wasn't ready to move on."

"He died a hero, and I couldn't serve." Biggins stared into his cup. "I was scheduled to report when I caught the Spanish flu. I was pretty sick, got pneumonia, and wasn't completely better until a week before the Armistice. Many people don't understand the circumstances, and I rarely explain them."

For the first time, Jax felt congenial toward Biggins. "No reason to explain, and I'm sure Ida doesn't think less of you for not being in the trenches. Bella wouldn't, either."

Biggins met Jax's gaze for a long moment. "What about you?"

Did the other man care about his opinion? If so, Jax wanted to be fair. "It doesn't matter. The only thing of importance to me is that you don't hurt Ida."

Again, Biggins hesitated before responding. "She's told me about her father's financial losses and about Brewster dying. She said Cecil Laheene courted her for a short time, and I already heard about him from talking with you and Bella when you were investigating his death. Ida has been through a lot in the past few years. I won't add to it." He traced the rim of his cup with one forefinger. "I love her, although I haven't told her yet."

The rueful expression on the other man's face and his ragged admission made Jax smile. "Don't wait too long."

A chuckle left Biggins. "I could say the same to you. It's been over two months since you've been home."

Heat rose in Jax's cheeks, but he held the other man's gaze. "Not because I wanted to be away so long." He drummed his fingers on the table. He hadn't wanted to be away at all. But he owed Mick O'Donnelly. "This is the first chance I've had to get back. I didn't expect Bella to be gone, since the resort is usually busy in mid-June." And she hadn't mentioned the trip in her notes to him.

"It's the only time all six could get together. Like I said, Mrs. Rogers is working additional hours and Mac is pitching in, which I think he enjoys." Griff took a long swallow of coffee. "Besides, the girls will only be away for a few days."

A few days when he'd be here. Jax didn't want to spoil Bella's reunion, but he yearned to see her. Despite feeling more amiable toward the other man, Jax wouldn't spill his guts out to someone he barely knew, so he tried for a benign topic. "It looked like you had rain last night. I drove through a little, coming through the state."

If the sudden change in conversation surprised the golf pro, he didn't let it show. "We had thunderstorms with heavy rain. It was bad enough that I'm not sure we'll get many players this morning. Still looks like more precipitation could be coming."

"I wonder how it was on the lakeshore and islands."

"I grew up in northeastern Pennsylvania, so you have more insight into lake storms than I do."

"A little more maybe, since my mother grew up in that area. Sometimes, they get storms we don't feel much here. Ten miles can make a big difference, and Winnabee is a few more miles north of the shore. It's an isolated island. If a gale hit, they may be without electricity and telephone. Mother said that happens often on the lake islands." He paused for a moment before going back to his earlier concern. "I'd still like to call the Remington home."

"The local operator should be able to connect you." Biggins glanced toward the window over the sink. "It's barely dawn."

"Bella is an early riser. I'll wait to call, though. They probably sat up late talking, so she may sleep in. They did that during their college days. I'll try in an hour."

"All right," Griff said. "The temperature's dropped after last night's rain and the course has to be wet, but we have guests in the cottages. Some may play. Hard to say. I'll run over to the shop and come back around eight-thirty. By then, one of our employees will be there."

"I'll stay here," Jax replied.

"Mac should be down shortly," Biggins said, before taking his leave.

The observation was correct since the old pro entered the kitchen about ten minutes after Biggins left.

A wide smile creased his ruddy face. "Lad, tis a great surprise to see ye."

Jax stood and shook the other man's hand. "Biggins made coffee. Let me get you a cup." After he performed the task, Jax joined Mac at the table.

"Be ye home for good?" the older man asked.

"I'm afraid not. I got a few days off, but I have to be back Tuesday morning."

A frown replaced Mac's smile. "The lass twill not be home until Monday night."

"Biggins told me. It's a long drive to Philadelphia, so I may have to leave before she's back."

"Tis sorry the lass will be to miss ye." Mac took a swallow of coffee. "A dreadful storm passed through here last night. Tis likely to have been worse on the lakeshore and islands. If so, she may come home." The grin was back in place.

Mac's good humor didn't resonate with Jax, who remained anxious over possible storm damage on the lake. Since he didn't want to worry the older man, Jax kept his demeanor and response casual. "Maybe so." When Mac spoke again, Jax realized he needn't keep his own counsel.

"The islands dinna be a good place during a severe storm. Tis true everywhere. I grew up on an isolated peninsula, and storms twere harsh." A twinkle returned to his gray eyes. "That be why my brogue tis not typical Scots, nay anything else. We be far from others."

Jax grinned. "It's unique. As far as weather, my mother's home was near the lake, and she often talked about severe storms—summer and winter."

"I remember ye mum, and tis true they get some wicked weather. Maybe we should call the lass and see how they fared."

"Biggins and I discussed the same idea, but we wanted to wait, since it's so early. We'll call when he comes back."

Mac nodded, and the two of them discussed more casual concerns until the other golf pro returned.

After he and Mac moved to the chairs by the lobby fireplace, Jax got a blaze going. When Biggins later came in, he immediately headed their way.

"The temperature is still dropping and there's a light mist." Griff seated himself in one of the chairs by the fireplace.

"I wonder how it is over on Winnabee Island," Jax said.

A grin curved the pro's lips. "I've been wondering, too. Maybe we should call now and see how the girls are faring. They ought to be up."

"Do you mind if I use the telephone, Mac?" Jax was already on his feet before the question was out.

"Nay, lad. See how they be," the older man replied.

Jax hurried to the desk. As was common with a long-distance call, he had to wait for the operator to ring back. Jax shifted from one foot to the other while he did. When he spoke with the woman again, he felt more frustrated than ever. He returned to his chair and sat down.

"You don't look happy. Didn't the call go through?" Biggins asked.

Jax leaned back and thrust his legs out in front of him. "The call didn't get through to Burnley Cove, let alone the island. Our local operator connected with someone just south of the Cove. The woman said damage is severe all along the lake shore, and she thinks the islands were probably hard hit. Chances are both electricity and telephone service are out on Winnabee and other islands. Maybe along the coast, too."

Biggins' brow creased. "You said it's about ten miles out in the lake. Right?"

"About that."

Worry lined Mac's face. "Will our operator call with news? If there be any."

"When our local operator couldn't reach anyone up there, I asked her to try connecting with the Burnley Cove constable when she can get a call through. She'll keep trying. I said we'd like to reach the Remington place or the constable. I want to talk to Bella." Anxiety joined with fatigue to lower Jax's spirits. He'd come home to see her. Now, he might have to leave before she got back, and he didn't like thinking of her on an isolated island with no way to get assistance, if needed. How could he go back to Philadelphia if they didn't get word about the women? His apprehension was hard to throttle, but he didn't want to cause additional concern for Mac, so he fought to maintain a placid demeanor. "I'm sure the house is sound, which is important. Even though it'll be inconvenient to be without telephone or electricity, the girls should be comfortable."

"I doubt if we'll have any golfers, but one of the twins is in the shop." Griff said. "I'd like to stay here and wait for a return call."

"Good idea." Mac got to his feet. "I called Mrs. Rogers earlier and said we would nay need her today due to the weather. I'll fix a bite to eat."

Once the old pro was out of earshot, Griff turned his attention to Jax. "You look even more worried now."

A half shrug lifted Jax's shoulder. "I am, but I don't want to alarm Mac. Maybe I'm worried for no good reason, but I keep remembering my mom's stories about some terrible storms on the lake islands and shore." Jax's hands tightened into twin fists. "Mac and Bella are close, and he's lost so many people already. His wife back in Scotland. Then, Bella's Grampa Stew died young. Her Gramma Stewart passed a few years later. And you know about her parents and brother. All of them were family to Mac."

"Bella is, too. I see every day how close the two of them are. I'm anxious, too. About Bella and Ida." Griff shifted restlessly in his chair.

Jax nodded. "I haven't been to the Remingtons' summer home, but Bella was years ago. Back during her college days. The only way to get there is by water." Possibilities and problems filled his thoughts. "I hope the boat was secured, and the dock wasn't damaged. Do you know how many friends went and how much staff is there?"

"Six friends," Biggins replied. "Florence told Ida there's a skeleton staff right now—a cook-housekeeper, a butler, and one maid. There's a handyman, too. He cares for the property and handles the boat."

Jax folded his arms across his chest. "Years back, Bella said there are only a few houses on the island."

"They told me the same thing. As far as getting there, the handyman picked them up, by boat, on Burnley Cove on Thursday afternoon. Ida called that night to say they'd arrived safely."

Jax folded his arms across his chest. "If he regularly deals with the boat, he likely got it out of the water before the storm hit. A good judge of weather would. If not, their return might be delayed even longer." The possibility further sunk his spirits.

Something akin to sympathy darkened Biggins' gaze. "I hope that's not the case."

"As do I," Jax said. But he couldn't shake his uneasiness. An isolated island wasn't a good location during a storm, and four servants weren't much help.

"If we don't get a call, we can try again in an hour or two. Since Jenny and Richard Jenkins are staying at your house, why don't you get settled here? The family suite on this floor is empty. I'm sure Bella would offer it to you, and Mac would agree."

The golf pro's certainty and hospitality kept Jax from disagreeing. "I'll grab my bag out of the Chummy and clean up. Will you stay close to the telephone, just in case?"

"Of course."

Jax hurried to get settled. When he returned to the lobby, Biggins was standing by the front desk. "Any news?" The other man's troubled expression didn't surprise Jax, but it bothered him. He'd like some reassurance that his own misgivings were misplaced.

"The operator called back. She was able to speak with an operator up there and found out few people are on the island. Most of the ten houses are owned by elderly folks who seldom go out anymore. She says only one home is occupied all season. The owner also has a

83

limited staff." Griff braced himself against the desk. "Our operator also said the constable from Burnley Cove, which is evidently the nearest town, will call when he can. A lot of telephone service is out, and many homes in his bailiwick were damaged. Rain is still falling, and there are gusty winds. Not a pleasant situation."

Jax's pulse pounded. "Did the operator have any idea about how the island fared? Did she say when the constable is calling us?"

"I don't know," Griff replied. "And I don't know how long before he'll call, either." He gestured to a chair. "You look exhausted. Sit down and try to relax."

Refuting the observation was impossible but, although Jax took a chair by the lobby's fireplace, relaxing proved to be impossible. Griff, who sat across from him, looked equally edgy. Although the pair talked about the resort, they both looked at the silent telephone periodically. Jax's mind remained on Bella, and he was sure Griff was equally preoccupied with thoughts of Ida.

Chapter Five

♥

At Ballantyne, not much changed over the next few hours. Steady drizzle fell and temperatures dropped. Griff and Jax took turns feeding the fire, but the chill never left Jax.

When Mac returned later to say food was ready, the two younger men joined him in the kitchen. All three men, and the twins who helped around the resort and lived in a suite at the back of the inn, chatted. The two boys peppered Jax with questions about his work with the Prohibition Bureau. He provided answers, as much as possible, but his mind remained on Bella.

After the twins left, Jax told Mac about the Burnley Cove constable. "The local operator will put him right through when he calls."

Mac nodded. "I hope twill be soon, but the man likely be busy if there's damage on the peninsula."

"I'm sure he is." Jax laid down his half-eaten sandwich. "If he doesn't call in the next few hours, I may drive up there. The storm was terrible, much worse than here. If there's a lot of damage on the island, the girls may come back sooner than planned. I could save them needing to take the train home."

"Tis doubtful they'll be able to cross the lake right now. When we get a bit of wind, they get a lot on the islands. At least, tis what I've heard over the years," Mac said. "I have nay been out on the lake. Too busy here during the season."

Before Jax replied, the telephone chimed. "I'll get it." He rushed to the lobby and snatched up the receiver. "Ballantyne Inn." When the voice on the other end identified himself as Constable Warren Amberly, Jax gripped the earpiece tighter and provided his own name and title. "Agent Jax Hastings, sir. Do you have news about the storm damage on Winnabee?"

He remained silent as the man quickly provided details, disturbing details. As he listened to the other lawman, Jax felt a growing sense of panic. Two of the man's phrases stood out. *Dead woman. Bad booze.* When the man finished talking, Jax swallowed hard over the lump of fear choking him. "I see. You don't know any more about the death. An identity or a description." Jax spoke in a low murmur so his voice wouldn't carry to the other two men. They'd need to know, but he wanted to break the news gently.

"I'm afraid not. The housekeeper is up in years. It wouldn't be a surprise if she was the one who passed," the constable said.

Jax inhaled and exhaled twice to gain composure. "I see."

"Since you're a Prohibition agent, there's one other important detail," Amberly said. "I've suspected bootlegging on Winnabee for a while, and the mention of bad booze disturbs me. Not that it can't be gotten a lot of places."

The revelation undid Jax's efforts to be calm. "There's bootlegging out there?" Some Lake Erie islands were used by rumrunners. Were Bella and Ida on one of them?

The idea made his insides knot. They could be in a more perilous situation than he'd first believed.

The constable's reply was terse and tense. "I believe that's likely."

Sweat dampened Jax's palms as he clung to the telephone. "I'd like to drive up, not to infringe on your territory, but because I'm friends with two of the young women at the reunion. If one of them is the..." While he'd been on the telephone, both Mac and Griff came to stand across the counter from him. Jax didn't want them to overhear the news, so he carefully shaped his words. "I could come yet today."

Again, the other man spoke in detail. At the end of the constable's monologue, Jax thanked him and hung up. For a moment, he bowed his head and struggled with the rising tide of panic inside him.

"What did he say?" Griff asked, his face tight with tension.

"Ye look troubled, lad." Mac's apprehension was obvious.

Jax needed to reveal Amberly's revelations. Disturbing revelations. With fatigue and fear threatening to overwhelm him, Jax gestured toward the fireplace. "Let's sit down." When they were all settled, Jax cleared his throat. "That was the Burnley Cove constable," he began, even though the other two men must realize the identity of the caller. "The operator up there got a call from the Remingtons' place earlier today. The line crackled badly, so making out the words was hard, but she relayed what she thought was said to the constable." He was repeating information gleaned from their own operator to soften the coming blow. "She thought the caller said a woman is dead."

All color drained from Mac's ruddy face. "Did she know who it tis or what happened?"

"No. She only got that phrase and another troubling one: *bad booze.* After the line went dead, the operator tried to call back with no luck. The telephone at the constable's office was out until a short time ago, but the operator sent word to him right away. Evidently, she didn't want to share all details with another operator. The constable says the telephones on the island go out frequently, even without big storms. The same is true with the electricity. As far as the Cove, a lot of docks and boats were damaged. Homes, too. He isn't sure how soon he or his deputies will get to Winnabee." Jax had kept his anxiety tamped down while talking to the man. Now, it threatened to surge out of control.

Mac went pale beneath his tan. "There is nay anyone who can check on the island?"

Griff ran one hand over his face. "Is the man at all concerned?"

A half-shrug lifted one of Jax's shoulders. "It's a private island, so not in the constable's jurisdiction. Or anyone else's bailiwick, either. He's gone out, or sent someone, after other storms, and he will get to the island as soon as it's safe to be on the lake. He promised that much." Jax looked at Mac. "You're right about the winds being worse up there. The constable said the water is choppy with a lot of white caps. When he goes, he'll get a doctor to go along."

"Good," Mac murmured, but his lined face remained pale and drawn. "'Tis a worry that a woman died."

"True." Biggins pressed his hands together, as if fighting for control.

"The constable mentioned the housekeeper is an older lady. Maybe something happened to her." But other possibilities haunted him. With no electricity, anyone could tumble downstairs in the dark. Or the high winds could have sent a tree crashing into the house. But what about the *bad booze*? Before Prohibition,

Jax had seen Bella drink on special occasions. So had he. Surely, she wouldn't be imbibing now, especially if bootlegged liquor was the drink of choice. The phrase *bad booze* shook him to the core because *bad* most likely meant *tainted.* In one brief note to Bella, he'd mentioned confiscating hooch poisoned with methanol. Surely, she'd remember and not drink the stuff herself. Or maybe she'd thought the liquor was safe. Drinking alcohol wasn't illegal, but he hoped Bella hadn't taken chances. Mac's worried expression made Jax offer additional reassurance. "That's probably what happened. Or the operator might have misunderstood whoever called. After all, the connection was poor." Jax wanted to ease Mac's mind. Unfortunately, it didn't ease his.

"Now that we have some details, maybe we should drive up yet today. I heard you ask the constable about doing that," Griff said.

"He'd rather we wait until tomorrow. Crossing the lake now would be dangerous, and he made it clear he doesn't support us doing so." Although Jax wanted to leave immediately, he knew the constable was right. Venturing out on the water with gale conditions would be foolish, not to mention that they needed a watercraft. "We may have trouble getting a boat due to the damage up there, but tomorrow, we can try."

Griff nodded before turning to Mac. "You're sure you can get along without me in the morning? I'd like to go, too."

"Of course. I'd be relieved to have ye two lads check on the lasses." The old pro got to his feet. "I think I'll rest now." Then, his back bowed, he shuffled away.

With one hand, Jax massaged his forehead. A headache was forming since lack of sleep and anxiety for Bella were taking a toll. "I didn't want to say anything in front of Mac, but the constable suspects bootlegging on Winnabee. He didn't offer details, but it wouldn't surprise me. Two accomplices in the Crabtree case last spring were involved with rumrunning, and they used a lake island. Winnabee is well situated for that type of operation."

For several moments, Griff stared into the fireplace. When he looked back at Jax, apprehension shadowed his expression. "I've overheard a few golfers talk about bootlegging. Bella told me she has, too. In fact, several men discussed bringing a few foursomes and renting cottages for a long weekend. Two of them had a source of booze on the lakeshore, so they figured on picking up liquor on their way here. At least, that's what she caught."

Fresh alarm stabbed Jax. So did a sliver of jealousy. Bella had shared the information with Griff, not him. Of course, he'd been hundreds of miles away. "Did she tell Mac?"

Griff shook his head. "No. She didn't want to upset him. She told me, so I'd be careful about booking large groups. Bella does most of that, but sometimes golfers talk to me, and I make the arrangements for them."

"How did she handle the situation?" Jax asked.

"She was in the little pantry off the dining room, so they were unaware of her presence. When they asked if they could reserve three cottages for a long weekend sometime this summer, Bella said we were fully booked up, which is true. Luckily."

Relief slackened Jax's muscles. "Good."

"I suppose they figured Ballantyne would be a nice, out-of-the-way place."

"Probably."

"You still look worried."

Jax braced his elbows on his knees and clasped his hands between them. "I don't like people wanting to use Ballantyne for parties with booze. That could attract the wrong clientele." It could draw gangsters, an idea that deeply disturbed him.

"I agree. We definitely don't want problems here, and I'll help Bella any way I can."

The strength and certainty in Biggins' voice gave Jax some peace, but he'd feel better when he returned to Moreley for good. Then, he'd be able to assist and protect her. "Thanks. Before I leave, I'll speak with Richard." Jax paused before he voiced additional concerns. "I admit I'm worried about the possibility of bootlegging on Winnabee. With so few houses and only one other place being occupied right now, it's ideal for an operation. The mention of *bad booze* in the telephone call keeps weighing on my mind. What if someone died from poisoned liquor?" What if Bella had died? Icy dread sent a shiver through him.

"I suppose it's possible," Griff said, "but is it likely?"

For several moments, Jax mulled over the idea. "Probably not. Working with the Prohibition Bureau must make me suspicious." He slumped back in the chair.

"You need some rest. There's nothing we can do right now, so why don't you take a nap? In the morning, no matter what the constable says, we'll head north."

On Winnabee, the rain finally subsided around four o'clock, but high winds continued. With little to do, the friends chatted and played cards. Everyone avoided additional references to Syl or booze. While Bella, like the rest of the group, worked hard to be pleasant and calm, her dead friend never left her thoughts.

When Stricket announced a light supper was ready, the young women went to the dining room. The lake was now visible through the mullioned windows, and so was more destruction. At least a dozen trees were down and smaller branches littered the ground farther from the house. The path they'd taken to the dock was cluttered with debris. As Bella gazed out, she felt a fresh wave of anxiety wash over her. How would they get back to the coast? When could they get back?

"The storm did tremendous damage. Even after the wind dies down, it looks like we can't get to the dock easily, and how will we get back to shore with the boat loose?" Ida echoed Bella's worries.

"We might have to rely on that cad Lauger, which I hate to do," Blanche added when she joined the pair at the windows.

"Me, either," Bella said. Avoiding the neighbor and his business partner seemed best, but how would they get off the island? If only, the constable would come.

Florence, who had gone to the kitchen to speak with her staff, reappeared. "Let's eat before the soup gets cold."

When Bella glanced at their hostess, she felt another trickle of uneasiness. Florence seemed remote and stiff. Was she struggling to hide her grief and shock over Sylvia's death? Or could she be responsible? As the five women took their places at the table, Bella looked around the group. The forced pleasantries of the afternoon had ebbed, and all of them appeared tense.

Once everyone had a bowl of the tomato bisque, Bella asked Florence about one issue circling through her mind. "The lake is still very rough, but it will surely calm down by morning. We need to alert someone on the mainland about the boat getting loose, if telephone service is restored."

Florence frowned. "The phone may be out for days."

"You mean we're stuck out here for an endless time?" Lina's voice held a note of alarm.

"Not permanently." Florence, once again, sounded snippy and dismissive.

"Of course not, but for how long?" Blanche asked. "We can't be here with Sylvia upstairs for days and days."

"She isn't up there any longer," Florence said. "I had Stricket and Monica move her to the cellar."

A hush fell over the group while, inwardly, Bella cringed. "Why there, of all places?"

"Yes, why?" Blanche echoed Bella's question.

With a sigh, Florence looked around the table before settling her attention on Bella. "Syl is beyond caring about her surroundings. Besides, it's only temporary, and I had Mrs. Longley and Monica wrap her in sheets and a blanket."

The last comment provided some solace, but Bella felt queasy. When she glanced at Ida and Blanche, Bella figured they felt much the same. Troubling thoughts assailed Bella. Putting their friend in a dank and dirty cellar seemed disrespectful, not to mention the constable—when he finally came—would want to see Syl as they'd found her. Since it was too late for that, Bella withheld criticism. She couldn't shake the impression Florence knew more about bootlegging than she'd admitted. She'd been anxious to make up reasons for Syl's death, and she still seemed impassive, but so did Lina. The rest of the meal passed quickly and quietly. Only brief bits of conversation took place, while long periods of silence ensued. Once they all finished, Bella folded her napkin and laid it on the table. "Since we got so little sleep last night, I'm going to turn in early."

"I'll come, too," Ida immediately agreed.

Blanche and Lina followed suit. Although Florence looked as if she was sucking on a lemon, she nodded. "If any of you need something, simply use the bell pull. Monica will come up as long as it's before nine o'clock."

The group dispersed. Lina and Blanche bid good evening to Bella and Ida on the upstairs landing and headed to their rooms. Bella and Ida were about to do the same when Monica, carrying an armful of linens, emerged from the door to the backstairs.

As soon as Bella saw the maid, she grasped Ida's arm. "I'd like to speak with Monica," she whispered.

A look of confusion blanketed her friend's face. "Why?"

"I'm wondering what she knows about the goings-on around here."

"What makes you think she'll tell us anything? She seems timid and meek, not that we've seen much of her."

"It can't hurt to try." Bella pulled her friend along.

As soon as Monica saw them, she bobbed her head. "Evening, misses."

"Monica, do you have a few moments?" Bella asked before the young girl passed by.

The maid paused. "Do you need something, miss?"

"Just information." Because Monica looked tense and ashen, Bella offered a reassuring smile. "Perhaps we could step into our room."

Monica looked up and down the corridor before nodding. Bella let the girl precede them and pulled her friend along. Once inside their chamber, she shut the door.

"Let's sit down," Bella said. She gestured to the group of chairs in front of the fireplace. When Monica hesitated, Bella went on. "It'd be more comfortable."

"Yes, miss." Monica's blue gaze went from Bella to Ida. With one hand, she brushed a loose lock of dark hair from her suddenly flushed face.

The maid perched on a chair while the two friends chose the ones across from her. Bella thought the girl looked as if she might flee, so she offered more reassurance. "There's nothing to worry about. I'm sure you already heard about Miss Sawyer."

"I did. Mrs. Longley and I tended to her before Mr. Stricket and I took her away. Wasn't easy to do either. I seen her room." The maid wrinkled her freckled nose as if she could still smell the stench of vomit. "Had to clean the mess up. Her and the room."

"I'm sorry you had to deal with it," Ida said.

Monica clasped her hands in her lap. "Weren't nice."

The mental images evoked by the maid's words and expression made Bella cringe. Poor Syl. Retching so much had to be miserable. After clearing her throat, Bella spoke again. "I'm sure it wasn't, but we didn't want to discuss that. We wondered if you knew anything about the liquor cabinet in the house. The decanters are empty, and I didn't see any bottles." She didn't want to reveal Florence's assertion that her parents had gotten rid of all alcohol. If that had actually happened, Monica would surely know.

The maid's gaze shifted downward. "The mister and missus didn't want no hooch around no more. Not after the law here changed in '19. Mr. Eyelers were supposed to get rid of the stuff."

"Did Mr. Eyelers do that?" Bella asked. When a wedge of silence ensued, she glanced at Ida.

Another moment passed before Ida spoke. "We won't tell anyone what you say."

Monica's eyes, huge in her pale face, went from one woman to the other as she wrung her hands. "I can't lose this job. I got no family and no place to go."

"Neither Ida nor I will say anything to get you in trouble," Bella assured her.

"But what if someone finds out?" Panic underscored Monica's question.

The girl clearly had troubling information, so Bella considered how to proceed. In all good conscience, she couldn't put Monica in peril without offering help. "If they do, and you're fired, we could use a maid at Ballantyne. It's a resort..."

Monica broke in. "I heard of it, miss. Could I really work for you?"

A smile touched Bella's lips. "The extra help would be welcome, since we've been very busy this summer."

"Even if nobody finds out what I tell you?" Monica asked.

"You don't want to stay here?" Bella exchanged a long look with Ida, who also seemed at sea. Why did the maid want to leave so badly?

"No, miss. I don't much enjoy being stuck on an island away from other folks." She chewed on her lower lip. "Mr. Stricket don't drink and neither do Mrs. Longley, but Eyelers takes more than one tipple whenever he can. He used to spend all his free time at a bar over on the mainland. Always come back drunk as a skunk, if the Remingtons wasn't around."

"Wasn't he reprimanded by Stricket?" Ida asked.

"Reprimanded?" Monica's confusion was obvious.

Bella tried a simpler word. "Didn't Mr. Stricket scold him?"

Monica shook her head. "Not that I know, miss. Mr. Stricket naps a lot. Not when folks is here, but he snoozes often otherwise. He's getting on in years, so I can't fault him. He makes sure the house and the grounds look nice, especially when the mister and missus come. And for miss and her company. Mr. Stricket wants Eyelers to be sober as a judge when he runs the boat."

"I see." Had Eyelers kept liquor for himself? Or was he selling the stuff? Bella still wasn't sure, and the uncertainty was troubling. "What happened to the Remingtons' liquor?" Would Monica give the same story as Florence?

A sharp breath left the maid. "Mr. Eyelers carried it off and stowed it in his hidey-hole," Monica replied.

Although she'd suspected bootlegging on the island, the answer surprised Bella. "Where is his hiding place?"

Once again, Monica clasped and re-clasped her hands. "The garden shed has a trap door. There's a dugout below. Plenty of room for booze and for anyone who tattles on him."

Dismay hit Bella hard. "Has Eyelers threatened you?"

The maid's breath came in gasps and, when she responded, Monica sounded breathless. "He did, miss. That's why I were scared to tell anything."

"Has he threatened Mr. Stricket or Mrs. Longley?" Ida asked.

"Maybe," the maid replied. "Mrs. Longley said we both need to hush up about whatever we see, especially at night. But she weren't trying to scare me cuz she sounded scared herself."

The women hadn't had much contact with the housekeeper, but Bella could understand Mrs. Longley's fear since Eyelers had likely threatened her with going to the hidey-hole, too. As for Stricket, he was nearing eighty, so his fatigue wasn't surprising. His habit of going to bed early made it unlikely the man had been in the hallway the night of the storm, which meant the figure must have been Eyelers? Had the man taken liquor to Syl? Bella wished she knew. Stricket could have been looking out for them. Eyelers, probably not. "Have you told Florence about Eyelers? Ida and I would go with you."

Monica's eyes widened. "No, miss, no."

Her dread was palpable. When Bella looked at Ida, her friend shrugged and frowned. "Why not?" Bella asked, not sure if she wanted an honest answer. The girl's reaction troubled her.

The little maid clasped her hands in her lap and stared down at them. "I shouldn't say." Her voice was a whisper.

Bella's anxiety increased. When she looked at Ida, she saw similar apprehension. "Neither of us will tell her what you say. Or tell Mr. Stricket or even Mrs. Longley."

"We won't pass anything on," Ida agreed.

Monica looked from one to the other. "Will you tell anyone else? Like Mr. Lauger or his friend? They was here yesterday. More than once."

Bella mulled over the comment. Monica hadn't been at the dock when the two men were. Had she been looking out a window? The dock was a distance from the house, so recognizing particular figures would be difficult unless she knew them well. "When have you seen them, besides at dinner?"

The girl shifted restlessly in the chair. "Last evening, they come to the garden and talked with Mr. Eyelers for a bit. Weren't too long after you ladies came upstairs. I were in the kitchen but hurried away from the window right off, so they wouldn't notice me."

"I see." Bella kept her voice calm, but her heart raced with dread. She'd earlier discussed her suspicions with Ida, who concurred. Eyelers, Lauger, and Darre bootlegging was one concern. Syl getting bad booze from one of them was another. The possibility of intentional poisoning was the worst. Those suspicions increased in validity as they learned more. "They must not have gone right to the Lauger house when they left here."

"Evidently not," Ida put in.

"Do the two of them come over often?" Bella asked.

Monica nodded. "Mr. Lauger usually comes to see Mr. Eyelers before one of his parties. We always know about them cuz lots of boats dock over there, and his place is all lit up overnight. Sometimes, a few boats hook up at our pier, too."

"Did you see if Eyelers went to the garden shed with Darre and Lauger?" If the group knew about Bella's relationship with Jax, and she feared they did, they might want to move the supplies right away.

"Not yesterday," Monica murmured, "but I seen them go in there before. More than once."

Bella needed to proceed with caution. Upsetting the girl wouldn't help, but she wanted to find out more. Once telephone service was restored, she'd call the constable and ask him to contact the nearest Prohibition office. That was probably in Toledo, which was more than an hour away. Would they come based on what Bella now knew? She hoped so. She wanted justice for her friend, and she wanted to keep others from suffering the same fate. Shutting down a rumrunning ring would be icing on the cake. "Does Florence ever speak with them when she's here?"

Monica raised her interlaced fingers to her lips. "A few times last summer and this spring, too. Both Mr. Lauger and Mr. Darre come over to see her."

"What about when Miss Sawyer visited? Did she speak with all the men, too?" Ida posed the question.

"She talks to Mr. Eyelers whenever she comes out to the island," Monica replied. Her brow furrowed. "Miss Sawyer goes off with him some, too. Over near the garden shed. I seen her there on Thursday morning when she first got here."

The observation solidified Bella's suspicion. "Did you see her go inside the shed?"

"Yes, miss. Then, I hurried off."

Bella and Ida exchanged a long glance.

"From what we heard, Florence and Sylvia often attend Mr. Lauger's parties," Ida said.

"They do. I don't think they've missed none in the past year. He has them every month from May through October." Monica wrung her hands as she spoke. "I don't know nothing more about them events. Mrs. Longley always says for me to stay in my room when Miss Florence and Miss Sylvia are getting gussied up to go over. They help each other dress, which is good cuz I got no skill at such things. Mrs. Longley lays low, too."

"What about Mr. Stricket?" Ida asked.

"He turns in early, like usual," the maid said.

Bella nodded. "And Eyelers? You said he always talks with Lauger before a party. Does he go over there, too?"

"Yes, miss. Any nights he's here, he gets drunk as a skunk in his room. Starts hitting the bottle after Mr. Stricket goes to bed. Mrs. Longley told him about breaking the law once and how Mr. Remington would get mad if he knew. Eyelers said to keep her mouth shut if she knowed what was good for her." A shiver rippled through Monica. "He's a mean man sometimes."

"Mrs. Longley was right to advise you about staying away from him, especially when he meets Lauger and Darre." Bella offered what she hoped was a reassuring smile. If possible, she'd have Monica leave when they did.

The maid nodded. "I should go. I don't want no one missing me."

Since Bella didn't want the girl to get in trouble, she agreed. "Of course," she said, but Bella had one additional question of importance. "Where is Mr. Eyelers now?"

"He left with Lauger and Darre last night before the storm. Haven't seen him since, but he don't always come back when he heads out in the evening. With trees down, it'll be hard getting here from over there. Hope he'll be gone 'til tomorrow at least." Monica's last statement rang with relief.

"Are you sure Eyelers didn't come back last night?"

"Yes, miss. He's not quiet coming in and out. He goes right by my door and wakes me by clattering around," Monica replied.

Bella wanted to get Ida's opinion as soon as the maid left. Something—some *things*—wasn't right. "How much liquor was in the Remingtons' supply? Enough for Eyelers to keep selling it over a long period?"

The girl looked from Bella to Ida and back. "When he were carrying them bottles out, he told me to scat. It took him a long while to tote it all away, though." When she put both hands to her face, they trembled.

"If there's something else important, please tell us," Bella said.

Monica focused on Bella. "I passed by the parlor that first night and heard you saying your beau is a lawman."

Color surged into Bella's cheeks. No one had used the word *beau*, but she didn't dispute the girl's observation. "We both have a friend who is a federal Prohibition agent." Although a grin curved Ida's lips, she said nothing. Bella glanced back at Monica.

"You planning to tell him all about Eyelers and Mr. Lauger and Mr. Darre?" the maid asked.

The question revealed almost as much as some of Monica's statements had. Did the girl believe there was something for an agent to investigate? So far, the evidence was sketchy. Bella planned to pass it on, but more details would help. "If Mr. Eyelers is selling alcohol, he's breaking the law."

"Yes, miss." The reply was solemn and succinct. "He must be, since he told Mrs. Longley to hush up or else. Maybe Mr. Lauger and Mr. Darre are, too. I don't ask no questions, but there are strange happenings out here nowadays. It weren't like that when I first took the job a couple years back. Mr. and Mrs. Remington are good folks. So was Mr. Lauger's grandparents. At first, I got sent over with apples from our trees in the fall. Got acquainted with some over there. The help were nice, but they're gone and new folks come. All men, as far as I can tell." She released a harsh breath. "I know about rumrunners, miss. I figure they do that and maybe more."

The additional information only increased Bella's dread and certainty. Her suspicions had not been amiss. "What else do you think they're doing?"

Monica licked her lips. "One time last summer, I heard talk about making the liquor go farther, so they'd have more to sell. It were Mr. Eyelers and Mr. Lauger. Not sure how they'd do it."

The information sent Bella's heart plummeting. She knew how they could do it, and she knew how dangerous that could be. "Thank you for telling us." Although the girl still seemed anxious, she was providing more bits and pieces as they talked.

"Will you tell your beau? Can he do something about them? I still want to leave here, but Mr. Stricket and Mrs. Longley will most likely stay on."

"He's in Philadelphia, but I'll get word to him." But what could Jax do without more details? How could she get them? Bella set that question aside and offered relief to the girl. "The operator will tell the local constable about Miss Sawyer, so he'll be out as soon as he can." Maybe the man would get help from Toledo right away.

Monica's eyes went wide again. "He hasn't done nothing yet about doings out here."

"Do you think he's aware of bootlegging going on?" Ida asked.

Monica shrugged. "He don't never come out. This here's a private island, so he's got no real say-so, but wouldn't lawmen like your beau?"

Bella sidestepped a direct answer. "He should come out about Miss Sawyer's death. If he suspects other wrongdoing, he can pass the word along to the Prohibition Bureau. That would be faster than me sending a note to Jax, but I'll tell him, too."

Monica put one hand to her mouth. "Do you think someone meant to hurt Miss Sylvia?"

While Bella did, neither Ida nor Blanche seemed as certain, so she answered carefully. "You said Eyelers and Lauger discussed making the liquor go farther. They could do that by adding poisons like wood alcohol. A lot of bootleggers do."

"And that's bad?" Monica asked.

"It can be deadly. In fact, people have died from it. We think it's possible that Sylvia did."

"That's awful." The maid's tone and expression were solemn.

"It is, but we won't know for sure until there's an autopsy," Ida said. "Even if Miss Sawyer drank toxic liquor, it could've been accidental, not intentional."

"An autopsy won't reveal which one," Bella said, but she was set on finding out.

For a moment, Monica gazed at Bella and Ida. "I should go before someone misses me."

Bella got to her feet. "Thank you for speaking with us. Before we leave, I'll give you my address at Ballantyne. I'm sure we can find something for you there." Depending on how things developed over the next day, Bella just might take Monica along, but she didn't want to further upset the girl if it didn't work out.

"Thank you, miss. Thank you." Monica stood up and bobbed a curtsy. "I'll be grateful to get away." She nodded to Ida before rushing out of the room.

Once the maid was gone, Bella sank back into the chair. "She's aware of much more than I figured."

"That's for sure. No wonder she wants to leave this place. I do, too."

"I'm with you." Bella stared into the empty grate. "We have a lot of details, but they aren't fitting together yet."

Ida, her expression grim, nodded. "We certainly do. Sylvia going to the garden shed with Eyelers when she first arrived is troubling."

When a headache asserted itself, Bella pressed a fore-finger to each temple but found no relief. "I agree, but it's hard to say exactly what he's doing. Selling booze, but only to Lauger, or also to nearby speakeasies, or to bootleggers who distribute more widely? Or maybe Eyelers, Lauger, and Darre have their own bootlegging operation. The last would be worst since they could come here to get the stuff from the hidey hole any time. We don't want to run afoul of them."

A sigh escaped Ida. "Too bad Jax isn't closer."

That sentiment echoed inside Bella, but not only because he was an agent. "He'd need authority to get involved, and we don't have enough information to make that likely. If Eyelers is only selling to Lauger, he might not be a target for the Bureau, since they have bigger operations to investigate."

"You're a lot better informed than I am." Ida shifted restlessly in the chair.

"Like I told Monica, I'll write Jax, but the constable might be suspicious when he gets here. Maybe he can get help from someone closer."

"What do you think we should do next?"

For several moments, Bella weighed the possibilities. One immediately arose. As she considered it, Jax's usual admonitions echoed in her mind—she wasn't a law officer, nor was she armed. But she had experience in investigations. Although she'd mostly accompanied him on interviews, Bella had also gone to the scene of three crimes. She'd helped sort through clues, too. She could delve into the current case right now. Bella glanced at Ida. Would her friend try to dissuade her? Possibly, but she voiced the idea anyhow. "I'd love to look under the garden shed. We could go after dark, so no one sees us. Florence's room faces the front, and Lina and Blanche look out on the side yard. Even if one of them is up and looking out, we wouldn't be visible. Plus, Eyelers is gone, which makes it a perfect night."

Ida didn't immediately respond. Instead, she clasped her hands in her lap and stared down at them. Finally, she said, "We both brought flashlights."

A grin curved Bella's mouth. "We did." Her expression grew solemn. "There are several shrubs in front of the garden. We can dart to the first line within seconds. Besides, after midnight, it's unlikely any of the group will be awake. We were all up most of last night. Same with the help."

"We can hole up here until midnight. I doubt if I'll sleep before then."

Amusement filled Bella. "You're very enthusiastic."

"I only got to help a little on your last case, and it was fascinating. I can understand why you always wanted to assist Jax. Other than for the obvious reason." Ida wiggled her eyebrows.

"I wish he was here," she replied, "for every reason."

Chapter Six

Bella and Ida dozed off, but they woke long before midnight.

"Has the wind died down?" Ida asked as she rolled off her bed and stretched.

After a peek out of the window, Bella turned to her. "Yes, but it's still cloudy. We should bundle up, since it was cooler today and is probably even chillier now."

"Good idea."

Ida pulled out a heavy sweater, as did Bella. They both retrieved their flashlights before sitting down by the fireplace. "It's only eleven o'clock, but I still think we should wait until midnight."

"I agree." Ida grinned. "It turns out your imagination wasn't running away with you."

"Maybe not, but it's affecting my sleep. I dreamed about Eyelers meeting bootleggers at the dock," Bella admitted after a moment. "When they asked if the stuff was good, he chortled and said some was."

Ida shuddered. "That's creepy, but it also sounds quite possible, from what we already know."

"I'm hoping we can get a few samples." She paused before voicing another of her concerns. "I know Syl could've been poisoned by accident, but I want to know for sure. She deserves justice."

"I agree," Ida said. "Maybe I'd rather it be accidental because I hate to think anyone poisoned Syl on purpose."

"I don't like thinking that, either, but several people make good suspects in an intentional poisoning," Bella pointed out.

"Let's wait and see what develops."

"We don't have much choice." Obviously, Ida's mind was still completely open. Bella reminded herself to keep hers open, too. Good investigators didn't let themselves go too far down any particular path until all the puzzle pieces were gathered, if not all in place. "We won't be able to tell ourselves if the booze is tainted, but we can keep them for when the constable comes out."

"Maybe that'll be soon. I hope it is. Today has passed slowly. I feel like we've been stuck here for an age."

A long breath left Bella. "I agree. I was really looking forward to reuniting with old friends."

"I was eager to get here. Now, I can't wait to get back to Ballantyne."

Bella echoed the sentiment. For the next hour, the pair chit-chatted about other things. When the hall clock struck twelve, she picked up the flashlights she'd laid out earlier. "We should get going."

"You were right to suggest bringing flashlights."

Bella shrugged. "Florence mentioned they lose electricity fairly often. The candles and oil lamps are charming, but not as functional."

Ida followed Bella into the hallway. The pair crept toward the staff staircase and tiptoed down it. When they reached the back door, Bella paused. "Let's not turn on the flashlights until we really need them. Just in case someone is awake."

"All right. Lead the way."

The friends slipped out and hurried across the lawn to the garden. Once they reached the other side of the box-wood row, Bella paused. "We could use one light now." She turned on hers and pointed it at the ground. The pair carefully wended their way to the shed. Dodging twigs and small branches slowed their progress. When they finally got to the small building, Bella exhaled sharply. "We made it." With one hand, she opened the door. As she aimed the flashlight, the interior came into view. Tools leaned against one wall, while two others had shelves holding pots of various sizes. A workbench, one that appeared to be an ancient breakfront, with soil and more pots, was in front of the fourth.

When Ida came alongside Bella, she looked around, too. "I don't see a trapdoor."

"Neither do I, so it must be under the cabinet." Bella studied the hulking piece of furniture. "It looks heavy."

"We can take the soil and pots off, and remove whatever is inside. That should help."

With that, they went to work. Even with the contents taken out, moving the workbench a few feet proved hard. Both Ida and Bella were panting by the time the hidden door was visible. After Bella opened the hatch, each pointed her light into the musty dugout. Multiple bottles were visible, as was a small table. "I'll go down first," Bella said and immediately descended the rickety ladder. Once she reached the bottom, Bella swung the flashlight around the cramped, dank interior. "There are crates and crates of bottles. Different labels and all kinds of liquor. Come on and see."

Ida joined Bella. "You're right. The place is filled with booze. There's enough for people to have parties every night for a month." She moved her flashlight around. "Look over there. What's in the smaller bottles?"

Three steps took Bella to the far side. She bent to focus on the vials neatly stacked on shallow shelves.

"There's rat poison, and some have homemade labels with skull and crossbones." She turned to her friend. "Those must contain wood alcohol or other poisons."

"I'd say you're right." Ida kept scanning the shelves. "These have other labels. Juniper oil, maple syrup, sugar, and glycerin."

As Ida spoke, Bella looked in the same direction. "I remember Jax saying bootleggers use those to mask the foul taste of tainted liquor. Gin is the easiest type to make and adding these ingredients is part of the process. Syl had gin bottles, but despite the labels, I feel certain it wasn't good gin. The original liquor was probably consumed long ago, maybe at one of Lauger's parties. Or Eyelers could've had it himself. Then, they reused the bottles."

"That seems likely. I told you about the parties from last Christmas."

"Did they serve mostly gin?" Bella asked.

"I'm not sure, but they had cocktails. Many people were drinking gin rickeys, whiskey sours, and highballs."

"All of them would be made with gin."

"I only had fruit juice. There were several kinds—grape, orange, apple."

"Which could be used to mix other cocktails, and to cover any vile taste of bathtub booze."

"You seem to know a lot about this," Ida said.

Bella shrugged. "Jax told me a few things before he left. Since then, I've listened any time guests discuss Prohibition. We never served liquor at the resort, but people talk about booze more often than they used to. Some are free in revealing they drink bootlegged liquor. Of course, they rarely realize I overhear them." And none knew about her association with a federal agent. She moved the beam of her flashlight around the interior. "There's a crate of empty bottles. I'd say Eyelers uses this place to mix and store alcohol."

"He's got quite an operation going. Do you still want to take a couple of bottles?"

A pause preceded Bella's response. "That may not be a good idea. He has a highly organized system and would most likely miss them. I was worried about the evidence disappearing, but I doubt if anyone will come to buy the stuff while we're here, and there's a lot to haul away quickly and easily. It's conceivable it could disappear but, with luck, the local constable will be out tomorrow. If he isn't, we may need to come back for samples."

"What if the constable is being bought off? Syl mentioned policemen in cities taking bribes. Prohibition agents, too."

"We have to hope he isn't, although it's possible." Once again, Bella wished Jax was at hand. He was better informed about how to handle evidence and investigate clues. But he wasn't nearby, and Bella reminded herself that she was a competent detective. Senior Constable Richard Jenkins thought so, and Jax agreed—albeit reluctantly at times. But that was because he worried about her, and he worried because he cared. Warmth dispelled the chill around her heart before she shook off the errant thoughts and faced her friend. Daydreams had to wait. "Let's leave everything, as is. We know what's here, and we can point authorities in the right direction."

"Whatever you say. You're the experienced sleuth," Ida said with a grin.

Thirty minutes later, the pair settled on their beds. Both sat cross-legged, facing one another. "I'm wide awake," Bella said.

"Me, too. Even though we found Eyelers' stash, I keep wondering how many of those bottles are filled with poison liquor."

"I also wonder if Syl got booze from him and, if she did, was Eyelers aware the stuff was potentially fatal?" Bella couldn't keep from bringing the idea up again because it stayed on her mind.

"That's two big *ifs*."

"True, but we have a few facts. First, Syl could get liquor on the island. Or so she said. With only two houses occupied, the potential sources are limited, and we know Eyelers is definitely one. Second, Lauger and Darre are not only business partners, they talk with Eyelers fairly often. And they've gone to the shed together. Third, there's a stockpile of booze and bootlegging ingredients in the shed dugout. Finally, Eyelers went to the Lauger place before the storm." Bella braced her elbows on her knees. "Considering the amount of booze and other supplies below the shed, it isn't much of a jump to believe Eyelers, Lauger, and Darre are rumrunners."

"I don't disagree, but it doesn't mean any of them meant to kill Syl. What motive would Eyelers have? Or Darre?"

"There's no obvious reason either of them would want to harm her. He could've given her bad booze at Lauger's request."

"Or maybe Syl bought it from him, and he'd mixed in too much wood alcohol by mistake."

Frustration gripped Bella. "Maybe, but Florence was furious with Syl for talking about her debts, and she's acted strangely since we got here. Not like her old self at all.

"Do you think Florence purposefully gave bad booze to Syl? I'd rather believe it was Lauger, if that happened."

"Florence was very upset when Syl brought up her gambling debts. Plus, she insisted Syl must've died from natural causes, which isn't sensible."

"No, it's not, but it's just as bad if it was accidental instead of intentional since diluting good liquor with toxins is risky." Ida paused for a moment.

"Florence insisted Syl must've had a lot of liquor, but you said she sounded sober when you overheard her around midnight." Bella reviewed their other gleanings. "Florence definitely wanted to quash the idea that Syl died from tainted alcohol, when that's the most likely scenario to me. After I tried to call the constable, she said he probably wouldn't hurry out here for a dead woman. Like Syl was a stranger. It gave me the creeps."

"What an awful way to refer to a friend."

"I thought so." A little shiver rippled through Bella as a new idea came to mind. "I should've thought of it before now. What if Florence had the body moved to the cellar so that it can be disposed of before the constable comes?"

"That would mean Florence was involved in Syl's death. She's acted oddly, but to kill a close friend? I still have trouble believing it," Ida said. "But I'm not discounting your ideas. You know a lot more about investigations than I do."

Her friend's observation eased Bella's mind. "Even though we don't want to believe it, it could be what happened."

"How would Florence explain the body disappearing? It would make her guilty," Ida said.

As her friend spoke, Bella nodded. "You're right. But what if Lauger got Eyelers to sell Syl tainted liquor? He has a motive to kill her."

"He does, but it'd be heartless. He might've wanted to make her sick enough to miscarry, although I'm not sure poisoned liquor would do that. Some folks in the temperance movement supported the idea that any alcohol is bad for an unborn baby. Blanche thought so, too."

"That's true, and it makes sense even though there's not a lot of proof." A moment passed before Ida went on. "What about Lina? She's still carrying a torch for Kenton, and he's the one who ended things. She wasn't sympathetic about Lauger brushing Syl off, either." Bella picked up her pad and pencil. "Until this weekend, I didn't realize Kenton ended their relationship."

Ida nodded. "Neither did I, and neither did Blanche. Florence must have, because she hoped Lina wasn't angry with Syl. It's worse because Lina's mother died around that time. In light of that and everything else, I wonder how much of a grudge she holds." A rueful grin pulled at one corner of Ida's mouth. "Your viewpoint about intentional poisoning is getting more and more viable to me."

"I know it's only a possibility, but a strong one. *Grudge* jogged my memory. Remember our first semester at college? Lina got very upset when her composition instructor gave her a *B*. She'd always gotten straight *As* in writing, and she complained to everyone."

"I remember the incident well," Ida replied. "Lina made a big stink about it for weeks and told all our classmates to stay out of the man's classes."

"That didn't work, but she lost some friends with all her whining." Bella offered a rueful smile. "If we hadn't known her better qualities before that, we might've felt the same way."

"True." Ida took a long breath. "But would Lina do something to Syl? Constant complaining is a far cry from poisoning someone."

"I agree, but maybe Lina only wanted to make Syl sick, not kill her. That seems possible with every suspect."

"I suppose. But how would Lina get bad booze from Eyelers?"

"Maybe she didn't. Maybe she brought it with her."

For a long moment, Ida stared at Bella. "She'd already have liquor because of her prescription waiver."

"She would, and she could've doctored it herself. Arsenic and strychnine are easy to get. Rubbing alcohol is a fairly new product, but she might have some, and it's toxic." Bella jotted down more notes. "It's unsettling to consider, but I can't dismiss the idea."

"Neither can I," Ida agreed. "Since Lina barely passed college chemistry, I doubt if she'd figure out how much poison would cause illness, not death."

"It would be hard for anyone but a chemist or druggist, and Lina was as vehement as Florence about Syl not dying from tainted liquor. Eyelers, Lauger, Florence, and Lina."

"And two possibilities. Accidental or intentional."

"That sums it up," Bella agreed. "Then, there's the *how*. Lauger gave a flask to Syl on the dock. She was alone on the boat with Eyelers on Thursday morning, and I can see Syl taking liquor from Florence, who must know about the bootlegging. But how would Lina get her to drink something? That seems harder, considering their impasse."

"You're completely ruling Blanche out, right?" Ida asked.

"Absolutely. I can't think of any reason for her to harm Syl. Besides, she shared a lot about the effects of methanol poisoning. Do you feel differently?"

"Not at all. I just wondered."

"I also doubt if Darre was involved. He has no personal stake, and no good opportunity to give booze to Syl." When she looked back at the notepad, Bella scanned her writing. "We've gotten a lot down. Pretty much everything. If there's more, my mind is getting too foggy to handle it. I don't know about you, but I'm getting sleepy."

A yawn escaped Ida. "Me, too."

Bella laid pad and pencil on the nightstand before taking the flashlight from Ida. "Let's get some rest."

Once in her bed, Ida whispered, "Sweet dreams."

"You, as well," Bella replied, but her dreams weren't sweet. Instead, the image of Sylvia's waxen face and still body haunted her.

When Bella woke the following morning, her eyes felt gritty. While she'd gotten some sleep, it was restless. The hows and whys of Sylvia's death hadn't left Bella's mind. Images of her friend floated through her dreams and lingered into her wakeful consciousness. Not wanting to disturb Ida, who was still dozing, Bella crept out of bed and tiptoed to the window. Blue skies and bright sunlight greeted her. Beyond the treetops, the lake looked as smooth as glass. The calm waters would allow boat traffic, so, surely, the constable would come today.

"Good morning."

Ida's drowsy voice reached Bella, who turned to her friend. "I hope I didn't wake you."

As Ida rolled to sit on the edge of the bed, she shook her head. "I've been half-awake for most of the night. What time is it?"

"Almost ten. I suppose we should dress and go downstairs."

Ida agreed, and the two friends quickly donned clothes and headed to the dining room where the others were already at the table. After greetings were exchanged, Florence gestured to the sideboard. "Mrs. Longley made toast and eggs. Coffee, too. The electricity is still off, and the telephone is out again. If you were wondering."

"At least the wind has died down," Bella said after procuring her food and taking a seat.

"I noticed the lake is calm, so someone may be out today. If they understood any of what you said to the operator, Bella." Blanche looked and sounded as hopeful as Bella felt.

"I wouldn't count on it," Florence said. "The constable on Burnley Cove doesn't consider Winnabee a top priority. Besides, he's probably still dealing with damage over there."

Their hostess' dour expression and dismissive words increased Bella's trepidation. Florence held little resemblance to their college friend. She didn't even seem much like the woman who had greeted them all on Thursday. She'd been a bit on edge then, but her entire demeanor changed after her debts were brought up.

"I don't see why a constable is needed," Lina said. "Syl drank too much. Way too much."

"She did, which isn't unusual," Florence put in. "I suppose drinking so much for so long, she developed a tolerance and had to guzzle more to drown her sorrows."

"She seems to have plenty of sorrows from what I overheard between her and Lauger." Lina pursed her lips. "When a girl is as wild as Syl, she's bound to reap trouble."

When she and Ida exchanged a glance, Bella felt another jolt of suspicion about Lina. But Florence was acting as callously. Why?

"There aren't any signs of Syl drinking too much the night she died," Blanche said. "She had very little on Friday, and she was sober when I spoke to her that evening. I don't approve of buying bootlegged booze, but that's a more likely cause, especially since getting legal liquor is difficult, if not impossible, nowadays."

"Lina gets it legally." Florence glanced at the small blonde.

Color climbed into Lina's cheeks. "I have a federal waiver. Did Syl? Neither of you ever said so." Her voice held a sharp edge.

"No, she didn't have one," Florence replied. "I was just making an observation."

As Bella listened to the by-play, she wondered if Florence was trying to push blame on Lina. She'd only do that for two reasons—she was guilty herself or she suspected Lina. Part of her wanted Syl's death to be accidental. But another part—a bigger one—suspected foul play.

After breakfast, Lina complained of a headache and returned to her room while Florence went to speak with Mrs. Longley. The other three friends adjourned to the parlor.

Once they settled by the fireplace, Bella planned to ask Blanche for her opinion of the changes in Florence and Lina, but the other woman spoke first.

"I hope the constable gets here today. Sylvia being in the cellar bothers me. I realize she's unaware of it, but it seems disrespectful." She folded her arms across her waist. "When Florence sent a note inviting me for this weekend, she made it sound like she and Syl were very close. I knew they'd paired up after the rest of us left for war work, so I wasn't surprised. They seemed friendly when we first got here...but since yesterday afternoon." She shook her head. "It's hard to understand why Florence isn't more upset."

"I agree with you completely," Ida said.

"So do I," Bella agreed. "Ida and I discussed it last night."

A rueful smile tugged at one corner of Blanche's mouth. "I figured you would." Her good humor dissipated. "I didn't broach the topic with Lina. She says she feels bad about Syl dying, but I'm not sure I believe her. Especially after her last couple of outbursts."

"It's not good that she still loves Kenton," Ida said. "I was grief-stricken when Alan died, but he didn't desert me for someone else, so I don't completely understand Lina still wearing the willow for a man who left her."

Bella's heart clenched. Ida had never realized her fiancé had fancied himself in love with a French nurse. Bella had only learned of the liaison herself in April when Jax had reluctantly revealed the situation. Because she didn't want to hurt her friend, Bella kept silent. She wondered if that was the right course. Now, Lina's lingering anguish, and the damage being done by it, convinced Bella that keeping the secret was best. Besides, she'd promised Jax she would. With effort, she brushed back those thoughts. "Lina can't seem to get past him ending their relationship. Kenton and Syl getting together while Lina went home to see her mother makes it worse."

"Evidently, they were smitten before then." Blanche leaned an elbow on the chair arm and braced her chin in her palm. "The two of you went for operator training before I joined the Red Cross in mid-March. Lina was still stepping out with Kenton. Of course, Syl flirted with him, like she did with all the boys. He seemed to be flattered, but I'm still surprised he took up with her."

Ida grimaced. "Lina should be angrier with him, not so much with Syl."

"I would be. I still think accidental poisoning is likely, but Lina and Florence are both acting strangely. We know Florence owed Syl money. Do you two think Lina's got something to hide?" Blanche looked from Ida to Bella.

"She's in the mix," Bella replied, "but some things going on around here make me wonder about other people."

Blanche's gaze narrowed. "Who else? Although I can probably guess."

"I'm sure you can," Ida agreed.

Bella's teeth toyed with her lower lip. "Last night, Ida and I did a bit of other digging."

"Really? What kind of digging?" Curiosity lit Blanche's gaze.

As Bella recalled Monica's fear, she proceeded carefully. "This information can't go beyond the three of us, and we all need to be careful what we say and to whom. At least until the constable comes. He'll have to know everything, of course."

Blanche's expression grew solemn. "I won't reveal anything you say. I promise you that."

Since Blanche had always been reliable and circumspect, Bella nodded. "We spoke with Monica. She had a lot to say about Eyelers." Bella summed up the details.

Blanche listened intently. "If he's threatening the staff, he must be in deep."

"Not only that, he met with Lauger and Darre that evening after we all went to bed. Monica only caught a glimpse from the kitchen, so she doesn't know what was said," Ida put in.

"That's interesting and troubling," Blanche said.

Bella nodded. "We found evidence that's even more revealing. Monica said Eyelers has a hidey hole under the garden shed, so Ida and I checked it out last night."

A low gasp left Blanche. "What did you find?"

After Bella shared their discoveries, she finished by saying, "We didn't bring any bottles back because everything was neatly organized, and I worried about Eyelers getting suspicious if he noticed some of his stock missing. Even though he was gone last night, he could be back any time."

"You were smart not to disturb anything. He's a slippery character, and we don't want to run afoul of him while we're stuck out here," Blanche said.

"I agree," Ida said.

Despite the other women concurring, Bella wished they had evidence in hand. "I hope the Burnley Cove constable gets here soon."

"So do I." Ida ran one hand over her face. "The whole situation is alarming. I looked forward to a fun weekend with old friends, and it's turned into a waking nightmare."

"It isn't that bad." Lina's voice penetrated the conversation.

The little blonde stood in the doorway. Close enough to have heard every word of Bella's revelations. Apprehension moved through her. How long had Lina been there? Several moments of dead silence filled the room.

Blanche found her voice first. "Is your headache better?"

"Somewhat." Lina crossed to perch on the loveseat facing the fireplace. "I thought I'd sleep, but I tossed and turned."

Bella focused her attention on the other woman. Was a guilty conscience keeping Lina from resting? While Bella empathized with Lina's sorrow over losing Kenton, she wished her friend would move forward instead of wallowing in grief. Previous cases had proven murder often resulted from bitterness and retribution. The logistics of Lina poisoning Syl were difficult, but not impossible. That thought stayed with Bella as the group moved on to reminiscing about their college days.

Chapter Seven

♥

An hour later, the front doorbell chimed. "I hope that's the constable," Blanche said immediately.

"Shouldn't he have his hands full with damage in his own jurisdiction? That's what Florence thought." Lina scowled.

"Someone dying is a top concern for a lawman," Bella pointed out.

"I suppose," Lina replied, but her tone lacked conviction.

"The lake was calm enough for boating, but the dock is partially gone. Getting from there to the house wouldn't be easy, either," Ida said. "But who else could it be?"

Bella got to her feet. "Maybe it's Mr. Lauger coming to check on us." She had no idea why the idea popped into her mind except that he might distract the women while Eyelers and Darre moved Syl's body. Almost immediately, Bella chastised herself for being too suspicious. She'd already agreed with Ida that a missing body would be difficult to explain.

"Possibly," Blanche said. "Let's see."

All four young women stood and headed to the foyer. They arrived to find Mrs. Longley, a rotund woman with frizzy gray hair, ushering two men inside. "I'll fetch

Miss Florence, gentlemen." She glanced at the clutch of friends. "Maybe you girls would keep our guests company while I do."

"Of course." Before Bella said more, the housekeeper scurried off.

"Thank you." One man stepped forward and doffed his cap.

As she took a better look, Bella recognized his attire as a uniform. Relief filled her. "You must be the constable from Burnley Cove."

"Yes, miss." His gaze swept over the young women. "I'm Constable Warren Amberly." He was a powerfully built man of middle years. While not tall, he had a commanding presence. "This is Dr. Marcus Kern."

The doctor was younger, perhaps in his late thirties. He was also slighter of build. Like the constable, he had an amiable expression on his clean-shaven face. "Good day," he said with a slight nod.

Amberly glanced at the girls. "Our operator only got bits of information from whoever telephoned."

Bella introduced herself and explained she'd been the caller before looking at her friends. In turn, each of the others gave their names.

By the time the four finished, Florence appeared. "Thank you for coming, gentlemen." A smile brightened her face as she spoke, and she was once again the congenial hostess. Her earlier dismissive attitude was gone.

"I'm sorry we didn't get here sooner, Miss Remington," the constable replied. "We've got a lot of damage over on the lakeshore, so telephone service is spotty. Even when a call goes through, the connection is often interrupted, as happened with your call."

Florence maintained her amiable expression. "We're quite used to both telephone and electricity going out after a storm. Of course, this time was inopportune."

The lawman nodded. "Indeed, it was. Can you give us a general idea of what happened? When I heard about a woman dying, I thought it was..."

"You thought it was our Mrs. Longley," Florence said. "Or perhaps, my mother?"

Dark color climbed into the constable's face. "I wasn't sure who might be visiting besides your friends, and I only learned about them being here yesterday. But I know Mrs. Longley." He turned his cap in his hands.

"And she's getting older," Florence observed. "But she's hale and hardy."

Abruptly, Bella realized the disjointed telephone conversation hadn't conveyed important details. Considering how bad the static had been, that wasn't surprising. Since Florence hadn't answered the constable's question, Bella hurried to do so. "Six of us are here for a brief reunion. We attended college together. Unfortunately, one of our friends died the night of the storm." Speaking the words nearly choked her. It was hard and hurtful to think of Sylvia being dead. She'd been so full of life.

Constable Amberly and Dr. Kern both focused on Bella. "What happened?" the lawman asked again.

"We aren't sure," Bella replied, "but we found her dead in bed."

"She'd been drinking heavily," Florence added.

"She certainly had," Lina said with a tsk-tsk. "She's a heavy boozer."

"I see," Amberly murmured, but he still looked taken aback. "I knew you'd requested a doctor, and that's common procedure with a sudden death. I had no idea that a young person had died."

"Syl drank a lot on Thursday, but she only had a little on Friday." Blanche looked directly at Dr. Kern. "I was a nurse during the war, and I've seen victims of methanol poisoning. So have my father and husband. Both of them are physicians. Syl told us about being able to get liquor on the island, and I'm guessing it was tainted. The symptoms of poisoning are like those of being heavily intoxicated, but she definitely wasn't drunk on Friday evening."

Dr. Kern, clad in a neat suit and bow tie, cleared his throat. "Indeed, the early symptoms of methanol poisoning are much like those associated with drunkenness."

The constable pulled a notepad and pencil out of his pocket. "What is the deceased's name?"

"Sylvia Sawyer," Florence replied.

"If someone can show me the way, I'll do a preliminary survey of Miss Sawyer's remains," Dr. Kern said. "Of course, we'll need more details."

As Bella glanced around the room, she noted her friends looked as unsettled as she felt. Perhaps, they'd all rest easier once Sylvia was in the physician's custody. Not that any of them would ever get over the past two days. The trauma would live with them forever. Bella felt sure of that.

"Miss Remington, where is your friend?" the constable asked.

Florence stiffened slightly before explaining where Sylvia's body was. To Bella, both men looked ill at ease as they heard the reply. When they failed to immediately respond, Florence went on. "I'll have the staff move her to an empty servant's room below stairs. You can make your examination there, doctor. For now, please make yourself comfortable in the parlor." Florence glanced at Blanche. "Will you show these gentlemen the way?"

Bella's attention returned to Florence, who still looked calm. Could she maintain such a benign demeanor if she'd had something to do with Syl's death? Bella didn't want to think so.

"Of course," Blanche replied.

As Florence turned away, Constable Amberly spoke again. "I'll need to talk with each of you individually. Is there a private space for me to do so while Dr. Kern examines your friend?"

Florence spun back to face the constable. "Is that really necessary? We know nothing more than we've told you. We found Syl dead in bed. While she wasn't drunk all day, she might've had a lot alone in her room. Syl drank often and heavily." There was a slight acerbity to her tone, although her expression stayed carefully schooled. "We've all discussed the tragedy already. Surely, you understand why we'd rather not talk about it again."

The constable's gray eyebrows pulled together to create a disapproving frown. "It would've been better if you hadn't discussed it among yourselves or moved the body, but we can't change what's happened. I'd like to see the victim's room before I talk with all of you." His gaze bored into Florence. "I hope it hasn't been disturbed."

Color rose in Florence's face. "It was a terrible mess since Syl vomited all over, so of course, I had the room cleaned."

Amberly's jaw clenched. "Again, I wish you hadn't done that. I'd still like to look. Then, I want to get each story separately." He glanced around the group. "Please refrain from further talk now. Both of my deputies are busy, so I'm alone and can't monitor your behavior. I'll have all I can handle getting your comments recorded." He clasped and unclasped his hands. "A bit of rheumatism makes that harder and harder."

His last statement motivated Bella to speak. "If you'd like to talk with me first, I'll take notes on the other interviews. I know shorthand and could quickly transpose the information when you finish. Or simply write things down for you."

Surprise widened the man's pale hazel eyes. "Remind me who you are. Hearing all of your names was a bit confusing."

"Bella Stewart. I'm a partner in Ballantyne resort near Moreley."

For several moments, Amberly studied her face. Finally, he nodded. "Miss Stewart. You've helped with several investigations in your area." His frown softened, and a smile replaced it. "Richard Jenkins is an old friend, and he sings your praises."

Heat climbed into Bella's cheeks. "Senior Constable Jenkins is more than kind." The retired lawman had helped in those cases, too, and he'd welcomed Bella's assistance even when Jax hadn't.

"He gives credit when credit is due," Amberly replied. "Help is welcome, so I'll speak with you first. Miss Remington, is there a room I can use?"

Florence looked as if she might object, but she finally answered. "My father's den should do." She escorted the constable and Bella out of the foyer and toward the back of the house. There, Florence opened the door to a small room lined on three sides with bookshelves. The fourth had a fireplace flanked by narrow windows. "Unless you need something, I'll take Dr. Kern to the body."

"Nothing else at the moment. Thank you," the constable said. "Miss Stewart can show me the room before we get started."

"Of course," Florence replied, but her voice sounded dismissive and her expression was hardly hospitable.

"If you'll follow me, I'll take you upstairs," Bella said. When the constable nodded, she led the way to Sylvia's room.

Once there, the constable put his hands on his hips as he looked around. "It looks like no one stayed here at all."

He was right. There was no sign of recent habitation. The bed was neatly made. Syl's clothes were gone, as was her valise, and the dresser top was bare. When Bella looked at the nightstand, she noted that the gin bottles were missing, too. "I told Florence not to do anything in here. I had no idea that she had until the maid said so."

Amberly turned toward her. "Your friend doesn't seem to understand that this situation needs to be investigated. Simply saying someone died is hardly enough. Even if it had been someone older, I'd want details."

The comment, while valid, disturbed Bella, who wondered if Florence had some other motive in clearing the scene. "It was a terrible mess."

"Please describe it to me."

"As we said downstairs, there was vomit everywhere—on Syl, the bed, the floor." She chewed on her lower lip. "And there were two gin bottles on the nightstand. One was full, and the other half-full."

A frown deepened the creases on Amberly's forehead. "I'd like to see those"

"They're not where they were. Maybe Florence had them taken away."

Amberly's nostrils flared with a deep breath. "I'll ask her."

Bella shifted from one foot to the other as she considered revealing the midnight foray to the garden shed. Perhaps, it would be better to wait until they were behind the closed den door. While the constable surveyed the room, Bella watched in silence.

After opening the drawers and looking under the bed, he rubbed his chin. "Not much to see here, so let's go down and get started on interviews."

Bella once again led the way. When they got to the den, Constable Amberly closed the door behind her and gestured to the two chairs facing the mahogany desk. "Please make yourself comfortable, Miss Stewart."

Bella sat down while Amberly settled behind the desk. Then, he retrieved his pad and pencil from his jacket pocket. "Let's start with your call. The operator only caught bits of what was said. She got the part about someone dying and about bad booze. Frankly, I thought Mrs. Longley might have imbibed. She's a sweet lady, but I know she used to enjoy a tipple or two before bedtime." His expression softened. "She was a friend of my mother. But let's get down to brass tacks. Why don't you go over the basics of what brought all of you to the island, what happened yesterday, and when you all found Miss Sawyer?"

"Of course." Bella explained that they'd been college friends, but hadn't seen each other for several years. She went over their arrivals on the island and the activities the first night and the next afternoon. When she mentioned Lauger and Darre, the constable stopped her.

"I'm familiar with Mr. Lauger, since he's been spending a good part of the year out here since the war."

"Was he in France?" Bella asked almost automatically. "Sorry, I'm supposed to be answering questions, not asking them."

"It's natural to wonder. He was in the army, but never left the States. Questions?" A grin lifted the corners of the constable's mouth. "After all, you're a good detective, from what I've been told."

Warmth again crept into Bella's cheeks, but passing up the opportunity to learn more was impossible. "What does he do for a living?"

Amberly's smile faded. "Nothing, as far as I know. His family is very wealthy. The parents died some years ago, but the grandfather on his mother's side still owns a factory. Young Lauger never worked there or anywhere else. His grandparents raised him, and they all spent summers on Winnabee until the last couple of years. His grandfather had a stroke, so he doesn't want to be far from medical help now." He tapped the pencil on the desk. "Did anything about Lauger stand out to you?"

"One thing is that he and his friend Darre said they're business partners with various ventures." She should tell him about the garden shed, but easing into it seemed like the smartest strategy. From personal experience, Bella knew lawmen didn't want amateurs poking around a case. While Constable Amberly had been friendly and reassuring, he was a virtual stranger.

One eyebrow lifted. "I'd like to know the nature of those businesses."

Bella would, too. "Mr. Lauger and Mr. Darre came to the dock on Friday afternoon and to dinner that night. Several of us asked them for details, but they didn't respond. Florence and Syl were vague about the type of businesses, too."

"Have your two friends attended parties at the Lauger place?"

"They have. Last summer and in May." Bella considered how to reveal the issues surrounding both women without sounding accusatory or catty. "Friday afternoon, Syl went out on the boat with Mr. Lauger. They were gone for almost two hours."

"Had they been drinking?"

A half-shrug lifted one of Bella's shoulders. "Maybe a little, but both seemed sober. They were arguing when they returned." Discomfort made Bella shift restlessly. She didn't like discussing Syl's delicate condition, but what choice was there? "From what some of us heard, Sylvia was expecting a child."

The constable's eyes grew wide as he stared at Bella. "You're sure of what you heard?"

Bella nodded. "Several of us are."

A long breath left him. "I'll tell the doctor. He can make a medical determination during the autopsy, which will be necessary under the circumstances."

Amberly scribbled away before posing another query. "What about your friend and Lauger meeting at other places?"

"I'm not sure, but that's how Florence made it sound. She said they'd gotten together in Chicago, where Syl has been living."

Amberly nodded. "And Mr. Darre stayed with you ladies the entire time that Miss Sawyer and Mr. Lauger were on his boat?"

"Yes. He mostly chatted with Florence." Should she say he'd been quite familiar with her friend? Overly familiar. Briefly, Bella debated revealing Darre squeezing on to the chaise lounge with Florence. Finally, she provided the information without being judgmental. Constable Amberly had accepted Syl's condition easily enough, so he was unlikely to be agog over Darre and Florence being close. "They seemed to be well-acquainted, and he sat with Florence on her chair."

Amberly, his gray eyebrows raised, looked up from his notepad. "A dock chair?"

"Yes, there are several chaises out there. We were using all of them when Lauger and Darre arrived, although there were two more in the boathouse. Mr. Darre said he didn't need one."

"I noticed a large diamond on Miss Remington's left hand. Is she affianced?"

The comment revealed an advanced level of scrutiny on Amberly's part. Evidently, he was a skilled detective himself. "Yes, she is. Her fiancé is a lawyer in San Francisco."

"How did they meet?"

"He's originally from Columbus, which you probably know is where Florence lives."

The constable's reply was a nod. "Do you know how long Miss Remington and Mr. Darre have been acquainted?"

"Not exactly. Since they were both at the Lauger parties last summer, at least that long."

"Did any of them offer details about those events? I've heard liquor is served."

Bella chewed on her lower lip as she considered his question. Did Constable Amberly think Lauger was bootlegging? Or was the lawman being paid off to keep away and worried that Lauger and Darre might let something slip? Amberly knew Richard well, but that didn't mean he was also honest and upright. Too bad Bella had no way to contact Senior Constable Jenkins and glean more information on Amberly. "Few details, although they mentioned drinking and gambling." What they'd really discussed was Florence owing money, but Bella wasn't sure about sharing that yet. More proof that, while she had detective skills, she wasn't a copper. Friendship shouldn't impede justice, but Bella felt torn and uncertain. Lauger was as strong a suspect as Florence or Lina. And the possibility of accidental poisoning remained.

Amberly ran one hand over his face. "This is a private island, so it isn't in my jurisdiction or subject to scrutiny by any local lawmen. We've never gotten sufficient information to get help from the feds regarding possible rumrunning." Once again, he tapped his pencil on the desk. "I didn't want to mention it in front of the others, but I also knew Jax Hasting's father very well. I met Jax a few times when he was growing up, and I spoke with him yesterday."

The last comment stunned Bella. For several moments, she struggled to maintain decorum. Simply hearing Jax's name sent her heart into overdrive. With effort, she focused on the current set of circumstances. Why would Amberly speak with Jax, who was far away working on a case that couldn't be related to events on Winnabee? Could it? "He's in Philadelphia."

"He's in Moreley for a few days."

Fresh shock hit her. A series of questions swept through her mind. Why was he home and for how long? Had he come back as part of his job or was his return for a personal reason? Why had he spoken with Amberly? "Do you know if something in that investigation brought him back?"

A puzzled look settled on the constable's face. "I don't think so. We spoke because he and..." Amberly looked down at his notepad. "Jax and Griff Biggins, your golf pro, were trying to reach you and Miss Byington. They were concerned about storm damage over here. When they finally got through to our local operator, she alerted me. I was out of the office and didn't get the message until late last evening. Jax was upset when I mentioned the death. I figured it was Mrs. Longley. I was unaware of the reunion until he told me, and I didn't know details until I got here today. When I revealed there'd been a death, he and Biggins were set on driving up here immediately. After I told them crossing the lake at night was a bad idea, especially as rough as it was until this morning, they agreed to wait. I called before I came out this morning. They'd already left, so they're on their way."

Once again, Bella's pulse picked up. "To the island?"

He nodded. "They may have trouble getting a boat since a number were damaged in the storm. According to your partner, Mr. MacLendon, Jax and Mr. Biggins took off about nine-thirty."

"Ida and I came by train, so I'm not sure about the driving time." Tamping down her interest in Jax's arrival wasn't easy. No matter why he was coming, Bella wanted to see him. She could pour out all the evidence, along with her suppositions.

"Close to two hours is my guess. That's under good conditions, though. Some roads leading to the Cove have trees down, so maybe closer to a few hours today. Add a little time for them securing a boat and for the ride over here. I wouldn't expect them to arrive until two o'clock at the earliest. I hoped to get here earlier myself, but it's been a hectic day-and-a-half since the storm hit us."

Bella nodded. "I would imagine so."

Amberly released a weary breath. "Now, I have a good idea of how you all arrived and what happened the first evening and day. There seems to be a difference of opinion on how much Miss Sawyer drank."

Actually, the viewpoints were contradictory, but Bella strove for honesty. Florence and Lina would have to explain why they disagreed with the rest of the group. "The first night, she drank a lot. She was sober yesterday morning at breakfast, but hung over. She took a hip flask to the dock, but sipped very little before the men arrived. If she and Mr. Lauger drank on the boat, it didn't show."

"Miss Remington and Miss..." His voice trailed off as he glanced at his notes. "Miss Hartley seemed to disagree. Is there some reason they feel differently than you and the other two?" He looked back at Bella.

"Blanche Carriger and Ida Byington." Bella supplied the information. "I'm not sure why they think Syl drank excessively after we all went to bed. She was upset. After dinner, she and Mr. Lauger took a walk in the garden. When they came back, they were arguing again—about him marrying her, I think."

"He didn't want to wed her?"

"No." Bella paused before revealing the rest. "He wasn't sure he was the father. Or so he said."

"I see."

When Amberly didn't continue, Bella spoke again. "Syl ran inside, and Lauger left with his friend, although

133

they didn't go far." She revealed what Monica had seen later.

Amberly braced his elbows on the desk. "A lot happened in a short time, and we haven't gotten to finding Miss Sawyer."

"After Syl left, the rest of us didn't stay up too long. Ida and I are sharing a room, and the storm woke us. We all came downstairs. All except Syl. Blanche checked on Syl before bedtime. Maybe if we'd checked on her again, we could've helped." Regret and remorse formed a lump in Bella's throat.

"That's unlikely. Whether she simply drank too much or ingested bad booze, you wouldn't have the means to save her. We've covered a lot. Is there anything else that stands out to you?"

"Ida went to the bathroom around midnight. She heard Sylvia and someone else chatting and laughing in Syl's room."

His eyebrows lifted. "So, Miss Sawyer was still alert at that time." He made the observation in an almost inaudible tone. "Did you hear the two women?"

"No, I didn't. Only Ida did, and she thought it was another woman. I must've been asleep when she went to use the bathroom."

"I'll definitely ask Miss Byington about it. Anything else?"

"Ida saw a man going toward the back staircase."

Amberly sat up straighter. "Did she recognize him?"

"She only saw a man of medium height and wiry build."

The constable put two fingers to his forehead. "Both the butler and the handyman fit that description. I planned to talk with them anyhow."

"Mr. Eyelers left before the storm, and I don't think he's back, so it must've been Mr. Stricket." Or Eyelers sneaking around.

"I'll ask him why he was upstairs at a late hour. Any idea of where Eyelers went?"

"To Lauger's place. The maid says he goes over there fairly often."

"I don't mind saying I'm anxious for Agent Hastings to arrive. Maybe he'll be able to convince someone higher up at the Bureau to look at the situation out here. There are odd goings-on that may or may not be related to your friend's death."

His sincere observation reassured her. Amberly seemed like an honest lawman, so she plunged ahead and revealed the rest of what Monica had shared, and what she and Ida had done as a result. Bella held her breath as she waited for his response.

"You went to the garden shed at midnight and poked around?" Both disbelief and disapproval were in his voice and expression. "What in the world were you thinking to do such a thing?"

The rebuff stung. Knowing she and Ida had taken a risk, but convinced they'd been right to do so, Bella lifted her chin. "Mr. Eyelers went to the Lauger place prior to the storm. He wasn't back last evening, and it was unlikely he'd come after dark. Not with so many trees and branches down. It'd be hard enough to make his way back in daylight."

Amberly's expression didn't soften. "Dr. Kern and I made it."

"But you didn't dock at the Lauger place, did you?" Bella realized she was being argumentative, but she pressed on. "You didn't have to come as far as Eyelers would."

Several seconds ticked away as Amberly stared at her. When he spoke, some—but not all—of the displeasure left his voice and countenance. "We docked here. However, you were still foolhardy to be poking around Eyelers' hiding place in the middle of the night. Miss Sawyer may have died as the result of methanol poisoning. I've suspected bootlegging out here for a while. I'm sure I don't need to explain to you that violence often accompanies rumrunning."

"No, sir, you don't." The urge to offer more excuses filled Bella, but she resisted. Antagonizing the man wouldn't help.

Amberly's jaw tightened until a tiny muscle twitched in his cheek. "You might as well tell me what you found."

Bella aimed to remain placid and brief. "Cases of empty bottles, cases of full bottles, and an array of other substances: wood alcohol, juniper oil, sugar, glycerin, and maple syrup. Rat poison, too."

A scowl darkened the lawman's face. "He was diluting the good stuff to make more money. The wood alcohol is dangerous, but it adds bulk so he could make one fifth into two or more. Some of the other items mask the nasty taste of toxins."

"That's what we figured, but what about the rat poison?"

"It's tasteless, but not odorless. Its presence on a shelf with bootlegging supplies is disturbing, since the taste could be hidden with some of the other ingredients." He tapped his pencil on the notepad. "Accidental poisoning happens far too often, but is there any reason Eyelers would want to kill Miss Sawyer?"

Bella shook her head. "I don't know of any, but Sylvia mentioned Florence gambling and losing a lot the day before yesterday. She also said Florence was deeply in debt and owed her money. Florence was furious. She quickly tried to cover up by laughing it off like it was a joke."

"Quite a few speakeasies run illegal gambling operations in back rooms. Both men and women bet in them, so that's possible. Was anymore said about the subject? Particularly the debt?"

"Both Lauger and Darre revealed she owed them money, too. Lauger said she might get even at his next party."

Amberly slumped back in the chair. "So, there's most likely a bootlegging ring and a gambling operation. I can't say I'm shocked, but I didn't expect to learn so much this morning." He narrowed his gaze on her. "I assume you and your friend left the supplies in the shed."

"We did. We had to move a cabinet that was on top of the hidden door to the dugout, but we put it back and left everything else as we found it. We even covered all footprints and marks from moving the cabinet."

"Good. You took a big chance, though. What if Eyelers had gone to his stash while you and Miss Byington were snooping? The man must have at least one weapon and, if he's involved in Miss Sawyer's death, even unintentionally, he may not have hesitated to kill the two of you."

Because what he said was true, Bella felt another sting of criticism, so she hurried to offer additional explanation. "We felt sure he wasn't here and wouldn't be back."

"So, you said." He glanced back at his notes before looking up again. "You haven't discussed all this with Miss Remington, have you?"

"No. Only Blanche, Ida, and I talked about everything."

"Why didn't you include the other friend in your discussion? It's Miss Hartley, right?"

"Yes, Lina Hartley." Bella stopped. Although she had no solid evidence about Lina's potential involvement in Sylvia's death, the constable should be informed about the rift between the pair. "A few years back, Lina's college sweetheart ended their courtship and became betrothed to Syl. I don't have details because I'd left school to serve in the Signal Corps. In fact, I only found out Lina hadn't spurned him this weekend. She blames Syl for the breakup."

"That presents a troubling additional aspect." Amberly ran a hand over his face. "I thought I'd be here a short time. Evidently not. I'll speak with everyone, including Miss Hartley."

"I made some notes last night that I'd be happy to share with you."

"Since I need all the help I can get, I'll take you up on the offer." He jotted down a few more notes. "Thank you for providing details. I know it can't be easy to lose a friend, especially under suspicious circumstances."

Her heart clenched as he spoke. Very suspicious circumstances. "It is."

"I'll go out and get the next person." He rose from the chair but paused. "Your maternal grandfather was Constable Moore, wasn't he?"

Bella nodded. "Yes, he was."

"I met him in passing when I was first on the job. Like Richard Jenkins, he had a great reputation."

Pride and warmth spread through Bella. "When he took the job in Moreley, he and my grandmother lived at Ballantyne. They stayed after he retired, so I spent a lot of time listening to his stories. The two of us even put together a memoir of them."

A broad grin creased Amberly's face and erased the last of his sternness. "No wonder you have strong detective skills."

Bella returned the smile. Her work with her grandfather was one of her initial points in convincing Jax to let her help on a case when she'd first gotten home. That and Richard Jenkins' support. "Thank you."

Amberly nodded. "Excuse me. I'll be right back."

Chapter Eight

♥

Within a few moments, Amberly returned with Ida. Once both of them were seated, the constable began, much as he had with Bella. Ida answered the questions with the same information until the constable brought up what she'd overheard shortly after midnight. "Did you recognize the other voice?"

"No. I didn't even recognize Sylvia's voice. It was her room, so I assumed it was her chatting with someone." Ida paused for a moment. "I thought Sylvia was most likely talking with Florence. They've stayed close over the years."

Bella kept scribbling until Amberly looked at her and back to Ida. "I'll ask Miss Remington if she checked on any guests after you all went to bed, but I won't mention you overhearing anything. I'd rather Miss Remington not realize you did, especially if she was the one in Miss Sawyer's room."

Bella nodded. "We've only told Blanche what Ida overheard."

A frown crinkled his brow. "Blanche is the one who was a nurse." Once again, his voice was stern.

"Yes," Bella replied. "She, Ida, and I discussed Syl's death. She won't tell anyone else." Maybe she should have revealed this tidbit when he'd asked about anything he needed to know. But Blanche wouldn't talk, so it really didn't seem like an important point to Bella.

Amberly didn't look convinced, but he returned his attention to Ida. "Miss Stewart mentioned that only Miss Remington and Miss Sawyer stayed in college during the war. Did you remain in touch with either of them?"

"I exchanged a handful of notes with everyone over the years, but not when Bella and I were in France," Ida said. "We barely had time to write home."

Again, Amberly glanced at Bella. "Richard said you'd served in France as a Signal Corps operator." His gaze went back to Ida. "You two are brave young women."

A soft smile touched Bella's lips. "We did our bit, which wasn't nearly as much as some."

"You did a lot, I'm sure. Miss Byington, are you and Miss Stewart the only ones in your group who went overseas?"

Ida nodded. "Yes, but Blanche served with the Red Cross here at home. She worked in a hospital back east. Lina is a secretary, but she worked with Red Cross canteens during the war."

"What about Miss Remington and Miss Sawyer? Did they volunteer at all?" the constable inquired.

Bella noted Ida's hesitation in replying. Neither of the others had done much in the war effort, which had come as a surprise to Bella. Thinking back, she recalled Sylvia and Florence saying it was foolish to waste time in the endeavor. Sylvia's attitude was especially inexplicable since her fiancé had fought and died in the trenches.

"I think they both went to fundraisers for the Red Cross and other charities," Ida said.

"They weren't full-time volunteers or workers any place?" the constable asked.

"No, they weren't." Ida shifted uneasily in her chair. "Both were always very involved in social activities. I'm sure they attended some events that raised money for soldiers."

"An interesting attitude."

The way Amberly said *interesting* made Bella think the constable found the behavior odd. Not that she disagreed. Both her brother Matt and Jax had been in the Ohio National Guard, so she'd realized long before America went to war that they'd be called up. The certainty had led Bella to look for ways to serve after April 1917, when President Wilson declared war. Most everyone else of her acquaintance had done the same. But not Syl or Florence.

When neither Bella nor Ida spoke again, Amberly continued. "As I said to the group, we won't know the cause of Miss Sawyer's death until Doctor Kern does an autopsy, but the symptoms and circumstances make me lean toward bad booze as a strong possibility. Miss Sawyer carried a flask or two with her. Where are they now? I didn't see them in her room."

"No," Ida replied. "I have no idea. Maybe Monica, she's the maid, took them."

"Many flappers carry hip flasks. Miss Stewart said both Miss Sawyer and Miss Remington went to speakeasies and such. Would you classify them as flappers?" Amberly asked.

"Not Florence, not as far as I could tell," Ida replied, "but Syl seems to fall into the category."

"What do you think, Miss Stewart? Are they flappers?"

Unsure why the constable hadn't asked when the two of them were alone, Bella hesitated to respond. Had it only occurred to him after hearing from Ida? The reason really didn't matter. Her opinion of Sylvia was low, but Bella felt sorry for her friend, too. Even though she'd acted foolishly at times, Syl didn't deserve to die. "On Friday night, Sylvia was definitely dressed in that style, but all of us dressed up. She shared her typical activities with us, which included going to illegal bars. When Ida and I joined the group around seven o'clock, Syl had been imbibing and was already slurring her words and acting foolishly. My opinion may not be shared by everyone, and I'm sure the others will tell you Sylvia and I disagreed over her drinking hooch and frequenting speakeasies."

"You disapprove of alcohol consumption?" Amberly asked.

His own opinion wasn't clear in words or voice, but many lawmen didn't support Prohibition. Some were on the take. She still wondered if Constable Amberly was among them. Just because he knew Richard Jenkins, and had known Jax's father and Bella's grandfather, Amberly wasn't necessarily the same sort of by-the-book officer all of them had been. He'd talked about being glad Jax was on the way, but was that a cover-up? She couldn't be sure. When Bella replied, she spoke cautiously but candidly. "I don't like people breaking the law. They're putting money in the pockets of gangsters who are violent and kill innocent people. Sylvia wanted me to take a drink, and I refused. She wouldn't take no for an answer and got snippy. That made me mad, and we had words."

"Understandable," the constable said.

"Did Jax explain why he joined the Prohibition Bureau?" Bella asked.

"We didn't discuss that," Amberly replied.

After briefly outlining the O'Donnelly case, Bella continued, "I didn't have powerful feelings about Prohibition until I heard about Jocelyn O'Donnelly's murder."

"That would move most people. Unfortunately, many folks circumvent the law—or break it outright. With violence on the increase, I hope that will change. We need more support from average citizens. The law is controversial, but it is the law." He leaned back in his chair. "It's no wonder you and Miss Sawyer disagreed.

Jax has a tough job, and people who engage in illegal activities only make it worse for agents like him."

The constable's words reignited Bella's banked anxiety. While Jax wasn't always at the forefront of her mind, he was always in the back of it. As was her worry for him. "I suppose I reacted quickly and sharply because of that."

"Did Miss Sawyer continue to flaunt her activities?" he asked.

"She and Florence both talked about going to high-class speakeasies. Florence tried to make it sound like she wasn't in favor of it, but she went when she visited Sylvia. Later, we learned about them attending parties at the Lauger place," Bella replied.

"Far too many people go along," Amberly said. "Miss Byington, is there anything else that you found interesting or important about their discussion?"

"Not really. Florence's parents had an extensive supply of liquor. Some of us visited when we were in college, and I recall the bar being well-stocked. Florence said her mother and father asked Eyelers to get rid of it when Ohio went dry." Ida laid her hands on the chair arms. "Sylvia said she could get booze on the island. Florence insisted Syl was kidding, but Bella and I didn't think she was."

"Miss Stewart mentioned that, but she also said the two of you checked the garden shed and found a stockpile of various items beneath it."

Bella glanced at Ida, who was looking back with dismay stamped on her face. "The constable needed to know."

Ida shrugged and looked back at Amberly. "He has a lot of liquor, along with poisons and other substances to cover up the nasty taste of hooch." Color bloomed in her cheeks. "Not that I've tasted bootlegged booze. It's just what I've heard."

A low chuckle rumbled out of Amberly. "Thanks for the clarification." Then, his amusement ebbed. "Miss Stewart, from your work with Jax and Richard, you recognize how important it is to be circumspect about case details."

"Of course," Bella replied, but she wondered why Amberly made the remark. Was he still upset that she and Ida had discussed their suspicions with Blanche? His next statement illuminated his concern.

"We've suspected someone on one of these islands is bootlegging. Eyelers might be involved, and I plan to look closely at him and Lauger. Since Eyelers tends the boat, he has a way to transport liquor, maybe over to Burnley Cove. Maybe others places, as well." He drummed his fingers on the desk. "He's also one of the few who stay on the island all year. Not much rumrunning in the dead of winter, but spring through late fall is the busy time. Stricket, the cook, and the maid arrive in May and leave in October."

Surprise filled Bella. "I didn't realize Eyelers was here alone at times."

Amberly nodded. "A few weeks early and a few later in the year. But, if he's involved in bootlegging, he can't be limiting his participation to those times, which means others in the household may harbor suspicions about what's going on. Like the maid, as you've indicated." He ran his fingers through his closely cropped hair. "I'll talk to her and the rest before I go. As for Lauger and Darre, I'll have to make a trip over there, too. It won't be right now since I need to go back with Doc." He focused on Ida again. "Miss Stewart mentioned you saw a man upstairs the night of the storm. I take it he didn't see you."

Ida shook her head. "He was disappearing down the servants' stairway when I came out of the lavatory. I stopped immediately because it made me uneasy."

"And you couldn't tell if it was Stricket or Eyelers?" the constable asked.

"I'm afraid not. It was a man. Medium height and wiry. I couldn't even determine his hair color. He was simply a silhouette," Ida replied. "But Eyelers was gone by then, according to Monica."

Amberly looked from one young woman to the other. "You've given me a lot to go on, and I thank you both."

Three hours later, Jax and Griff were nearing the end of an arduous trip from Ballantyne to Winnabee. "It looks like Amberly is still on the island since that's the boat his deputy described," Jax said as he gestured toward a craft already tied to the battered dock. "After talking with Richard, I feel better about the man, and I'm glad he and the doctor are here." Even so, tension knotted his insides. Upon arriving in Burnley Cove, he and Griff learned the local constable had already left for the island, but no additional details were known. After he and Biggins secured the boat, Jax jumped to the dock and looked around. "Amberly was right about the damage. There are a lot of trees and limbs down."

Griff pointed at the mansion in the distance. "At least the house looks okay. From here anyhow."

"That's a relief." Jax had been on edge ever since they'd gotten word about the storm. Hearing about a death had escalated his apprehension. What if it was Bella? The question hadn't left his mind. He shook off the fear and kept going forward. In a few minutes, he'd know.

The two men moved toward the dwelling. Their progress was slow as they had to walk around or climb over debris. By the time they reached the garden, both were panting.

"That was a tough trek," Griff said.

"I won't argue." Although the air was cool, sweat beaded Jax's forehead. A memory of marching to and from the trenches hit him, but he forced it away. He had plenty to handle in the present.

The pair moved forward and entered the house through what was likely to be the servants' entrance, since it was in back. Two sets of stairs were just inside the door.

"Which way?" Griff asked.

"The kitchen is most apt to be downstairs." Jax pointed to a narrow set of steps. "The main part of the house has to be up this flight." His theory proved right, and the men arrived in the foyer within a moment.

"No one's here." Griff looked around the spacious entry. "Should we scout around? I'm eager to find out details about what happened."

Jax saw his own anxiety mirrored in Biggins' eyes. Neither one needed to say what details. "I am, too." He glanced around the main floor. "There are several doors. Let's peek in the open ones to start. Why don't you take the left side, and I'll take the right?"

Before Jax and Griff had time to check even one room, an older man ambled into the foyer. "Who might you gentlemen be?" A slight edge was in his voice and tension laced his wiry form.

The man's tone and expression indicated no genuine desire to help, but Jax forced a smile. "I'm Agent Jackson Hastings, and this is my colleague, Griff Biggins. Constable Amberly is expecting us. Where might we find him?" Although he wasn't here on official business, Jax didn't think they'd get far by admitting they were looking for Bella and Ida. When the older man failed to respond, Jax reached into his jacket pocket and extracted his credentials. "Now, could you point us in the right direction?"

"He's using the den for interviews. Please follow me." He led the way down a corridor that extended from the foyer. When he reached a closed door, the man briefly turned back to them. "I'm Mr. Stricket, the butler. If I can be of additional assistance, you need only ask." Then, he rapped on the door.

Jax's pulse pounded in his ears, while hope and terror warred in his mind. *Be safe, Bella. Be safe.*

A different man's voice called out, "Come in."

Stricket poked his head inside. "Two gentlemen to see you, sir. Agents Hastings and Biggins."

"Thanks for the promotion," Griff whispered to Jax.

Jax managed a weak grin. "It was the quickest way to find Amberly and, hopefully, Bella and Ida." And, with luck, find both of them hale and healthy.

When the door opened wide, Jax took a step before stopping dead in his tracks. A man of middle years, probably Amberly, sat with Bella and Ida. Surprise and relief filled Jax. Despite the smudges beneath Bella's beautiful, dark eyes, she looked as lovely as ever. But even more important, she was alive and well. Words failed Jax and, beside him, Griff seemed to be in much the same state.

Long moments passed before the other man rose and moved toward the newcomers. "I'm Constable Warren Amberly. I was expecting you two, although I didn't think you were both Prohibition agents."

Jax, his heart in his throat, was still watching Bella, whose gaze had widened. He forced his attention to Amberly and thrust out his hand. "I'm Agent Jax Hastings." He cocked his head toward his companion. "This is Griff Biggins. He isn't an agent, but telling the butler that seemed like the fastest way to get to see you."

Amberly nodded before exchanging handshakes with the men. "I was just wrapping up my interviews with

Miss Stewart and Miss Byington. Since you're all acquainted, come on in."

Griff was quick to take the only empty chair and pull it next to Ida. With an ottoman being the lone available seat, Jax put it by Bella's chair and sat down. "Are you all right?" he asked in an indistinct murmur. Clearly, she was still alive, but her fatigue was obvious. Who had died? One of her friends or the elderly housekeeper? As compassionate as Bella was, any death would pierce her heart.

"I'm better now," she whispered.

His heart pounded so hard that Jax feared it might beat right out of his chest. Concern disappeared, and he grinned. "So am I. When Constable Amberly said a woman was dead..." Jax cleared his throat of the emotion threatening to choke him. "I was...that is, we were all terribly concerned."

"Especially Jax," Griff put in. "He wanted to drive up last night."

Heat flooded Jax's face as he looked at the golf pro. "You wanted to come, too." He wasn't sure why he felt a need to offer an excuse. What Biggins said was true.

A low laugh escaped Griff, but he was gazing at Ida, not Jax. "I sure did."

The constable cleared his throat. "Ladies, our interview is at an end, so I'll take a break and speak with Dr. Kern. I'll be back shortly."

Once Amberly was gone, Bella reached out and grasped Jax's hands. "I'm so glad you're here, but you look exhausted. Are you getting any sleep?" As happy as she was to see him, Bella couldn't ignore his fatigue or his weight loss. He was almost as thin as he'd been in France. "Are you eating properly?" When he hesitated to reply, she hurried on. "The answer must be *no* to both questions." Even though Amberly had said Jax and Griff were on their way to the island, Bella had been caught off-guard by their appearance. Or maybe by the simple sight of Jax. Two months apart was too long. She hoped he agreed.

Griff offered an explanation. "He drove all Thursday night to get to Ballantyne. After we realized there'd been a terrible storm up this way, we were all worried. Mac remembered a bad one from some years back, and when we found out you'd lost telephone and electricity, that caused more concern. Finding out a woman died, but not knowing who, was much worse."

Ida squeezed his hand. "Thank you for worrying and for driving up here."

Griff moved his gaze back to Ida. "It's a relief to find you safe and sound."

Bella wasn't sure where to focus or what to say, so she started with Griff's first revelation. Puzzled, she looked back at Jax. "You drove all night getting home? Why?"

Jax's gold lashes fluttered down to hide his eyes. "I only have four days off. I left right after work on Thursday, so I didn't want to waste any time." His gaze met hers. "Of course, I figured you'd be at Ballantyne, not up here."

"Oh, Jax. Why didn't you mention you were taking time off in your last note?" They'd already missed being together during most of his leave.

A shrug moved one of his shoulders. "Derringer didn't give final approval until Wednesday. If I'd written then, I would've arrived before the note. I thought about calling, but I was worried that something would happen in Philly, and I'd get stuck. I didn't want to get your hopes up and dash them at the last minute."

The explanation made sense. "I'd love to go back to Ballantyne right now, but I'm not sure when we can leave. Constable Amberly is looking into Sylvia's death by himself, and some complications have arisen." Bella chewed on her lower lip.

He gazed back at her then. "It was your friend Sylvia who died?"

Both Ida and Bella nodded. "I was the one who told the operator that a woman was dead, but the line was filled with static, and the call was lost after only a few minutes. I'm really sorry everyone fretted about us," Bella said.

Griff and Jax exchanged glances. "We thought maybe the housekeeper, because Constable Amberly said she was on in years. Or possibly someone fell down the stairs in the dark," Jax said. "Is that what happened?"

"Unfortunately, it's not that simple," Ida replied.

The two men sat stock-still as Ida and Bella took turns telling the story of how Blanche had found Sylvia the previous morning. They offered the grim details bit-by-bit.

After she relayed Monica's revelations, Bella gave Ida a slight shake of the head to warn her friend not to mention their foray into the garden shed. Ida's reply was a smile. Bella thought their silent, surreptitious message hadn't been noticed until Jax spoke.

"What are the two of you leaving out?" Jax asked as his gaze went from one friend to the other.

Bella released his hand and avoided his steady perusal as she considered how to respond. He knew her too well, and he wasn't apt to let the subject drop, so she relented and revealed their midnight excursion. Jax listened without interrupting. Once she finished, Bella fully expected a lecture from him, but Griff spoke first.

"What were you thinking?" he asked in a voice laced with disapproval. "That was risky. You two could have been hurt or even killed. You've helped Jax with investigations, but he wasn't here. No lawmen were, and you put both yourself and Ida in grave danger."

It wasn't until Griff made his last point that Bella realized his chastisement was directed at her. For several moments, she simply stared back at him. The golf pro was always amiable, which made his outburst stunning. Although she was one of his bosses, Bella felt defensive. "We told you about Eyelers being gone. It was a good time to look, and we discovered important evidence."

"But he could have come back. And what about the neighbor and his partner? What if they have more accomplices? Risking your life is one thing, but encouraging Ida to risk hers is where I draw the line," Griff shot back. His usual calm countenance was gone. Dismay gleamed in his eyes.

"Griff, I wanted to go," Ida said. "Bella didn't make me."

When he looked at Ida, Griff's expression softened. "You went to France with her, too, and that was perilous. Bella puts herself in harm's way too much..."

Jax's voice cut into Griff's statement. "Bella is a good detective, maybe better than I am. And she's not foolhardy. She's intuitive and intelligent." His voice was as cold and hard as a sheet of ice, and his eyes held green frost as he stared at Biggins. "She'd never try to talk Ida, or anyone else, into taking an unwarranted risk. She'd go on her own before doing that, and you've got no business finding fault with her."

Amazement and gratitude spread through Bella. Jax was defending, not reprimanding, her. He believed in her abilities. He believed in her. And he'd evidently gotten past his penchant for issuing warnings to her about staying safe. Progress. A lot of progress. As for Griff, his primary concern seemed to be Ida, and Bella couldn't fault him for that.

"Jax is right, Griff. I went because I wanted to go. That's the same reason I joined the Signal Corps. Because I wanted to do my part, not because Bella talked me into it," Ida said. "I appreciate you wanting to make sure I'm safe, but you went too far, and you owe Bella an apology."

Griff's jaw tightened as he searched Ida's face. A long moment of silence ensued before Jax spoke again.

"I agree about Bella deserving an apology. You were out of line, Biggins. Way out of line." Jax's nostrils flared with a sharp intake of breath.

The two men stared at each other for what seemed like an eternity. Bella wasn't sure what message passed between them, but she soon heard Griff saying he was sorry.

"I was out of line, Bella," the golf pro said. "For criticizing you and for suggesting Ida can't, and doesn't, think for herself. I won't make either mistake again. I promise both of you that." His attention went back to Jax. "I promise you, too."

"I'll hold you to that," Jax said, but his voice once again sounded normal and his expression held little tension.

After Bella and Ida agreed they expected Griff to keep his word, he smiled at Ida. "I've been as worried as Jax. That's not a good excuse, but it gives me the shivers to think of you falling victim to foul play."

Ida beamed in return. "It's all right to worry, but not to be overly protective."

"Well put." Bella noted a guilty look sweeping over Jax's face as she spoke. He'd been guilty of that on more than one occasion.

"Ida and Bella proved their mettle in France and, while we can't help but worry about them, they don't need us hovering." Jax addressed the remarks to the other man, but his attention was on Bella.

She smiled. "Also, well said. But we need to get back to the goings-on here. Constable Amberly will speak with Blanche, Lina, and Florence. And the household staff. He wants to talk to Lauger and Darre, too." Bella explained about Syl's relationship with Lauger.

"The bounder," Griff said.

"And worse," Jax added. "If he gave her a flask on Friday, she could've had a little that night."

"They were sober when they got off his boat," Bella said. "Darre and Lauger brought some liquor to dinner, but no one drank. Blanche is convinced that Syl didn't die from too much booze. So am I."

"From what you've said, I agree." Jax ran a hand over his face. "When we left Ballantyne this morning, I didn't expect to run into such a complicated situation."

The comment echoed inside Bella. "This weekend hasn't turned out at all like I figured." An understatement, to be sure.

Warren Amberly's return prevented further conversation among the group. "I spoke with Dr. Kern. He'd like to get Miss Sawyer back to town for an autopsy as soon as possible. I shared what you ladies revealed. He isn't prepared to issue a cause of death yet, which isn't surprising, but he's leaning toward methanol poisoning based on what you've told me. Symptoms are similar to drunkenness, but a big issue is your friend getting liquor illegally. It wouldn't take a lot to kill her, depending on the composition, of course. Almost all bootlegged booze is tainted, and you ladies found ingredients that are toxic."

Jax ran one hand over his face. "We just heard about the ties between Sylvia and Lauger. That adds complications."

The constable nodded. "It does. After I left Doc, I tried calling my office and got through. Unfortunately, one of my deputies broke his arm moving debris, so he needs Dr. Kern himself. Once the boy gets his bone set, he'll cover the office." Amberly rubbed his chin. "I planned to go back with Doc and return here. Now, that may not be today. It's tricky because Winnabee isn't actually in my jurisdiction. I can't assume Miss Sawyer's death resulted from a crime. At least not at this point."

"Even if it was accidental, whoever gave the liquor to her could be held responsible," Jax said.

"True," the constable agreed, "but I've got to get back to my office."

"Does that mean you aren't investigating any further?" Bella asked. "You haven't even talked to Florence, Lina, and Blanche. Or the staff here. Or Eyelers, Lauger, and Darre."

Jax heard the dismay in Bella's voice and saw the alarm on her face. She naturally wanted justice for her friend, but he understood Amberly's situation. The man was balancing a lot, and an accidental death wasn't a top priority for him. If it was an accident.

"Not right now. The preliminary autopsy results will be important," the constable replied before turning to Jax. "I'd like to speak with you in private, Agent Hastings."

Jax rose. "Of course."

After bidding goodbye to the others, Amberly led Jax out of the room and down the hall. He stopped at the far end. "I assume the young ladies told you quite a lot."

"You'd be guessing right," Jax admitted with a smile. "I'm sure there's more, though."

Amberly rubbed his forehead. "I understand them wanting their friend's death thoroughly investigated, and I agree there's more to it than immediately meets the eye. An autopsy to determine if it was methanol poisoning is important, but deciding whether it was accidental or intentional may be difficult. I'd like to dig deeper, but

I have responsibilities in town right now. Although we're shorthanded and overburdened, I'll try to get back or send my other deputy."

"I completely grasp your problem," Jax assured the other man.

"An important factor is the liquor, poisons, and other substances under the garden shed. I assume you heard about all that."

"Bella admitted she and Ida went to investigate after talking with the maid. They revealed what they found."

"She and her friend have plenty of pluck, but you're aware of that already."

Jax couldn't help but grin. "I am." Too much pluck at times, but he withheld that observation. Bella wouldn't be Bella if she was reticent.

"I can't say I was shocked by what they found. Rumors have circulated about bootleggers using this island for a while. I've never been able to get details, and I don't have the authority to search for rumrunners out here."

The explanations made sense and offered insight into why Amberly wanted to talk privately. "Bella mentioned you not having enough evidence to get the Bureau to act in the past."

Amberly released a pent-up breath. "I haven't until now."

A plea clearly underlined the statement. "I can't get involved without permission from my boss, but I can ask." Jax considered how Amos Derringer would react to his request to stay and investigate. Maybe positively, but maybe not. The senior agent was also balancing a lot of responsibilities with a lack of resources. Finding Jocelyn O'Donnelly's killer was at the top of his list.

"I didn't think you could," Amberly replied, "but would you consider staying on and investigating if you get the go ahead?"

Jax drove his fingers through his hair. "What will you do if I can't?"

The older man shrugged. "Wait for the autopsy and see if Dr. Kern rules the death homicide. I'm guessing he will. At that point, I'll do what I can to determine if it was intentional. Right now, I don't have a gut feeling about it. Some signs point that way. Others don't. I'd like to nab Lauger if he gave bad booze to Miss Sawyer. I don't like a man who takes advantage of a woman and shirks his responsibility."

"Neither do I." Jax took a long breath. "He has a powerful motive to get rid of her."

"That's my thinking, too, and the timing is right, since it takes anywhere from hours to a day for someone to die after consuming tainted alcohol. The victim was found mid-morning, which means Miss Sawyer could've consumed the toxin any time between Friday morning and the middle of that night. Someone talked with her around midnight when Miss Byington heard laughter and voices. Probably another woman, which adds to the possibilities."

"Interesting," Jax said. Bella and Ida had revealed a lot before Amberly interrupted, but there were more details. Maybe many more.

"There are plenty of threads to unravel, and it's likely to take a while."

"I'm sure that's true. Do you plan to ask the girls to stay here?" Jax asked.

Amberly drove his fingers through his closely clipped hair. "I can't expect them to wait for autopsy results. Even a preliminary finding will take some time."

"The bootleggers could move the evidence below the shed soon." Frustration hit Jax hard as he considered the genuine possibility that Eyelers, Lauger, and Darre would get away with not only rumrunning but with causing Sylvia Sawyer's death. At least Lauger stood as a likely suspect. Eyelers could have abetted him. Or perhaps the men weren't responsible. Potential scenarios abounded. "Even if no one planned to kill Sylvia, those who provided bad booze could be arrested and charged. It's already happened."

"I hope it happens to more of these rumrunners. They're risking lives to make money." Amberly's jaw tightened. "Will you ask your boss about staying? Like I said, the telephone is working."

"Senior Agent Derringer may go along with the request, or he might send another agent. If someone is free. We're shorthanded, too, so I can't be sure what he'll decide."

"You won't find out unless you ask."

The statement was valid, so Jax let Amberly show him to the telephone alcove. Making the call proved more cumbersome than usual. While Jax waited on the line, he turned to Amberly. "The operator says it will be a few more minutes."

"I'd like to wait until you speak with your boss. When I get back to town, I'm apt to be caught up with problems there, so you won't catch me in my office until late this evening. If the line keeps working." He gestured to the candlestick and earpiece in Jax's hands.

While he waited, Jax considered how to sum up the situation and his request. When Amos Derringer finally came on the line, Jax breathed a sigh of relief. Finding his boss in the office wasn't always easy. Persuading the man to let Jax work an additional case might not be, either, so he presented the facts succinctly before explaining the complications surrounding local law enforcement. Finally, Jax got to his own involvement. "As you can tell, there's good evidence to believe a bootlegging ring is operating from Winnabee. Miss Sawyer got liquor here. From *who* is the major question. In any case, the doctor

157

agrees that methanol poisoning is a very strong possibility. He'll have details after the autopsy."

"I understand." Derringer's deep voice rumbled down the line. "I don't like Miss Stewart and her friend Miss Byington poking around. The girl has worked on other cases with you, but her midnight foray was foolish."

Jax yearned to jump to Bella's defense, but he didn't want to upset his boss. Besides, she and Ida had taken a risk, although a calculated one. "I realize that, sir."

"I'm sure you do. The question is, will she get in your way if you stay?"

Due to Derringer's phrasing, Jax could honestly answer in the negative. Bella would want to be involved, but she'd be a help, not an impediment. Such an admission was apt to aggravate his boss, so Jax sidestepped it. "She won't be in my way." Silence echoed through the earpiece. For a few moments, Jax braced himself for a rebuff. The senior agent knew a little about Jax's relationship with Bella. Not that much of a relationship currently existed. But Jax had hope for the future. Sooner or later, he'd be back in Moreley full-time. With any luck, it would be sooner.

"All right. The large supply of booze, poisons, and other additives is troubling, since it could mean a significant rumrunning operation is going on there. We definitely don't want bad booze harming or killing anyone else. It's happening far too often in too many places. The neighbor's parties are of interest. It's too bad there won't be an event in the next few days."

Jax felt the tension in his neck and shoulders dissipate. He'd be able to stay. "I'll see what I can find out anyhow."

"Good. I'll be in Washington for the next week. Call me early in the morning. We can go over what you've discovered."

"I will, sir."

A moment passed before Derringer spoke again. "You don't need to be told how to investigate, but be careful. As you already know, bootleggers can be brutal, and you're pretty much on your own out there."

Jax repeated his assurance. "I'll be cautious, sir." After they wrapped up with a few other issues, he put the earpiece back on the holder and returned both to the shelf. When he looked at the constable, Jax saw the man smiling. "You got the drift of our conversation."

"I did, and I'm relieved." His good humor disappeared. "I don't like bootleggers operating so close to my town. I feel sure they're supplying at least one bar in my jurisdiction, which causes problems by attracting folks from far and wide. Folks who don't care about keeping Burnley Cove peaceful and pleasant. Neither does the saloon owner who's buying the stuff."

"I'm afraid it's like that in a lot of places nowadays. First, speakeasies open. Then, illegal gambling becomes part of the action. Later, like you say, trouble follows." Jax ran one hand over his face. "Before you go back to town, I'd like to discuss what you've unearthed to date. Bella and Ida probably shared most of it, but your perspective would help me. In addition, I'd like to check out the garden shed."

Amberly readily agreed. "Let me talk to Dr. Kern and let him know I'll be longer. I'll meet you back in the den afterward."

Chapter Nine

♥

When Jax returned, Bella felt relief spread through her. He'd been gone over thirty minutes and, during that time, both Florence and Lina had come to the den, where Bella was trying to explain Jax's and Griff's presence.

Jax looked at Florence and Lina before nodding. "It's been a long time, ladies."

Florence put her hands on her hips as she spun to face him. "What are you doing here?" Her caustic tone clearly revealed her displeasure.

"I already told you about Jax and Griff coming to see if Ida and I were safe." Bella had trouble maintaining a benign tone. Florence had been friendly to Jax in the past. Now, at the very least, she could be civil.

"That's right," Ida added. "I'm sure your betrothed would do the same if he knew about the storm and Sylvia's death."

Griff put a hand on Ida's shoulder, but he glared at Florence, who glared back. "We were both worried. Everyone at the resort was."

A harrumph left Florence. "You're a golf professional," she said to Griff before staring at Jax. "You're a prohi, and we all know how they like to poke around in things that don't concern them."

If the derogatory term bothered Jax, he didn't let it show. "As everyone has said, Griff and I came out of personal concern." He paused for several heartbeats. "But I'll be staying because I am a Prohibition agent, and some activities on this island definitely interest the Bureau."

Bella thought he put a slight emphasis on *am*. As a lawman, Jax had the upper hand. Clearly, he wanted Florence to recognize that. Why was she so upset? Had she given the bad booze to Syl? The question continued to plague Bella, but so did other potentialities. But Jax's revelation evoked a wave of relief. Now, the reason for Jax's lengthy absence made sense. He must have called his boss. At least she figured that was the case. She'd definitely ask when they were alone.

All color drained from Florence's face as she continued to gape at Jax. "What are you talking about? There's nothing suspicious happening out here. Nothing to concern a prohi."

Jax shrugged. "If there isn't, I won't be around for long."

The statement didn't placate Florence, whose expression remained stony, but Lina spoke first. "I have medicinal alcohol. I don't have the federal prescription waiver with me, though." She wrung her hands.

"There are larger issues at play, so that's not a concern," Jax replied. "I'll need to speak with everyone since Constable Amberly wasn't able to do so."

"He doesn't have jurisdiction out here." Florence's voice dripped with disdain. "Neither do you."

As she spoke, Jax straightened to his full height, squared his shoulders, and looked directly at Florence. He backed his posture with words. "That's where you're wrong. I'm a federal agent, so I have jurisdiction in all forty-eight states. Constable Amberly will be back in a few minutes. I'll speak with him again before he leaves. After that, I want to talk with both of you and with the staff. Please don't wander far off and ask them to be available, too."

Florence pursed her lips. "Since our boat was set adrift during the storm, none of us will be going anyplace." With that, she spun on her heel and left the room. Lina followed her.

When Jax again sat on the ottoman, Bella clasped his hand. "I'm glad you're staying, but sorry Florence was so rude."

His lips softened but didn't quite form a smile. "She's not as rude as some folks I've run into over the last two months. But she isn't like I remember her."

Whatever else he might have said was cut off by the constable's return. "Agent Hastings, I talked to the doctor, so I'm free now. If the rest of you will excuse us."

Bella understood the statement dismissed others in the room. She rose and turned to Ida and Griff. "Let's adjourn to the parlor." They followed her out of the den.

"Dr. Kern is ready to leave, so I won't accompany you to the shed. I'm sure Miss Stewart will show you the way."

Jax detected a note of amusement in Amberly's expression, but he didn't acknowledge it. Bella would be happy to be involved, he was sure. "That's fine. Before you leave, I'd like a few more details. You've suspected bootlegging out here for a while. Do you have any reason to think Lauger and his friend Darre are involved? Other than what the maid told Bella and Ida about seeing them with Eyelers and such?"

"I've suspected Lauger of some nefarious doings. Eyelers, too. I'm not as familiar with Darre, and he's not on the island as often as Lauger."

"What do you know about Eyelers?"

"I first met him when he took the job with the Remingtons about four years ago. He's close-mouthed about his background, and I've found nothing on him. Before Ohio went dry, he spent time in a couple of saloons on Burnley Cove. Drank pretty heavy but never caused trouble."

"Are both bars still open?"

"One closed up, but the other is going strong. Supposedly, they only serve soft drinks." Amberly's emphasis on *supposedly* spoke volumes.

"Is it the place you think is buying from bootleggers?"

Amberly nodded. "The owner is a shifty, sly character. I've only got two deputies, and we're plenty busy during summers with tourists. We haven't been able to catch him breaking the law. Or nab Eyelers selling to him, and I'm pretty sure that's what's happening. My guess is he started small and probably soon after the law went into effect. With almost no one else on the island until May, he had a couple of months to make runs to towns with booze from the Remingtons' bar. I didn't know until this morning that they'd asked him to dispose of the stuff. Miss Stewart shared that news."

"Lauger wasn't involved right away?"

"I don't believe so. He started having parties last summer. Around then, Eyelers might've started selling to him. The bits and pieces fit together to indicate that's what happened. Since I don't have authority out here, I contacted the Bureau then. You're busy with bigger operations, so I understood why no agents were sent. My deputies and I tried to nail the bar owner, but he was always a step ahead of us."

"It's tough to catch these people." Jax massaged his temple. "You didn't say if you suspect Darre of any crimes."

"Eyelers isn't the sharpest fellow, so he can't be running a big operation. Lauger is plenty smart, and I figure he took charge eventually, since there's a lot of money to be made. I haven't crossed paths with Darre. He and Lauger told the girls about being business partners but avoided revealing what sort of business."

"What about Lauger's parties? Bella and Ida mentioned Florence owing money to Sylvia, Darre, and Lauger."

"That bothers me in a couple of ways," the constable said. "Rumors around the Cove indicate gambling goes on. Folks don't like losing money, and those are the ones who talk."

The last statement evoked an intriguing possibility. "Do they think the games are fixed?"

A shrug lifted one of the man's muscular shoulders. "One of my deputies heard complaints about that. No solid proof, though."

Jax blew out a long breath. "I won't be surprised if the games are rigged, and it could be part of how Florence got deeply into debt."

"Most of the guests aren't locals. They're fancy folk who sometimes come for a weekend. The Lauger house is a sprawling mansion, so he can put them up. He lays out some enjoyable meals, from what I've heard. Plenty going on during the party weekends, according to local gossip." The constable's dark brows lowered as he studied Jax. "Your boss sending anyone to help you?"

"Not yet. I need to see what I can uncover. If there's enough evidence, he may send another agent or more."

"I don't envy you the job you've got. It's a darn chancy one."

Since he couldn't refute the obvious, Jax simply said, "I'm very cautious."

"Good. I don't need another death out here."

With that, the two men shook hands and Amberly went on his way. Jax returned to the den, where Ida, Griff, and Bella were talking. They stopped when he came in.

"The constable and doctor need to leave, but I'd like to look under the shed. Bella, would you show me the way?"

"Of course." Within a moment, they were headed out of the house and into the garden. As they made their way through storm debris, she spoke again. "I take it you called your boss, and he approved of you investigating?"

"Amberly asked me to stay and, since there's good reason to believe bootlegging is going on out here, Derringer agreed I should look into it."

"What about Syl's death?"

"Since she probably died from ingesting toxic liquor, I'll pursue the case from that angle."

By then, they were at the garden shed. Jax opened the door and let Bella precede him.

"The trapdoor is under the cabinet," Bella said.

Jax looked from the bulky piece of furniture to her. "Moving it couldn't have been easy."

"It wasn't," she agreed.

He surveyed the floor. "There are no marks in the dirt from shoving it around."

"Since we didn't want to alert Eyelers that someone was snooping, we covered them."

"You did a great job of disguising your tracks. Not a footprint or mark from moving this thing. Well done."

"I've learned a few things from our previous cases." Bella grinned as she spoke.

He couldn't help but smile back before turning to the cabinet. "I'll need your help to get this out of the way."

Within a few moments, the pair was in the cramped, dank dugout.

"This place is a bootlegger's dream. All kinds of supplies to doctor liquor." Jax studied the neat rows of bottles. "You were smart to leave everything, as is. Eyelers would surely detect even one bottle being gone from the shelves."

"That's what I figured."

Jax bent to survey the crates on the floor. After pulling a bottle out, he turned it over and around. "This one appears to have been opened." He pointed to the neck. "This isn't what the original seal on this type of liquor would look like. It's similar, but not identical."

"They teach you how to detect differences in caps and seals at the Bureau?"

"It's not part of the training, but I've been on a few raids with more experienced agents. It isn't what I do on a daily basis, since I'm primarily working on the O'Donnelly case. Sometimes, more manpower is needed and, if it's in the Philly area, I get called. I've learned a lot that way."

"You raid speakeasies, or gangster hideouts, or both?"

When Jax glanced at Bella, he noted the concern darkening her gaze. Maybe he shouldn't have made the admission, but it was too late to retract his words. "We've raided a few bars. No hideouts."

"Don't raids take time away from finding Mrs. O'Donnelly's killer?"

"Not much time. Besides, we always hope to find people who know something about the shooting."

"Have you?"

Jax shook his head. "So far, no one has the right details for arrests. Or, if they do, they don't want to say."

"For fear of ending up like she did."

Her reply didn't surprise Jax. "You're correct. I can't reveal much but I'll say this: the hit was meant for Mick and it was ordered by someone high up in a big operation. There were two shooters, a driver, and a lookout man. They seem to have spread out. We've followed leads, but with no luck yet." When Bella bit on her lower lip, Jax took one of her hands. "I promised Mick to see the case through."

"I know."

"I didn't think it would take so long."

"But you would've helped him anyhow." Her voice was firm with certainty.

Jax couldn't argue the point. "I would have."

"Which is as it should be. If not for Mick O'Donnelly, you might not be here now."

"We'll get to the bottom of his wife's death. For now, I want to focus on the current situation." He released her hand and turned to search the corner of the dugout. "There are a bunch of bottles in these stacked crates. I can use one to replace this tampered bottle." He lifted the one in his grasp. "I doubt if Eyelers will do a thorough examination of the crates right off."

"You don't think he'll try to move the stuff?" Bella asked.

"He'd need a lot of help, which he may have for the bootlegging operation, but getting them out here could be a challenge." Jax glanced around the interior. "They could take just the liquor and leave the poisons and other ingredients."

"The booze is what has value, so you're probably right." Bella shifted from one foot to the other. "From what Monica said, Lauger replaced his grandparents' staff with all men. I don't know how many there are."

The revelation troubled Jax. "If they move the booze, any case against them will be weaker." Not only that, without another law officer, he'd have little chance of stopping a group. Finding out the number was critical. "I'll call my boss back and confirm the stockpile of booze and bootlegging ingredients." He grabbed one bottle and replaced it with another. Then, Jax carefully stacked other crates on the one with an empty slot. "Even if Eyelers doesn't notice I've moved things around, my guess is he and his partners will get the liquor out of here as soon as possible. Moving to the Lauger property would be easier than getting it off the island, and there's ample help to do it."

"I suppose so."

"Let's get back to the house. I'd like to go over your notes and Amberly's after I call Derringer. Will you meet me in the den in thirty minutes?"

"Of course."

The pair headed up the rickety stairs. Once in the shed, they replaced the cabinet and hid all evidence of their foray.

"I hope your boss will send agents right away." Bella fell into step beside Jax as they walked through the garden.

"Everything considered, I think he will. There's a lot to investigate with bootlegging. Then, there's figuring out who's responsible for giving Sylvia Sawyer poisoned alcohol."

"And determining if it was accidental or intentional."

Jax nodded but said nothing more. Neither did Bella.

A half-hour later, Jax talked with Amos Derringer again. After explaining what he'd found, he listened to his boss with interest. By the time they finished their exchange, a plan was set. Now, he needed to share part of that plan with Bella. He entered the den to find her perched on the edge of one chair.

"What did your boss say?" was her immediate greeting.

Jax took the seat beside her before replying. "Since I spoke with him earlier, he did some digging. One call was to the nearest Bureau office. He learned from the head agent there that Warren Amberly isn't the only one who's suspected bootlegging out here. His initial calls weren't in vain. Even though no agents were sent, they have had the information on the back burner."

"Have they been investigating?"

"Not actively. That office doesn't have enough man-power to pursue gossip and guesses." He drove his fingers through his hair. "The Bureau doesn't have enough agents to handle blatant activity."

"Does that mean he won't send anyone to help you?"

"Not at all. Derringer will have two agents come as soon as possible. Probably from the nearest Bureau office since they already have suspicions."

"Will they get here today?"

"I doubt it. The drive will take a couple of hours, maybe longer. Some roads leading to the lakeshore are almost impassable due to debris. Of course, no one will start out until the assignment is made, which will take a bit of time. They should be here early tomorrow."

She leaned back in the chair. "Good. What are we going to do until then?"

The question didn't surprise Jax. He'd already said they could review the notes, so that was where he began. After retrieving them from the desk, he returned to his seat. "I'd like to clarify a few things."

"Great."

When she beamed at him, Jax couldn't help but smile back. For now, she was safe and so was he. "You didn't use shorthand for most of these notes."

"Ida and I were talking last night when I put some information in my notebook. I wasn't in a hurry, so I used longhand. Today, Constable Amberly took notes when he talked to me, and I followed suit when he spoke with Ida. Can you decipher everything?"

His grin deepened. "My handwriting is what needs deciphering." He absently massaged his right shoulder.

"How are your shoulder and arm doing?"

Being wounded twice in France had caused problems, problems that had forced Jax to relinquish his dream of being a golf pro and to accept the job as Moreley's constable. The same wounds made it hard for him to write for long periods, which had led to Bella helping him in previous cases. Although he'd like to be back to normal, Jax didn't discount opportunities to renew his ties to Bella. "About the same."

"Griff said you drove all night to get to Ballantyne. Not taking breaks couldn't have helped."

"You're right, but I let him drive up here." Mostly because his bicep had hurt badly.

"Good," Bella replied. "I still think you should reconsider surgery. The doctors said it might not help a lot, but it could make some difference."

"After the O'Donnelly case is solved, and I'm done with the Bureau, I may have the operation."

"Really?" Her surprise was obvious.

He nodded. "Really. The best time would be right after I resign and before I go back to being town constable. Richard will stick around for a few weeks more."

"Did you ask him before you left in April?"

"No, I talked to him before Griff and I came up here. I wanted to get some information on Amberly."

Her expression grew pensive. "The constable said he knew Richard. He knew your dad and my Grandfather Moore, too. And he met you when you were a boy."

"I vaguely remember him, but Richard offered a vote of confidence, which was important."

"Were you wondering if he was being bribed by bootleggers?" she asked.

"I was, since it's all too common, but he's a straight arrow. He wants to quell any rumrunning in the area because it causes a lot of trouble for him and his deputies."

Bella laced her fingers together and laid her hands in her lap. "I didn't have powerful feelings about Prohibition until you told me about Jocelyn O'Donnelly. Ever since, I've been alert to people breaking the law. Some say it's foolish because liquor was legal only two years ago, and it's still legal in most of the world. In fact, that's what Sylvia told me when I wouldn't take a drink the first night we were here."

A frown furrowed his brow. "Were all the girls drinking?"

"Only Syl was the first night. Florence had a little the following evening, but she also admitted to going to speakeasies when she visited Syl in Chicago, and you're aware Lina has a special prescription waiver for medicine with alcohol."

"Do you believe Lina about the waiver? Doctors write them regularly. But I don't know her well," Jax said. "Would she lie?"

"She says it's helping her sleep, and she's had issues for a while. Do you remember her sweetheart, Kenton?"

Vague memories of the times he visited Bella at college returned. "I met him. Evidently, they didn't marry?"

"No. He dropped her after Ida and I left for operator training. We didn't know he'd ended their courtship until this weekend. We just knew they split up, and Kenton started stepping out with Syl later. Before he left for France, they became betrothed."

Jax frowned. "But he and Syl didn't marry?"

"He died in the trenches," Bella replied, "but it seems like Lina mourns him more than Syl did. Although Syl and Lina didn't exactly argue, things were uneasy between them, and Lina was highly critical of Syl's behavior with Lauger and her drinking."

Jax rubbed his chin. "Which means Lina has a motive to harm Sylvia, but what about means? Are you thinking she poisoned some of her prescription medication and put it in Sylvia's hip flask? How easy would it be for Lina to do that?"

"Not too easy, so I'm not sure about that possibility, which is why I didn't tell you right off," Bella admitted. "Lina and Sylvia had a couple of harsh exchanges, and Lina didn't mince words when talking to the rest of us about the situation, either. As strange as it might seem, she's still carrying a torch for Kenton after over three years."

Jax's eyebrows lifted a fraction. "I don't think it seems strange at all. I've been carrying a torch for you much longer." The admission was out before he gave it proper consideration. Since it was the truth, he didn't regret the words. They'd already wasted too much time.

Amazement rounded her dark eyes. "You have?"

"I said so before I left Moreley two months ago." He hadn't admitted quite so much, but almost.

"We both said we'd had crushes on one another since high school," she murmured. "That's not quite the same as carrying a torch."

He shrugged. "My feelings started as a crush, but they grew into a lot more by the time I left for France. Despite the big barrier created by Matt's death, I never stopped carrying a torch for you. Not even when I figured we'd never be more than friends, if that."

"That barrier was only in your mind," she assured him.

Because Jax had harbored guilt about her brother's death in the trenches, he'd kept his distance from her afterward. Only last spring had he revealed details about Matt dying, and about his own remorse and regret. Once Jax realized Bella didn't hold him responsible, he'd finally revealed some of how he felt, and so had she. Now, he was letting her know more. "In my mind, the gap got larger and stronger." A short, quick breath left him. "Anyhow, I understand Lina not getting over her beau. It might be even worse because her friend got together with him. Then, he died and Sylvia went on, seemingly unaffected."

Bella grimaced. "It appears that way."

"It certainly puts an interesting new light on the situation, although Lina would still need to doctor her prescription alcohol and get bad booze to Sylvia. But I won't rule her out." He drummed his fingers on his thighs.

"I just remembered something. The other morning when we all went to the dock, Lina talked privately to Eyelers. Not for long, but they moved far enough from the rest of us that we couldn't hear. I didn't think of it before now."

"Maybe because a lot has happened since then. You know how it's been in previous cases. People remember things in fits and starts, and we figure them out in a similar manner."

A slight smile touched her lips. "You're right. Eyelers looked hung over Friday morning and when he picked us up on Thursday. That might have made Lina think he had booze. Bootlegged booze. Of course, Syl had already told all of us about getting liquor some place on the island, and there aren't many people here at present."

"Very interesting," Jax agreed.

"I've also wondered about her needing a drink to sleep. According to what Lina told us, she's been having a nip at night ever since Kenton took up with Syl. That's been a few years. Do you think the same amount would be enough to help her now?"

Jax mulled the question over. "I'm not an expert on alcohol, so I can't be sure. She may have an increasing desire to drown her sorrows. I'll ask her more, but she's only one suspect." He glanced back at the pad of paper. "Florence spends enough time on Winnabee to know about rumrunning. That fact keeps standing out to me."

"And she's gone to parties at the Lauger place. So did Syl."

When Jax again scanned the notes, he frowned. "What did you mean by saying Darre acted familiarly with Florence? They must have met at some of Lauger's parties. Do you think they're friends?"

Bella wrinkled her nose. "Mr. Darre squeezed next to Florence on the chaise lounge. He sat very close and put his hand beside her bare leg. We were all in bathing suits." She shook her head. "I sound like a prude."

"Not at all. You're a very modern young woman, who has a sense of propriety. That's admirable in these times."

"Thank you." After a brief pause, Bella went back to explaining the situation between Darre and Florence. "She looked uncomfortable when he got so close, but she didn't push him away or ask him to move. It's hard to explain, but it seemed creepy."

"It sounds creepy." Jax's gaze widened as he read more of the notes. "He said there were ways she could repay her debts without money? It doesn't say here how Florence reacted."

"She flushed and tried to hush him up," Bella replied.

"Did he hush up?"

"He finally dropped the subject."

Once again, he looked at the pad of paper. "You said Florence drank at dinner?"

"On Friday night. Lauger and Darre brought liquor with them. When they offered it to her, she took it. She didn't drink a lot. Certainly not enough to be intoxicated."

"And no one else was drunk." She'd said as much earlier, but he wanted to confirm the facts.

"No one." Bella laid a hand on her head. "It was a rather stilted conversation. Syl said little at the table and neither did Florence nor Lina."

With a sigh, Jax leaned back in the chair. "I remember seeing Florence several times when Matt and I went to your college for events. She always seemed very sweet, even a little shy. I was surprised when she was curt with me today."

"Florence acted more like her old self when we first got here, although she seemed uneasy and stiff. It wasn't until Syl teased her about gambling and losing money that Florence got annoyed. Comments about her debts from Lauger and Darre made the situation worse." Bella scanned his face. "I'm sorry she called you a prohi. She should've been more courteous."

A chuckle escaped him. "It's become common shorthand, so I didn't mind."

"You're a federal agent, and you deserve respect." She looked upset on his behalf.

Jax reached out and clasped her hand. "Thanks. I appreciate your support more than you know."

"I'm not doing anything you didn't do earlier."

He cocked his head. "You mean when Biggins criticized you? He had no business finding fault and, not only that, he was dead wrong."

Bella grinned. "More than once, you've said I'm too headstrong and need to be more cautious."

He couldn't deny her honest assertion. "I've said it because I worry about you and don't want you getting hurt." The image of Mick O'Donnelly rose in his mind. The man was devastated by his wife's death, and Jax empathized.

"Constable Amberly chastised me about going to the garden shed, too, but you didn't." She let a brief silence fill the space before continuing. "Do you disagree?"

"With him?" Jax asked. "Or with you and Ida snooping after midnight?"

She pursed her lips. "Your last question indicates you side with Griff and the constable."

"I don't side with anyone chastising you. You're a grown woman, an intelligent and capable one." He squeezed her hand. "What I've said in the past, and what I still say, is you aren't a law officer. You aren't armed, so you can't easily protect yourself if you run afoul of crooks. Bootleggers can be brutal, and I don't want what happened to Jocelyn O'Donnelly happening to you." He couldn't be any clearer.

"I appreciate the sentiment. I don't want that to happen, either, but last night was the perfect time to check Eyelers' hidey hole since he was gone. We wouldn't have done it otherwise."

Jax laced his fingers with hers. "That's good, but I'm here now, so you won't need to go digging for clues on your own."

His last words made her beam. "But I can do it with you."

Before letting go of her hand, Jax brought it to his lips and pressed a gentle kiss to her palm. Then, he sat back in the chair. "I'm not planning to scavenge for more evidence until the other agents get here. You can assist in other ways."

"All right. What are your plans before help arrives?"

Relief spread through Jax when she didn't argue. "Talk to Florence, Lina, and the staff. If Eyelers comes back, I may speak with him but mostly about Sylvia's death. I don't want to make him suspicious. I'll continue to emphasize Griff and I came for personal reasons, which is completely true."

"All the girls know you're a federal agent. I don't think Blanche is involved, but any of the others might have warned Eyelers about you being a Prohibition agent. Syl could have told Lauger when they went for a boat ride." She clasped her hands together and rested her chin on them. "I don't think you should go looking around the island until you have other agents here, either."

"I'd like to check out the dock more carefully and get a feel for how easy it would be for bootleggers to get on and off Winnabee with booze. I'd like to see if any other islands are visible in clear weather. I'm definitely not planning to head to Lauger's house, sneak in, and survey the place."

"Good."

He grinned again. "Before I look at the dock, I should talk with your friends."

"I'll see if they're still in the parlor. Do you have a preference about who is first?"

"Do whatever you think is best. You'll take notes for me, won't you?" While Bella couldn't take part in much of the coming investigation, she could help him now.

"I will," Bella replied before heading out of the office.

When she was gone, Jax slumped back in the chair. A few hours ago, his primary interest had been Bella's safety, not that it wasn't still of top importance. Unfortunately, although he'd found her safe and sound, he was embroiled in a complicated investigation—two, really. Nailing down details about what had to be a bootlegging ring was one; discovering the exact reason for Sylvia Sawyer's death, and who had caused it, was the other. Of course, he still couldn't be sure if it was accidental or intentional, which actually made three questions to answer.

Chapter Ten

Within a few minutes, Bella returned with Florence, whose expression was blank but whose eyes flashed with anger or possibly resentment. Since her current attitude was at odds with her college personality, Jax was increasingly dubious about her innocence. Despite her earlier rudeness, he stood when she entered the room. Good manners couldn't hurt. "Thank you for speaking with me, Florence. Bella probably already told you she'll take notes."

Florence's narrow chin rose a fraction, making it look as if she was looking down her nose at him. "We talked already."

"That was a casual conversation, not an interview." Jax maintained a calm demeanor. "Please sit down."

Florence perched on the edge of the chair farthest from Jax and folded her arms over her abdomen.

As Bella took a seat next to him, she rolled her eyes. Jax had to repress a grin. Bella seemed as disgusted with her friend as he was. But she'd been reluctant to highlight Florence's potential involvement in Sylvia Sawyer's death. Maybe because Bella had already had time to scrutinize and assess the current evidence, she'd drawn that conclusion. Or maybe she couldn't accept that a friend might be implicated. His good humor subsided. With any luck, Warren Amberly would return, or his deputy would, and take over the death investigation, leaving Jax and his fellow agents to deal with potential bootleggers. Not that Florence was in the clear there, either. At least she wasn't in Jax's mind.

He cleared his throat. "I want to go over some points with you. Sylvia Sawyer has visited here a few times, hasn't she?"

"Yes." Florence met his gaze with a stony stare.

"How often did the two of you attend parties at the Lauger house?" Jax formed the question to require more than a *yes* or *no* answer.

Florence blinked rapidly, although that was her only outward reaction. "I didn't count the number of times."

Frustration nipped at Jax. The woman was being obstructive, which only increased his dismay. Unwilling to be thwarted, he tried another tack. "Sylvia went out on Lauger's boat with him, so she must have felt comfortable in his presence. That indicates some level of familiarity."

Florence's nostrils flared with a sharp intake of breath. "Sylvia was friendly with a lot of attractive young men."

At that comment, Jax shot a glance at Bella, who was frowning. Was she thinking what he was? That the remark rang with criticism and disloyalty? So much for not speaking ill of the dead. "What about Mr. Darre? He stayed and chatted with you, right?"

Color flared like twin flags in Florence's cheeks and her mouth dropped open. "He didn't stay because of me. He stayed because Barton and Sylvia clearly wanted time alone. A lot of time. That was nothing new."

Since subtle questions weren't gleaning much information, Jax tried being blunt. "Didn't Mr. Darre mention you could repay a debt to him in ways other than money?"

The color in Florence's face intensified. "He's a tease and was trying to be funny."

"Really? It's an odd way to tease a betrothed young lady," Jax said.

Florence scowled at him. "Sylvia said you were always a dull stick, and she was right. Not only that, you still are."

Because he didn't care a jot about her opinion of him, or Sylvia's, Jax let the criticism roll off. "Some of us have a sense of propriety." He glanced at Bella, who winked in return. He yearned to wink back, but Florence had a knife gaze on him. No sense in shifting the woman's anger toward Bella. He was about to continue with another question, when she spoke.

"The other night you said your fiancé wants to become a judge. Surely, he's very proper." Bella paused for several heartbeats. "You used to be, too."

Jax watched as the anger seeped out of Florence's expression. When she blinked rapidly, he wondered if she was fighting back tears. "I still am, in most ways." She looked at Jax. "I'm sorry for being so rude."

Since she looked and sounded sincere, he nodded. "Apology accepted," he replied. "I know you must be terribly upset by your friend's death and by the possibility that bootlegging is going on out here. I'm simply trying to get information, so I would appreciate your cooperation."

A shuddering breath left Florence. "As Bella said, I'm engaged. My fiancé lives in San Francisco, so I'll be moving there after the wedding. I arranged our brief reunion because I won't get back to Ohio much after my marriage."

"When will you be married?" Jax asked.

"It's planned for October in San Francisco," Florence replied, but there was no joy in her tone or expression.

"You said you don't get to the island a lot. When were you last here?" The notes indicated Florence had entertained Sylvia frequently in the past year or two, so Jax listened carefully.

"I used to spend all summer," Florence said. "When I was in school, I'd be here from late May to early September. My older sister and my mother came, too, of course. My father joined us on weekends and for the month of July."

She hadn't answered his question, but Jax was careful in how he sought a forthright response. Usually, people were hiding something when they didn't reply directly. "Is this the only time you've been out this year?"

Florence shifted in the chair as if trying to get comfortable. "No, I was here in early May."

"Were more houses occupied then?" Jax asked.

"No, none except the Lauger place. Only Sylvia and I were here. With our help, of course. By then, the other houses had some staff on site, but no families were on the island. That's not unusual, though. Early May has never been a busy time."

Once again, she hadn't completely answered him. "Did you and Syl go to a party at the Lauger place then?" Jax asked.

Florence swiveled toward Bella. Her mouth tightened before she looked at Jax again. "We did. Bart is on Winnabee from early March until Thanksgiving." Florence folded her hands in her laps and gazed down at them.

"He and his friend Darre are in business together." Jax made it as much a statement as a question.

Two splotches of red again formed in Florence's pale cheeks. "They are."

"What kind of business?" he asked. The question hung heavily in the air for a long moment.

"I don't know any details." Florence kept her gaze on her clasped hands.

Fresh frustration filled Jax because he figured she was lying. He returned to a previous point. "Was Lauger also teasing about you owing him money, and Sylvia, too?"

"They think they're being funny." Her head came up, and her expression once again grew stormy. "None of that concerns you or your Bureau."

It was more than obvious that she wouldn't admit to gambling debts or to knowledge of bootlegging. He'd have to gather more information some other way. "Since the Bureau sometimes looks into deaths resulting from bad booze, that gives me jurisdiction to investigate Sylvia's passing. You must want to know what caused her tragic death."

Florence said nothing for what seemed like an eternity. "Of course."

Jax studied her for a moment. Then, he rose from the chair. "Thank you for your time and assistance. I appreciate both."

Florence gaped at him. "Is that all?"

"For now, yes."

"I can go?"

"Sure," Jax replied in what he hoped was a reassuring tone.

The woman wasted no time in hurrying away.

"You didn't ask her very much," Bella said. "You didn't press her on gambling debts or anything else."

With a sigh, Jax collapsed back into the chair. "She wasn't going to tell me anymore right now. Besides, I can't risk her getting suspicious and warning Eyelers, Lauger, and Darre. That's too likely already."

"I should've taken that into account." Bella tapped her pencil on the notepad. "You made it sound like Sylvia's death is your biggest concern."

"It's definitely a major issue," Jax assured her. "Like I said, if she died from bad booze, we'll thoroughly investigate the case. It won't matter if it was accidental or intentional. Far too many folks perish that way, and part of the Bureau's job is to keep it from happening."

A shuddering breath escaped her. "I hate having been at odds with Syl over how she talked about Prohibition and..." Her voice trailed off.

"And how she criticized me?"

Bella nodded. "It made me mad, but I didn't want her to die."

"I know you didn't," he said, "but thanks for defending me. I appreciate that." And he did. More than he could say. Being town constable hadn't been his first choice of jobs and being a liquor agent ranked below it. Jax absently rubbed his wounded arm. Would he ever be able to pursue his lifelong dream of being a golf pro? It didn't seem likely.

"What if Eyelers comes back yet today? What if Lauger and Darre come along? Eyelers must know you're an agent by now."

"Probably so." A rap on the door interrupted, and Jax called out. "Come in."

A young girl, perhaps seventeen or eighteen, peeked inside. "Miss Ida said Miss Bella was here, and I wanted to tell her something."

Bella extended one hand. "Monica, sit down." She gestured to the chair beside her before introducing the maid.

Jax rose. "Yes, please do."

Monica perched on the edge of the chair and clasped her hands in her lap. When she didn't speak, Bella did. "What did you want to tell me?"

The girl's gaze darted to Jax, who smiled. "If it's something personal, I'll leave you to speak with Bella alone."

Monica shook her head. "No, sir. I heard you was a lawman, and I thought I should tell Miss Bella, so she could tell you."

"I see," Jax said, his amiable expression still in place. "Why don't you tell both of us?"

"Yes, sir. I were upstairs cleaning. One window were left open, and water come in during the storm, so I were wiping around there and closing it when I looked out." She pulled her clasped hands to her chin. "I seen the Remington boat by the dock. It got set loose the other night, but it's back and it looked like Mr. Eyelers on the deck."

"Was he alone?" Jax sat up straighter and focused on the girl. Had Eyelers hidden it for some reason? Or had he been on a bootlegging run?

Tremors rippled through Monica. "No, another boat was pulling up. It were Mr. Lauger's. Sure looked similar, at least. I didn't stay to see no more. I wanted to let Miss Bella know."

"I'm glad you did, Monica." Bella's voice was soft and reassuring.

"Miss Florence knows I were coming to talk to you," the maid said. Apprehension shadowed the girl's eyes. "But I didn't say why."

Bella patted her arm. "Don't worry. We just spoke with her, and she knows Agent Hastings is looking into Miss Sawyer's death. If she, or anyone else, asks about why you wanted to talk with me, just say you wondered about cleaning my room."

Monica blinked rapidly before nodding. "Yes, miss."

Because he could see the girl was frightened, Jax hurried to offer reassurance. "There's nothing for you to worry about, but don't let anyone else know what you saw. For now, we'll keep it among the three of us. All right?"

"Yes, sir." Monica stood up. "I got chores to do, so I best be about them."

"Thank you, Monica," Bella said, "and I haven't forgotten about you working at Ballantyne. If you want to go back with Miss Byington and me, we can arrange it."

Relief spread across the girl's face. "I'll get my things packed," she said before disappearing from the room.

When the maid was gone, Jax turned to Bella. "The girl is going to work at the resort? How did that come about?"

"She's unhappy here, and not only due to Eyelers and his activities. With so few people on the island, it isn't an ideal place for a young girl. Since we need more help, I offered her a job at Ballantyne."

"Good idea." Jax looked back at the notes.

"Do you want to speak with Lina now?"

"No, not yet. I'll talk to the rest after I look at the dock."

"You're not going down there when those men are around."

The concern shadowing Bella's expression was genuine and valid, but he had to see what was happening. "There must be a good vantage point where I could observe the area without actually going there. Some place closer than an upstairs window."

Her brow furrowed. "There's an abandoned lighthouse about a hundred yards from the Remington dock. We could see a lot from there."

"I noticed it. Can people still get inside?"

"The first night, Florence told us it has wonderful views. We were going to look around yesterday, but with Sylvia dying and the storm damage, we didn't go."

"Do you think you can find the way?"

Bella nodded. "Lina wasn't keen about going, so Florence explained it wasn't far and where the path starts in case any of us wanted to head there. I could show you where it is."

"Can we get there without exposing ourselves to possible scrutiny from anyone near the garden shed or boathouse? I don't want bootleggers seeing us."

"There's a path on the north side of the house, away from the garden and not near the dock, either."

Jax hesitated for a heartbeat. "Okay. Let's go."

Bella led the way to the French doors and turned right. She understood Jax's desire to see what the three men, likely three bootleggers, were doing, but anxiety plagued her. Constable Amberly wouldn't be back today, and the other Prohibition agents weren't likely to arrive until tomorrow. A deputy might come, but that was little solace. If alcohol was moved, would Jax think he needed to monitor the transport? Or worse, stop it? Knowing him, Bella didn't consider the answer for long. He would and, despite his intention to keep her well out of harm's way, she'd be right behind him, since he wasn't going into danger alone. Since discretion was wiser than disclosure, Bella kept her plan to herself. Perhaps, they'd see nothing to evoke Jax's curiosity. Then, he could wait until help arrived.

As they made their way down a narrow path littered with small branches, Bella and Jax were silent. Once they reached the clearing around the lighthouse, he stopped. "It looks to be in decent shape. I wonder why it was abandoned."

"The owners on the island had it built, and they own it as a group. According to Florence, it was never needed since there are other lighthouses in the area. About five years ago, a decision was made to vacate it. The keeper stayed on for a couple of years and finally moved away early last year."

"Then, the stairs should be solid."

"Florence said they are."

Jax opened the door and let Bella precede him. Light poured in through a series of windows circling the main floor. On the far wall, a wood stove stood next to an old cabinet. In the middle of the room was a table with two chairs and, to their left, was a frayed couch. A stairway wound upward. "I'm going to head up and look around. Do you want to come along?"

Bella grinned. "Of course."

The pair mounted the steps. Within a few moments, they were at the top. "Quite a view," Jax said as he looked across the lake. Since the lighthouse was on the north side of the island, the shore wasn't visible, but several other islands, mere dots in the water, were. "No wonder the keeper stayed on for a while. It's very peaceful."

"And beautiful."

Jax pivoted so he could see the Remingtons' dock, and Bella did the same. "The craft Griff and I used is gone."

She immediately came to stand beside him. "What do you think happened to it?" Several ideas came to mind. None were good.

"Maybe Griff and I didn't tie it up well."

"You're too careful to make a mistake like that, and I don't think Griff would, either. He's pitched in with securing our boats a few times this season, and he knew what he was doing."

He ran a hand over his face. "Like I always say, you're very astute. Now, there's no way for any of us to get off the island today."

The compliment was nice, but worry filled her. Untying the boat indicated the bootleggers knew about Jax. Otherwise, they'd be likely to lie low. "I don't see anyone around the dock, but the other boats are there. Do you think they took yours to transport booze away?"

"I doubt they'd do it until after dark. Probably long after sunset." He shifted from one foot to the other. "Eyelers may know I'm on the island by now. Or, since the telephone is working, someone in the Remington house could've called Lauger. Calls between houses on the island would probably go through the operator at Burnley Cove. I wonder if she'd tell Amberly. I'll ask when I call him. Hopefully, she listened in."

The comment made Bella frown. "I know people think operators eavesdrop, but I never did, and neither did anyone in our group."

"You were handling calls as an important part of the war effort. Civilian operators don't get critical information about troop movements."

"True."

He shook his head. "I should call Derringer and tell him the bootleggers may be on to my presence, since I don't want the other agents walking into a trap. I'll call Amberly, too. He and his deputy need to know."

After a moment, Bella looked out the glass again. "When Ida and I came over on Thursday, I noticed another dock in a cove on the other side of the Remington property. From what Florence told us, Lauger's place is there. The house wasn't clearly visible, although the gables at the top were. Did you see any of the place?"

"Griff and I noted the buildings when we arrived. I wasn't thinking about bootlegging or parties at the time. The cove by Lauger's place is visible, and the top of the house is, too. The proximity to this dock would make it easy to transport liquor over for his parties. An added benefit is that both houses are on the north side of the island."

"That's a good point. You probably saw the homes on the south side, which is the widest part of Winnabee. There are four homes."

"And I noticed two facing east." He glanced at Bella. "What about the west side?"

"Two are there, as well."

"So, even when all ten places are occupied, the other visitors wouldn't have a good view of activities at this end of the island."

"No, they wouldn't."

"Florence indicated she's been the only family member out here this season. Do you know if that's really the case?"

"When she wrote notes inviting us, she mentioned her mother having heart problems now. She doesn't want to be far from her doctor, so she no longer travels, and her father won't leave Mrs. Remington even overnight."

"Florence admitted to being here in early May."

"I think that's the only time this year, since Sylvia was with her. Florence wouldn't come all alone."

"You're right. It wouldn't make sense for Florence to come by herself." He braced his arm against the wall. "What about her sister? Is she older or younger?"

"Several years older. She and her family live in Boston, so I doubt if she's been here for years. Maybe when their mother could still come. Probably not since her last babies were born. She had two when I was still in college, and she's had three more since then."

"I can understand why she wouldn't make the trip from back east with five children in tow."

Bella grinned. "Me, too."

"Amberly thinks the bootlegging started about a year or two ago. With the houses here being vacant much of the time, Eyelers has had free reign."

"Lauger and Darre, too."

"My understanding is that Winnabee doesn't have as many visitors as it once did."

"That's right. Most of the owners are older than the Remingtons, according to Florence. More the age of

Lauger's grandparents. She told us people are likely to be here in July and August, though."

"So, the prime times to transport booze would be March through June and September through November."

"You're convinced there's bootlegging." Bella wanted to make sure she knew exactly where he stood.

"Aren't you?" Jax asked.

"Yes, I am. But who gave or sold it to Syl? That's the part puzzling me."

"Even though we need to shut down the bootlegging operation, I won't forget about your friend."

Sad realization assailed Bella. "I don't know that we were actually friends anymore. Syl changed after our first semester of college. She stayed part of our group, but the two of us weren't close. The first night we were talking about how she flirted with all young men back during our college days."

"Really?"

A snort of laughter left Bella. "Yes, really. She turned her sights on you after Matt ignored her."

A look of bewilderment crossed Jax's face. "She wasn't shy. I remember that much."

"You must remember more. I certainly do."

A smile tugged at one corner of his mouth. "That sounds like you might've been jealous."

Warmth bloomed in her cheeks. "Looking back, I was really peeved with her. Almost as peeved as I was Thursday night when she was blathering about how Prohibition was stupid and so were..." Abruptly, she stopped.

He laughed out loud. "And so were the agents trying to enforce it. I appreciate you being miffed with her on my behalf."

"I couldn't help it, but I feel bad because she was very upset with Lauger, and for good reason. Then, she died.

And she was so ill." Bella put a hand to her mouth. "I wish we'd known. Maybe we could've helped her."

"You're trying to get justice for her, so you have nothing to regret."

Bella gave one nod. "Thank you."

"It's the truth," he said with a slight smile. "I've seen what I wanted, so we should get back."

Chapter Eleven

♥

Shortly before they reached the house, Jax clasped Bella's forearm. "We should tell Ida and Griff about our boat being gone, but I'd rather the others didn't realize."

"All right. It's a bad sign, isn't it?"

Jax shrugged. "It's a potential problem. Tomorrow, we'll have another boat with the other agents. Tonight, we're stuck with no way to get off this island. We need to consider what to do overnight. Two people staying in the house are suspects, and we're confident bootleggers are around. I'd like everyone to stay downstairs tonight. Maybe the ladies in the parlor and the gentlemen in the den." His odds of getting rest weren't good, since he planned to keep watch. Biggins would help him, but the elderly butler wasn't apt to be useful. He completely discounted Eyelers.

"We all slept in the parlor the night of the storm. It'll be more crowded with Mrs. Longley and Monica, but we'll manage. You won't be as comfortable in the den." Concern etched her lovely face.

"I'll be fine," he assured her. "It's only one night."

Bella nodded and continued back to the house. They walked the rest of the way in silence. When they stepped inside the French doors, Bella turned to Jax. "Do you still want to talk with Lina, Blanche, and the staff?"

"Maybe briefly. Especially Lina. First, I need to see if I can catch Derringer in his office. The other agents may leave early tomorrow, and they need to know the situation beforehand." Tomorrow morning, two other agents would arrive to help him. The old saying *there's safety in numbers* came to mind. Unfortunately, three was a low number. How many accomplices did the bootleggers have? He couldn't be sure, since more help came for parties. But how far ahead did they come?

After he and Bella returned to the house, Jax placed a call to Derringer. His boss was waiting to hear about the availability of additional agents. When that conversation ended, he spoke with Blanche and Lina. Neither added any new information, but Blanche confirmed her certainty that Sylvia died from methanol poisoning.

When he and Bella were again alone in the den, Jax slumped back in his chair. "I'm eager to get the preliminary autopsy report. Blanche is right that the amount of wood alcohol in Sylvia's system will reveal a lot. If it's high, there's a very good chance her death wasn't accidental. I'm not sure if the doc can tell right off, though. He'll probably need lab work done."

The assertion wasn't surprising, but it added to Bella's worries. "At first, both Ida and Blanche thought it was accidental poisoning. I never did, for some reason."

His gaze rested on her face. "You have great insight and intuition. More than most people, and you know Richard Jenkins always says not to dismiss gut feelings."

"You agree with me?" Bella wanted Jax's support.

"Accidental is still a possibility. We don't want to forget about it."

His words were a reminder, and she nodded. "Of course, we don't. But we've already talked about motive. Lina had one."

"As did Florence. Sad to say, Lauger might have, since he wasn't eager to marry Syl despite her condition."

"No, he definitely wasn't." Another piece of information came back to Bella. "At dinner the other night, Darre said Lauger wasn't a one-woman man. Evidently, he was seeing other girls all along."

"To my way of thinking, that's an additional reason for him to give her bad booze."

"Do you think he might have only wanted to make her sick?"

Jax shrugged. "It's hard to say. Anyone could have that motive." Jax pulled out his pocket watch. "I didn't reach Constable Amberly, so I have to call back."

"What did Constable Amberly say?" Bella, who had followed Jax to the alcove, asked as soon as he hung up.

"He called a couple of local police departments for help. Several officers are already there, so he and his deputy are heading out here."

"Because he's concerned about the booze being moved tonight."

Jax nodded. "He is, and so am I."

"Most bootleggers are well-armed. Lauger, Eyelers, and Darre probably aren't any different. And Lauger may have men at his place. He often does. By now, they must know you're here and be watching for you."

"Amberly thought the same thing, so he and his deputy are tying up by the old lighthouse. He said the dock over there was in decent shape, and it's not visible from the Lauger place or the Remingtons' dock. He's calling the Prohibition office in Toledo about the plans. I'll ask Florence for details about Lauger."

"She hasn't been a lot of help to this point."

"No, but her attitude may change if she realizes I suspect her of being involved."

"I hope so," Bella murmured.

After leading a stoic Florence into the den, Bella got out her pad and pencil. Her friend appeared neither cooperative nor cordial, which did not surprise Jax.

"Lauger, Darre, and Eyelers are rumrunning from this island." Although he didn't have proof enough for charges, Jax made it a statement.

A flush surged into Florence's cheeks. "That's ridiculous."

Jax gritted his teeth. Her response didn't surprise him, but it boded ill for getting to the core of the situation. "You know it isn't. The question is, are you involved? If you are, and you refuse to cooperate, I won't hesitate to arrest you, so it's in your best interest to be completely honest. In that case, I'll do what I can to help you." He kept his voice well-modulated. Being too tough might scare her off, and she was already scared. Her hands were in her lap, but their shaking was obvious. When seconds of silence passed, he nodded at Bella. Maybe she could get through to her friend.

"Florence, if you're only aware of what they've been doing, but not part of it, now is the time to say so," Bella said. "Otherwise, you may be in worse trouble."

All traces of stoicism vanished. Florence's lower lip trembled as she turned to Bella. "I didn't have any part in Syl's death. I wouldn't harm her. She talked about my debts, and I was furious. She wasn't drunk then, so she knew exactly what she was saying."

Bella laid a hand on her friend's arm. "Help Jax, please. The more details he has, the safer he and the other lawmen will be."

For a long moment, the two women looked at each other. Jax watched without interfering. With luck, Florence would respond to Bella's plea. But cooperation wouldn't mean she was innocent. One issue at a time, he reminded himself. Right now, catching the bootleggers before they moved their stock was foremost.

Finally, a long sigh left Florence, and she glanced back at him. "Eyelers didn't destroy my parents' liquor. They still don't know that, and I didn't until last summer." She clasped her hands more tightly together. "I visited Sylvia several times last year. She talked me into going to speakeasies. I'm not proud of my behavior because I drank and gambled. At first, I won money, which was fun."

"I can understand that," Jax said. "Many people want to see what the places are like, and it's easy to get caught up in the atmosphere."

A slight smile formed on Florence's pale face. "I wanted to have a little fun. My parents are sedate, serious people. That's why they wanted all the alcohol destroyed."

"Drinking at home, especially liquor bought prior to prohibition isn't illegal," Jax said.

"But they didn't want to do anything wrong. My father is a retired attorney. He considered running for public office before my mother's heart attack, so appearances are important to him. My fiancé is equally priggish. Not that it's a bad thing."

Bella's brow furrowed. "I thought you got engaged this spring."

"We did," Florence replied, "but we were courting last year. He's wanted to be a judge ever since we first met. He's a good man who needs a proper lady as his wife. I felt fine about that. After all, I was never wild."

"No, you weren't." Bella's tone was reassuring.

As Jax watched the by-play, he knew he'd been right to have Bella take part.

"I didn't think I'd miss any fun after my marriage. When I went to see Syl, she kept saying I deserved to enjoy myself before getting tied down. I shouldn't have listened to her, but she's so persuasive. Was so persuasive. It's hard to accept that she's gone." Florence shook her head. "Like I said, I won money the first couple of times. After a while, I lost a lot and had to borrow from Syl. I was afraid to ask my father because he'd wonder why I needed funds, and he wouldn't approve of gambling."

"That's understandable," Jax said. "Lauger and Darre also mentioned your debts, right?"

Florence's gaze fell to the floor. "Bart began having parties at his house last year, and he invited Syl and me to come. I thought I might win enough money to pay Syl back. At first, I did, but it ended up the same as in Chicago. Parker was at the party when I first lost a lot, and he loaned me money. When I said I'd repay him, he told me not to worry. Fool that I am, I believed him."

"The other day on the dock, he sounded like he wanted to be repaid," Bella said.

As tears formed in Florence's eyes, she wiped them away with the back of her hand. "At the party last month, Parker suggested another way for me to get rid of my debt. Like he did Friday. I couldn't do that so, when he mentioned it in May, I quit borrowing from him, which is how I got in debt to Bart."

When Bella looked at him, Jax saw both disgust and dismay in her dark eyes. Although he felt the same emotions, he didn't let them surface. Florence's gambling debts had led her into trouble, but they weren't his focus. "I'm guessing Lauger threatened to go to your father for repayment." That was the most likely scenario. The one sure to keep her on the hook.

Florence nodded. "He did. I begged him not to. By then, I realized the three of them were running a bootlegging ring and using my parents' liquor as part of it. He and Eyelers threatened to implicate my father, and he knew nothing about it. Nothing at all. I was so scared."

Jax leaned back in his chair. Her plight was worse than he'd figured. Not only was Florence being blackmailed, so was her father. Not that he knew it. "You kept quiet about the parties, the illegal gambling, and the rumrunning to protect your family and yourself." He didn't pose a question because the answer seemed obvious.

She nodded again. "I did. But Bart kept pressuring me. He knew I didn't want my parents or fiancé to find out. He also knew I was inheriting money from my grandmother, who died last winter. I should get my quarterly share next month. He wants to be repaid, but he still made threats—to tell everyone about my gambling and to involve my father. I had no idea what to do, except keep quiet and pay when I could. There won't be enough from my grandmother to settle my debt to him and Parker, and Bart is aware of it."

Jax wondered just how much she owed. Evidently, a great deal.

"Oh, Florence. I'm so sorry." Bella's heart went out to her friend. What a mess Florence had made.

"I don't deserve pity. I was stupid." She looked at Jax again. "Will I be arrested?"

"You aren't part of the ring, and you weren't caught in a speakeasy," he replied. "I wish you'd told someone sooner, but you're helping now. As far as owing money, you'll be off the hook for that once they're all under arrest. Unless there are others involved. Are there? If so, I'd like descriptions of them. I know Lauger has employees—all men—but are they regular staff or are they bootlegging accomplices?"

Florence chewed on her lower lip. "The men work at his house regularly. They're always at the parties. Three are security, and they look it. All are at least six feet tall with bulky builds. Maybe in their twenties or early thirties." She narrowed her gaze as if trying to picture the others. "There's a chef. He's a slight man. Shorter than I am and thin. Probably fifty. I doubt if he takes part in bootlegging, but the booze comes from the kitchen during parties. The other one is the boatman, who usually stays at the dock during parties. He also has a handgun. I'm guessing he's in his fifties. Medium height, medium build. Bart hires a few extra people working when guests are there. To serve food and drinks, and to run the games."

"The five are always at the house?" Jax asked.

"As far as I know."

"Are the three who act as security heavily armed?" He hoped she had some idea.

"They wear holsters with guns whenever I see them," Florence replied.

"Do they have shotguns?" Jax asked.

"I'm not sure, but I've seen two hunting rifles in Bart's den."

Before Jax responded to Florence, Bella posed a crucial question. "Are there shotguns or hunting rifles here?"

"My father never hunted, but there's a shotgun locked in his closet upstairs," Florence replied.

"Do you have the key?" Jax asked.

"Stricket does, but I can get it from him."

"I'd appreciate that. I brought my sidearm. Constable Amberly and his deputy will bring handguns and shotguns." Unsure about revealing everything, Jax hesitated. Finally, he presented the rest of his plan. He'd watch Florence carefully, just in case she was in deeper with the bootlegging that she'd admitted. Griff could help with that. "I called my boss back, and he's sending two more Prohibition agents. They probably won't be here until tomorrow morning."

Florence put both hands to her mouth. "You're going to arrest Bart, Parker, and Eyelers?"

"That's my intention. We have evidence under the garden shed," Jax said, "and Constable Amberly has several witnesses who were at Lauger's parties. They're willing to testify about the booze and gambling. I hope you will, too."

"Testify in court." Shock underscored each of Florence's words. "If I do that, my parents will find out. My fiancé will, too."

"They'll find out anyhow since there's a lot of the booze on this property, and that will be part of our case." Jax watched the play of emotions on the woman's face and felt a stab of pity. "I'm sorry, but your father will be questioned after we wrap up the arrests."

A shuddering breath left Florence. "Of course. I hoped to keep it all secret, but I should've known it was a futile hope."

Jax cleared his throat. "I'd like to ask a few more questions." When Florence nodded, he went on. "Are any of your employees involved in the operation?"

"Only Eyelers," Florence replied.

"Not Stricket. Not even being bribed to ignore what's happening under his nose?"

For a moment, Florence just stared at him. "Probably not. Mr. Stricket is slowing down. He rests often. My parents have wanted to pension him off for a few years, but he's resisted the idea. He seldom talks with Eyelers. Mrs. Longley and Monica avoid him, too."

"You mentioned a chef at Lauger's place. Is that his only role?" Jax asked.

"He cooks and tends to the garden at the Lauger place," Florence said. "Nothing more as far as I know."

Jax nodded. "Do you know if there are shotguns on the boat?"

"I haven't seen any," Florence replied, "but Syl and I were out with Bart and Parker one time, and Bart asked Millington—he's the Lauger boatman—if the big cupboard was locked."

The number of weapons didn't surprise Jax, since bootleggers were usually heavily armed. Being out-manned and outgunned was far from ideal, but allowing the men to haul off all evidence wasn't an option. They might take some to the Lauger place, but a lot could be moved on boats right away.

"Florence, how could you ignore so much? Didn't you worry about them having so many guns?" Bella asked, her dismay clear.

Once again, moisture filled Florence's eyes. This time, it spilled down her cheeks. "I was in debt to both Bart and Parker by that time, so I felt like I had to overlook everything. Or at least pretend I didn't realize what was going on."

"What about Syl? Did she say anything to them?" Bella asked.

"Syl was part of a fast crowd in Chicago. She went to speakeasies almost every night, so bootlegging wasn't new to her. Besides, she was interested in Bart right off. She ignored his behavior, even when she knew he was stepping out with other women." Florence wiped fresh tears from her face.

Bella inhaled sharply. "Were you aware of Syl's condition before Friday?"

"No," Florence replied. "She said nothing to me when she was here in May."

Bella frowned. "She knew back then?"

Florence nodded. "She must have. Bart was in Chicago in March."

The exchange made Jax want to throttle Lauger. Although he wasn't eliminating Florence as a suspect in

Sylvia's death, Jax thought the man had a stronger motive to kill her. Stronger than Florence or Lina.

"I appreciate you being so forthright, Florence," Jax said.

"I'm sorry I ever went to Chicago or to any parties at Bart's place. That was foolish," Florence said.

Jax agreed with her assessment, but he replied with, "We all make mistakes, and we're lucky if we're forgiven for them." When Bella caught his gaze, he knew Matt was on her mind. Her next words confirmed the supposition.

"The only genuine error is in not being honest as soon as possible." Bella smiled at Jax before again looking at her friend. "You've done that now."

"Thank you," Florence murmured.

"I don't have other questions, but please reveal nothing we said here." Jax got to his feet. "Again, I'm grateful for your honesty."

Florence, all anger gone, nodded before leaving the den.

"Do you believe Florence isn't involved in Syl's death?" Bella asked when she and Jax were alone.

"I'm not completely convinced," he replied.

"So, you're still keeping her, Lina, and Lauger as suspects?"

"Yep. Eyelers could have been an accomplice, but he doesn't have a motive himself." Jax leaned forward and braced his elbows on his knees. "I'm hoping to learn more after we make arrests in the bootlegging operation. One of Lauger's employees may know something and talk to avoid being charged in the death. Right now, any of them might be implicated."

"There are eight of them, and only three of you when the other agents arrive."

Her concerns were valid, so Jax responded with care. "We can probably catch them when they're moving the booze. A couple are apt to be on the lookout. One will probably stay at the dock. The rest will have their hands full. Literally."

"You said they'd probably start moving it this evening. What if they get it all out tonight?"

Bella had a good sense of what he planned. Too good. He wouldn't let her get involved in the actual arrest because the danger was great. How to fob her off was the question.

"Not telling me what you're going to do won't keep me from worrying."

He shrugged. "The other agents might make it this evening."

"What if they don't?"

Jax slid to the front edge of his chair and reached out. When Bella laid her hands in his, he gently squeezed them. "Wait to worry, okay? It won't be dark for a while. Nothing is likely to happen before midnight. Even when it does, I've been on several raids, and I know what I'm doing. Please trust me. I won't do anything all alone."

"I do. You're very good at your job."

He grinned. "How can you be sure when you haven't seen me do it?"

Her lips twitched. "Because I know you, and you've been conscientious in everything you do." Bella grasped his hands more tightly. "But you also put others before yourself. You take risks that can put you in harm's way. That *have* put you in harm's way. For example, you got shot again in March."

His smile disappeared. "I wasn't taking chances then. I was working a case—with you." Jax released her hands and leaned back in the chair. Before he said anymore, a knock interrupted. "Come in."

The door opened to reveal Monica. "Constable Amberly, his deputy, and some other men is here."

"Thank you," Jax replied. "Send them in." When he looked back at Bella, he grinned again. "Help has arrived, and sooner than I'd hoped."

"Good."

Within moments, Amberly entered the den. "Good evening."

Jax got up and shook the constable's hand. "I'm glad to see you." He glanced at the other three. "All of you."

As Amberly introduced the group, Bella took careful note. Zeb Stanley, of medium height and build, was the deputy. He was probably younger than the rest, maybe in his early twenties. The Prohibition agents, Lou Finnagin and Tex Yankton, were in their mid-thirties. Finnagin, taller and heavier than Jax, had red hair and freckles, giving him a boyish look. Yankton had a more compact build, dark hair, and dark eyes. All the newcomers shook Jax's hand and nodded to Bella.

"I should let you gentlemen talk," she said, her tone tentative.

Because he felt certain Bella was dying to hear their plans, Jax grinned. Since she'd be cut out of the actual arrests, he offered an excuse. "We'll go over the notes, and you took some in shorthand. I can't read that, and I doubt if anyone else here can."

When the men agreed, Bella beamed at him. "All right."

Amberly glanced around the room. "We're short a chair."

"The ottoman is large enough for Bella and me to share," Jax said. "So, let's get going."

Chapter Twelve

Once everyone was seated, Jax asked his fellow agents how much Derringer had shared. As he'd expected, his boss was thorough.

"I filled Zeb in," Amberly said.

"The constable told us about the girl's death on the way over," Finnagin said. "Any further developments?"

Jax summarized the latest interview with Florence and summed up with, "So, we've got three suspects and an accomplice to anyone of them in Eyelers."

Yankton frowned. "We're taking down the bootlegging operation first, aren't we? The two of us left right away with that idea in mind." He glanced at Bella. "Of course, you want justice for your friend, but Finnagin and I have plenty to do in the city. Our boss said Derringer approved Hastings staying on a little longer, but we need to go back."

Beside Jax, Bella grew tense but said, "I completely understand."

"My deputy or I can help Agent Hastings with the death investigation," Amberly put in. "I've got the go-ahead on that. Our local doctor is doing a preliminary autopsy as soon as possible. Unfortunately, some folks were injured in the storm clean-up, so he's tending to them first."

"Understandable," Yankton replied.

"Once we nab the bootleggers, we may get information about the death. One is a top suspect, and the other is a possible accomplice. Their crew may have details," Jax said.

Finnagin nodded. "And you're hoping to pressure one or more to reveal information leading to the killer?"

"That's exactly what I hope," Jax agreed.

"It may work," Yankton said. "Now, what's the plan for nabbing them?"

Jax revealed what was in the dugout, Eyelers' hidey hole.

"That's darn good evidence," Finnagin said. "If we catch them moving it, we'll have a strong case for the courts."

"How far is it to this Lauger place?" Yankton asked.

"Maybe a half-mile," Jax replied. "Does that sound right, Bella?"

"I haven't actually been there, but it's not far. Lauger and Darre said it only took them ten minutes when they came for dinner on Friday night. With debris from the storm, it's apt to take a little longer," she said. "But they might come by boat. They were at the Remingtons' dock a while ago."

All four of the newcomers focused on her. "Were you down there?" Yankton asked.

"Bella and I were at the top of the lighthouse. I haven't met any of them, but she identified Lauger, Darre, and Eyelers as the men on Lauger's boat, which was tied up there. The Remington craft was alongside it, despite it supposedly being gone after the storm. The boat Griff and I used was gone." Jax looked around the group. "Did you pass the dock coming in?"

"No, but Zeb went to the lighthouse and looked from the top," Amberly replied, before turning to his deputy.

"Only one boat there, and I'm sure it belongs to the Remingtons," Zeb said.

Jax drummed his fingers on his knees. "The Lauger boat was there earlier, and they took the one I used, too."

"Do you think they already started moving their stock?" Finnagin asked.

"Not from below the shed. That's too close to the house. Someone here would have seen them," Jax replied.

"True," Amberly added.

"Then, what were they doing?" Yankton asked. "Was any booze stored down around the dock?"

"Possibly," Bella said.

Jax shifted to look at her. "What makes you say that? Do you think Eyelers put some of his supply on the Remington boat ahead of the storm, so he could transport it to Lauger's place?"

"When we went to the dock on Friday, Eyelers was getting chairs out for us," Bella replied. "Ida and I started to help him, and he told us to stay out of the boathouse because there are bad planks. He said the same when we came over on Thursday. He was very adamant, which I thought was odd."

"He had booze in there," Finnagin said with certainty.

"I agree," Jax said. "I took a peek when Griff and I got here. The door was ajar. Nothing except empty shelves, but I didn't see any rotten flooring."

"That explains the Remington craft being gone, but reappearing," Deputy Stanley said.

"It sure does," Yankton agreed. "If they take their stock to the Lauger place, where can it be stored?"

"It's a very large house," Amberly added. "There's a gazebo, a greenhouse, a garden shed, a tool shed, and a caretaker's cottage, which hasn't been occupied for a couple of years."

"We need to catch them moving the stuff under the shed," Yankton said. "Once they get it over there, we'd have a tough time getting in unnoticed and finding their stockpile. They'd surely have the stuff well-guarded, if they get it away from here."

Jax nodded. "Agreed. We can't let them scatter it around on Lauger's property and on a couple of boats."

"Especially not when they can set up a vigorous defense to protect it and themselves," Finnagin said. "Besides, we'd have trouble getting an okay to search the entire property. Besides, simply having liquor isn't illegal. They aren't likely to haul the extra ingredients, just the booze."

Once again, Bella stiffened. Jax wanted to reach out and reassure her, but hesitated. Before the group headed out later, they would talk again. With that in mind, he laid out his strategy for catching the bootleggers. When he was done, the others agreed with the plan.

"Where will we put them once they're under arrest?" Yankton asked. "We can't take them back across the lake in the dark."

"Our best bet is to keep them in the house tonight," Jax replied. "I looked downstairs, and there are several empty staff bedrooms. We can split the group up. We'll have to take turns guarding them, of course."

"That's no problem," Finnagin said. "The five of us can manage."

"Griff Biggins, who came out with me, will help with that," Jax said. "While we're out tonight, he'll stay here with the ladies." Out of the corner of his eye, he saw Bella turn toward him. He knew exactly what she was thinking. Something else to discuss when they were alone. A tap on the door interrupted. "Come in."

Florence peeked inside. "Mrs. Longley will have supper on the table shortly. We should have rooms ready for you, as well."

"Thank you, but we don't need rooms," Jax said.

"No, we don't," Amberly agreed. "None of us will get much sleep tonight."

The men wrapped up their discussion. Afterward, the agents left with Amberly and his deputy. The door had barely shut when Bella stood up. "I should clean up for supper."

Jax's hand on hers kept her from going far.

"Let's talk."

She looked at him and nodded. After sitting in the chair next to the ottoman, Bella spoke again. "You didn't tell me all of your plans for tonight." She knew better than to insist on taking part. Her presence would distract Jax because he'd be worrying about her safety, and she might get in the way. All the same, she wished he'd told her before the others.

"I would have, but we were interrupted, remember?"

"I do," she replied. "Sorry, but..." Her voice trailed off as she considered how to explain.

"You thought I was hiding something again? I wasn't, and I won't." His gaze narrowed on her face. "You're still uncertain."

"Not about that. About the plan. It seems dangerous."

"Every raid has risk involved, but it's calculated risk. Finnagin and Yankton are experienced agents. Amberly is a long-time constable."

"And his deputy looks wet behind the ears."

A low laugh left Jax. "He's about the same age as Nolen Rogers, my deputy, and you have confidence in him, don't you?"

A warm flush rose in Bella's face. "I do, and your point is understood." Not that it kept her from fretting. She'd known Nolen since he was a boy, and he'd been Jax's platoon sergeant during the last weeks of the war. Amberly's deputy was a virtual stranger. A boyish stranger.

"You heard my plan. The others agreed it was sound. What do you think?"

The question caught Bella off-guard. "I'm not a lawman, experienced or otherwise."

Jax smiled. "You're a good detective, as I've said many times. You're very perceptive, so I'd like your opinion."

Pleasure spread through Bella at his confidence in her. "It sounds like an excellent plan. You're certainly right that they won't move anything until after dark. Probably long after dark." An idea occurred to her. "You need a lookout here to alert you when they arrive. Someone who could be in the attic, since it would offer the best vantage point. They'll have to use lanterns or flashlights coming up the path from the dock. The lights would be visible."

"You're right, and I was going to ask you and the maid to do that, if you think she's up to it. Maybe go up to the attic and watch. When you see something, let us know. Then, we can be stationed at doors and ready to go as soon as the two of you alert us. I'd like Griff and Ida to stay with Lina and Florence in the parlor, since they're still suspects in Syl's death. Not to mention Florence being aware of bootlegging all along." He grimaced.

"You don't think Florence kept quiet out of fear?" Bella wanted to believe her friend. Did Jax think she'd been actively involved in the bootlegging operation? Did he think she'd warn the others? The idea made Bella cringe.

"It's most likely she did, but we can't be sure. Just to be on the safe side, I don't want her wandering around."

"What about Stricket?"

"I'll have him, Mrs. Longley, and Blanche stay in the parlor, too."

"What if he or any of the others won't stay?"

A corner of Jax's mouth lifted. "Amberly was going to bring an extra shotgun and another hand gun. Plus, we can use the two here. Griff can use a weapon since he started army training before getting influenza. I'll see that he has a sidearm."

"I didn't think about him handling a gun." Although Bella knew Jax carried a gun in his job, the thought of Griff keeping people in line with a weapon disturbed her. With luck, everyone would cooperate.

"He knows enough to keep people from leaving," Jax said.

"You've got everything figured out," she replied. "I just wish it was over."

"It will be in a few hours."

A few hours seemed like an eternity, but she forced a smile. "Good."

After supper, Jax asked the staff to gather with the others in the parlor. The lawmen were together near the door, while Griff—now armed—was beside him. Stricket, arms folded, stood next to the fireplace. The women sat on the loveseat and couches.

"Everyone except Bella and Monica will stay here with Griff while we're outside." At dinner, he'd introduced the golf pro to his fellow agents and provided the basic scenario, so no one was left to guess what was going on.

"You'll all be out of harm's way here." Jax took time to look directly at the guests, staff, and Florence.

"How long will we be stuck here?" Lina asked.

"I'm not sure," Jax replied, keeping his voice calm. She'd issued several complaints at dinner, too. If he didn't know better, he'd suspect her of being involved in the bootlegging ring. As things stood, he was still looking at her for her friend's death. But how would she slip bad booze to Sylvia? He hadn't figured that out. "We'll wrap up as soon as we can. Bella and Monica, would you step out into the hall?"

The two rose and left the room. When the other lawmen also departed, Jax turned to Griff. "Thanks for handling this part."

"It's no problem. You need all the lawmen to nab the bad guys," the golf pro said. "The least I can do is keep watch here."

"Like I said, we'll be back as soon as possible." Heaven knew, none of them wanted to be waiting all night for something to happen. When Jax started toward the door, Griff's voice stopped him.

"Good luck."

"Luck is always useful." Jax went to where Bella and Monica were waiting in the main hall. "As soon as you see any sign of them, tell us. Yankton and I will be by the French doors at the back of the house. Amberly, Stanley, and Finnagin will be near the door by the kitchen. If one of you come to me and the other goes to the kitchen, that'll be great."

"Of course," Bella said before leading the way to the garret at the top of the house, where part of the path leading from the dock was visible. She perched on an old crate and gestured for Monica to sit on another one. "We might as well get as comfortable as possible. It could be a while."

"Yes, miss."

A while proved to be a relative term. She made small talk with Monica to pass the time, but kept her attention outside. In the distance, Bella heard the clock on the main floor strike ten, eleven, and twelve. When a faint beam of light appeared in the distance, she sat up straighter. "Monica, do you see the light?" Bella, heart in her throat, gestured toward it.

"I do. Should I run to the kitchen now?"

Before Bella replied, she saw two more dim flashes—one close to the first and the other some thirty feet away. "Tell them the group looks to be spreading out, but they're at least a hundred yards from the garden right now."

"Yes, miss."

Monica rushed out and Bella followed her downstairs before turning toward the French doors. When she approached, Jax and Agent Yankton got to their feet. "You saw them," Jax said.

Bella, nearly out of breath from her mad dash, nodded.

"Thanks, Bella."

When he started away, she grabbed his arm. "We saw three lights. Two were close together, and another was about ten yards away from them. More toward the house than the others. The closest was maybe three hundred feet from the garden."

His jaw tightened. "Okay. Now, why don't you join the others in the parlor? We'll be in when it's all over."

She'd fought her fear down for hours, but it returned full-force. "Be careful. You have a solid plan and good men to help you, but don't take unnecessary chances. Please."

"I'll meet you in the kitchen, Hastings," Yankton said.

"Be right there." Jax laid one hand on Bella's cheek. "Try to stop worrying."

He was asking for the impossible, but she nodded. "I'll try."

213

"Good." He brushed his lips over hers before stepping away. "See you soon. In the parlor."

With her heart in her throat Bella watched him walk away. Once he was out of sight, she went back upstairs. She might not be able to help now, but she planned to watch what happened and pitch in, if needed.

In the kitchen, Jax found the other lawmen ready. "Monica told you they looked to be splitting into two groups?"

The men nodded.

"You planned for that," Amberly said.

"And you were right," Finnagin added. "A couple are likely to come to this end of the garden to keep watch."

"They probably didn't see the four of you arrive today, but we're prepared for that potentiality," Jax said.

"Planning and preparation are key," Yankton put in. "Now, it's your call. Do you want us to move out?"

"Yep. Just as we discussed." Jax paused. "Thanks to all of you, and good luck."

With that, the five lawmen crept out of the house and toward the garden. Although they carried flashlights, none pulled one out. Staying in the dark as long as possible was to their advantage. The row of boxwoods was certainly well-placed, Jax thought as he inched alongside it. He'd put himself in a solo position, one where he'd be closest to the garden shed. After all, the strategy was his and he couldn't—in all good conscience—ask someone else to do the most dangerous part. A finger of guilt traced his spine. He hadn't been completely forthcoming with Bella, but she'd looked so anxious. Besides, he'd be fine, so why make her worry even more? With that, Jax returned his focus to the task at hand. His experience with raids revealed things happened fast, so he needed to stay alert.

He pulled out his handgun and crept closer. Navigating the debris and darkness made it slow-going, but the same was true for the bootleggers. When barely audible voices reached him, Jax stopped. The garden shed was about thirty yards away. So were four men. Immediately, he wondered where the others were. Had the chef come along? If so, he'd be most likely to stay on a boat. The boatman might be there, too. Uncertainty was a wild card.

Three of the four by the shed door went inside. The other swiveled from one side to the other, as if on watch. No surprise, Jax thought. Still no sign of any additional help, but they had to be out there. If only one was visible. Jax and his group figured some bootleggers would be at the opposite end of the garden. He only hoped they hadn't figured wrong.

Waiting for the crooks to appear with cases and bottles was the hard part. They had to be caught with the contraband in hand. Derringer had made that clear. Finally, after a seemingly endless time, two men emerged from the shed with cartons. Another one followed. With their arms full, the three were currently no threat. The rest might be, but Jax didn't wait any longer.

"Stop where you are," he shouted. The men froze in place before gunfire erupted from the other side of the garden, exactly where they'd figured the extra bootleggers would go. He carefully wove his way along the row of bushes still shielding him from view.

More shots went off, this time from where he'd stationed his team. When a moment of silence opened, Jax shouted again. "You won't get away. We've got people at the dock." Surely, Deputy Stanley was there by now. He was only one person, but he could easily pick off anyone trying to escape. As long as he hadn't been spotted by one of their cohorts. The silence lengthened. Finally, a strange voice called out.

"I'm hit. If I come out, will you help me?"

"We will," Jax hollered, "but toss your weapon down."

"I'll shoot you myself if you surrender." This bootleg-ger's voice rang with command.

"Ain't making enough to die for you," a third voice called out. "All out of bullets, so I'm coming, too."

Someone in the group of lawmen turned on his flash-light. "Over this way, guns down and hands up." Amberly's voice cut through the night, as did several flashlight beams.

When two men emerged, they did as the constable ordered. Within moments, they were in handcuffs. Jax glanced back to the garden shed where two crates of bottles were now on the ground, and only one figure remained visible. "You by the shed, put the crate and weapon down."

Low cursing was the reply.

"Do it now," Jax shouted before firing over the man's head.

The figure let the crate drop, and the sound of shatter-ing glass filled the air. Then, two hands went up. "Don't shoot no more," the voice said.

"How many of you are there?" Jax carefully moved forward.

Another disembodied voice replied. "Three run off—that'd be the boss men—and the chef and boatman is at the dock waiting. Three of us is still here."

The remaining trio had to be Lauger's security men. "Did you hear that?" Jax called to his fellow lawmen. "Eyelers, Darre, and Lauger ran to the boats."

"Yep." The reply came from Amberly.

"Finnagin and I will take these three inside," Yankton called out.

"All right," Jax called back, "let's get the others, constable."

Jax and Amberly raced down the path as fast as darkness and debris would let them. When they got close to the dock, they paused. "I hope your deputy disabled the boats."

"I'm sure he did."

From there, they crept closer and closer. All three boats had lanterns on them, and three figures were visible on one. Jax and Amberly stopped again.

"What do you mean, the engine is dead?" An angry voice sliced through the night. "Eyelers, get on another boat and try it. We gotta get out of here."

"Okay, Mr. Lauger."

When the man jumped onto the deck, young Stanley stood and whacked him with an oar. A splash followed. Jax grinned. "Let's help your deputy."

Subduing Lauger and Darre, at least Jax figured that was who they were, wasn't difficult. They were busy trying to start the boat and didn't see either Jax or Amberly until it was too late. With their pistols in their waistbands, the bootlegging partners were easy targets. While Amberly held a gun on them, Jax secured the handcuffs.

Meanwhile, Lauger hollered again. "Where's my boatman? Get up here on deck and do it now."

"He's bound and gagged." Despite the low light, the grin on Deputy Stanley's face was clear. "He and the other one were playing cards on deck. It wasn't hard to get 'em in custody. I took care of the boat motors after that."

"Good job, my boy," Amberly said. "Now, let's pull the other one out before he drowns and get cuffs on him."

Jax let the constable and his deputy take care of that. Within a few minutes, they were on their way back to the house.

Chapter Thirteen

Bella again left her vantage point in the attic and hurried to the kitchen as soon as the Prohibition agents entered the back of the house with the first group of prisoners. All three were tall and brawny, much as Florence had described Lauger's security men. She'd hoped Jax was with them, but he wasn't. "Where is everyone else?" The knot in her stomach tightened. Waiting had been ghastly, especially when gunfire had erupted. The period of silence afterward had only increased Bella's dread. Now, the dread was escalating.

"Down at the dock. We're headed there right now," Yankton said. "One of these two got hit. It's a flesh wound, but it needs cleaning."

"Is he the only one who got shot?" Bella asked.

The agent turned toward her. "Yep. Hastings and Amberly followed three others to the dock. The deputy is down there, too."

"Thanks," Bella replied. "Blanche is a nurse. I'll fetch her."

"We'll get them secured in chairs before we go."

By the time Bella returned with Blanche, she was a ball of raw nerve ends. Griff, gun in hand, came along and watched the prisoners.

Although Bella helped her friend tend the wound, her mind was on Jax. Once they were finished and the man was secured again, she began pacing.

"Bella, Jax will be fine. He knows what he's doing," Griff said in a kindly voice.

A sigh escaped her, but she stopped. "But waiting is hard."

"Agreed." After that, Griff engaged her in small talk.

As she struggled to respond sensibly, Bella stopped mid-sentence when she heard voices outside the back door and steps on the stairs. Darre, Eyelers, and Lauger entered ahead of Amberly and Stanley, which sent her heart racing. When Jax appeared, relief nearly took her to her knees. He looked fine. Was he?

His gaze immediately met hers, and a grin formed on his handsome face. "I told you we'd be back soon."

She smiled in return. "You did, and you're a man of your word."

Chuckles left several of the lawmen, but Bella didn't care. Jax was safe, and she was happy.

"Let's secure this bunch and get some information," Amberly said.

"You've accosted innocent citizens, and you have no authority out here, Constable Amberly." Lauger's eyes flashed with anger as he fought against the handcuffs.

"Since three of us are federal agents, we have jurisdiction here," Yankton said, "and the constable and his deputy were given the go-ahead to help us shut down a bootlegging ring."

Lauger snorted. "There's no bootlegging here. Not unless someone else is doing it."

"You've been bootlegging and having parties with gambling. I've got witnesses who'll testify to both," Amberly said.

"And we caught you red-handed moving your stock," Jax added.

"That booze was in Remingtons' shed," Lauger shot back.

"You mean you were stealing it?" Jax's voice held a note of amusement.

"You can't prove it's mine." Lauger glared at Jax. "You can't prove anything."

"I believe we can." Yankton's gaze ran over the first three prisoners. "I'm guessing a few of your men will testify against you to get a break themselves."

A chorus of *I wills* followed the statement. Lauger cursed them out.

Yankton glanced at Jax. "Do you want to keep watch on these two," his head jerked toward Lauger and Darre, "up here while we secure the others in those extra rooms?"

"Yep. If the four of you will escort them, Biggins and I will stay here with these two. Securing them to kitchen chairs will keep them from going anyplace," Jax replied.

"Sit down, gentlemen," Amberly said to the pair.

Darre immediately dropped into a chair, but Lauger had to be helped. The deputy used extra sets of cuffs to secure the pair before he and the other lawmen escorted the other prisoners out.

"You're making a big mistake," Lauger said.

"You're sore because you got caught," Jax replied. "Now, we've got evidence and witnesses."

"We won't be in custody for long. We've got talented attorneys." Unlike his business partner, Darre looked calm and composed. "They're experts in representing people wrongly accused of bootlegging. Getting in front of the right judge will help."

The man's pomposity set Bella's teeth on edge. By the *right judge*, he meant one who was on the take. Disgusting, but she hoped all the others would testify against Lauger and Darre, and she hoped the charges stuck. Surely, no judge could let them off in that case.

"But you won't simply be charged with bootlegging," Jax replied.

Lauger's brow furrowed. "What happens at my parties isn't cause for legal action."

"Maybe, maybe not. However, when someone dies from bad booze, the supplier can be found guilty of manslaughter." Jax leaned against the door jamb and folded his arms across his chest.

Did Jax hope Lauger would confess to giving Syl toxic liquor? Or was he watching for a reaction? Bella studied the man but saw only confusion in his dark eyes.

"I have no idea what you mean. Nobody died," Lauger replied.

"He's trying to upset you, Bart," Darre said.

"I'd think both of you would be upset about your boot-legged hooch killing someone," Jax put in.

Unable to remain silent, Bella spoke. "Especially when it's someone close to you. You should be ashamed of yourself, but you evidently have no shame."

"What do you know about any of this?" Darre asked.

"Quite a lot, since it was one of my friends who died," Bella shot back.

"I have no idea what you two are talking about. No one died at any of my parties." Lauger was insistent.

"Not a party. Right here. Upstairs." Bella found forming complete sentences difficult. The image of Syl's dead body filled her mind's eye, and her insides clenched with sorrow and anger. What sort of man didn't care that the mother of his child had been killed by drinking adulterated alcohol, probably alcohol from his supply?

"Somebody died here?" Darre asked. He looked every bit as confused as Lauger.

Suddenly, Bella realized they didn't know about Syl. Not feeling a need to spare either of the men, she blurted out what had happened. "Syl is dead. Most likely because of methanol poisoning from drinking your poisoned liquor."

Lauger's mouth dropped open, and all color drained from his face. He shook his head repeatedly, but made no reply.

Darre looked almost as stunned, but he quickly found his voice. "Syl can't be dead."

"She is," Bella shot back. "She died the night of the storm."

Lauger continued to stare at Bella. Finally, one word came out in a rough whisper. "No."

If his reaction was to be believed, Lauger hadn't intentionally poisoned Syl, but unintentional poisoning was almost as bad. Maybe he'd wanted her to get sick and lose their child. "She drank a little when she went out on the boat with you, and Syl got more liquor on Winnabee. All signs point to her having ingested bad booze. Booze that most likely came from your stockpile."

A shudder rippled through Lauger's lean form. "I didn't poison her. I wouldn't do that."

Jax stared at the two men. "It doesn't matter if you meant to harm her or not. If we can prove she died of methanol poisoning, and I'm sure we can after the autopsy, we've got witnesses who heard Miss Sawyer say she got booze out here. Most likely from your colleague, Mr. Eyelers."

Sweat beaded Lauger's brow. "I've told Eyelers repeatedly not to dilute the good stuff with too much methanol."

"Shut up, Bart," Darre said.

Lauger's head dropped forward. "I didn't want Syl to die." His voice was rough and ragged.

"You cared little about her feelings when she told you about the baby." Anger coursed through Bella. How dare this man act contrite now?

As Lauger looked up, the dark color surging into his cheeks became obvious. "I'm sorry everyone heard us."

"I'm sure you are, since you obviously didn't want to be held responsible," Bella said.

"I was surprised, but I would've married her." His voice was barely audible.

A harrumph left Bella. "That's not what you said by the dock or in the garden."

"I didn't want to give in too soon because she might've figured she could control me. Now, I regret being so harsh." Lauger's voice was rough.

"But not as much as you'll regret having contributed to her death," Jax suggested.

When Bella glanced at him, she saw his hands clench into fists. Jax would never hit someone, unless he got hit first, but he was fighting to restrain himself.

Lauger's dark lashes fluttered down, and he again bowed his head. "If Syl got booze out here, it wasn't from me. Except for what we drank on my boat, which wasn't much and the small flask I gave her. And all that is from my grandparents' bar. None of it has been touched by anyone else, so it isn't tainted. Same with what we brought to dinner."

"Stop talking," Darre said.

His partner shifted to look at him. "Shut up yourself. Syl and my baby are dead, and I'll say whatever I want because I had nothing to do with it. What about you, Darre? Did you give her some of the diluted stuff?"

Darre's jaw tightened, and he looked away. "I didn't see the girl except on the dock and at dinner. How would I get liquor to her? That's if I had access to booze."

"It's more than obvious you both have access," Jax said. "Bootlegging charges are grave, but murder or manslaughter is worse."

Finally, Darre blanched. "Like Bart said, we only shared liquor from his grandparents' stock with Syl. Nei-

ther of us drink anything else. We can't be held account-
able for the girl dying."

"You can," Jax replied. "Others have been. If you
weren't involved, you'd be smart to say who might have
been."

Darre released a long breath. "If you're looking for the
culprit, try Eyelers. He brought all the girls over on the
Remington boat, from what I've learned."

"He did," Bella agreed.

"You're right. Eyelers could be the one who gave Syl
more booze. Or sold it to her. I've suspected him of
making money on the side and not letting us know,"
Lauger said.

"You're talking too much," Darre said.

"I'm not taking the fall for killing Syl and my baby. If
you had anything to do with it, you won't need to worry
about going to trial. You won't live that long, Parker."
Lauger's assertions were explicit threats.

"I didn't harm her, Bart," his partner insisted.

Bella wasn't sure if she believed him or Lauger. Only
time would tell.

After Lauger and Darre were secured below stairs, Jax
suggested Bella and the others get some sleep, but she
insisted on staying up. Since he was glad of her company,
he didn't protest. Jax turned to Griff. "You might as well
find a place to rest for a while."

The golf pro nodded. "Good night."

Once he was gone, Bella moved to an armchair at the
far end of the kitchen, and Jax joined her. Naturally, she
had questions.

"You didn't say how you caught Lauger, Darre, and
Eyelers before they escaped."

"The deputy has a lot of experience with boats. Both his father and grandfather were fisherman, so he had no trouble disabling the crafts before those three got back to the dock."

"Didn't Lauger have someone on the boats?"

"He did. His boatman and the chef. The two of them were supposed to be on different boats, but Finnagin said they were playing cards when he got down there. They'd been drinking, too, so he could put the engines out of commission before subduing the men. All prior to Amberly and me arriving."

"That worked out well."

"Definitely. He'll head down and fix the problems right after sunrise. Then, we'll get our prisoners to the jail on the Cove."

"Lauger and Darre provided some important information."

"I was surprised," Jax said.

"I was, too, but Lauger seems to have feelings for Syl. More than I would've guessed from his behavior."

Jax slumped back in the chair. "If he wasn't being honest, he's a great actor."

Bella nodded. "I thought the same thing. I've also wondered all along if Syl got booze from Eyelers. If she did, her death was likely accidental, since he has no motive to want her dead. But I really thought it was intentional poisoning."

"Until he found out about Syl's death, which clearly came as a shock, I figured Lauger to be the culprit," Jax said.

"I did, too. He had means, motive, and opportunity."

"I agree. I can't completely absolve him, but he's way down my list."

"Which isn't very long unless you added someone."

"I haven't. Eyelers is ahead of Lauger but not too far up," Jax said. "The bootlegging and Syl's death seem to be separate issues."

The comment gave Bella pause. "Lina and Florence are still suspects."

"What do you think? You're an able detective."

The amused glitter in Jax's eyes made Bella smile. "Despite her protestations, Florence's debt and her anger at Syl for mentioning it, are motives. But she still owes Lauger and Darre."

"Maybe she only wanted to make Syl sick, to get even."

"That would be mean. Florence has changed since our college days, but it's hard to see her doing something so cruel. And dangerous."

"True, but she had motive, means, and opportunity. Ida heard two women talking in Syl's bedroom the night she died. Since she and Florence both drank at dinner, and they've gone to speakeasies and parties, Syl wouldn't have been suspicious if Florence brought more booze to her, would she?" Jax asked.

"Probably not," Bella replied.

"What about Lina? Have you thought more about how she could've gotten bad booze to Syl?"

"With their harsh exchanges, I doubt if Syl would've taken liquor from Lina. Not when Lina had such hard feelings. They barely spoke when in the same room."

"Which gives Lina plenty of motive. As far as means, she could've brought rubbing alcohol with her. Many people use it for massages and such. She might've gotten the idea to poison Syl after she got here. But opportunity. I don't see how she had any."

For a long moment, Bella searched her mind. Suddenly, an idea came to the forefront. "Lina got badly sunburned and didn't come to dinner the night of the storm. She really was burned, and she was in bed with a cold pack when Blanche checked on her. But she was upstairs alone for two or three hours."

"Rubbing alcohol is sometimes used on sunburns, although it may not work well. In any case, I'd like to talk with Blanche."

"I'll get her."

Within moments, Bella returned with her friend.

"Thanks for coming," Jax said after the two women sat down. "I have a couple of questions for you."

"I'm happy to help, if I can," Blanche replied.

"You checked on Lina after she got sunburned," Jax said.

Blanche nodded. "She was miserable, so I suggested cold packs. She'd brought a little first aid kit with her and used something, but it hadn't worked."

"Did you see her kit?" Bella put forth the question.

"It was on the nightstand," Blanche replied, "but I didn't look in it."

"I want to look." Jax got to his feet.

"I'm coming along," Bella said.

"I'll show you where it was." Blanche got up, too.

The trio was upstairs and in the bedroom within moments. "It's still on the dresser." Blanche gestured toward the piece of furniture.

Jax hurried to open the kit and held it up so Bella and Blanche could see.

Bella's hand flew to her mouth. Beside her, Blanche gasped. "Lina brought rat poison and glycerin with her."

"There's no good reason to bring strychnine," Bella murmured.

"None at all, since it's very doubtful Lina worried about rats being here. It's tasteless, so the glycerin wasn't really necessary," Jax said. "It would dissolve well in her prescription liquor. All she needed was a chance to swap whatever was in Syl's flask with her toxic concoction."

Bella felt sick at heart. "We knew she had motive. When I remembered her being up here alone on Friday evening, I realized she had an opportunity."

Jax released a pent-up breath. "And now we know she had means. I'll talk to the other lawmen before I confront her. For right now, don't reveal any of this to the others."

Both women, grim faced, nodded.

When Bella and Blanche returned to the parlor, Ida sat up. "Did Lauger admit to giving Syl bad booze?"

"He had every reason to want her dead, and she probably drank a lot after getting rejected. She got booze from someone out here," Lina said.

Her friend's attempt to push the blame on someone else sickened Bella almost as much as the premeditation involved in the crime. It was all she could do to hide her feelings. "Jax will be in shortly, and he can answer questions. He'd like us to wait here until then." Bella went to sit by Ida. More likely, he'd be asking very few and arresting Lina. She looked at the staff. "All of you can go to your rooms, but stop in the kitchen. The bootleggers are secured in some of the vacant ones."

The three nodded and left while Blanche took a seat on the other side of Ida. Florence, who sat on the other couch, ran a hand over her face. "What did the bootleggers say?" she asked.

"Several are eager to testify against Lauger and Darre," Bella replied.

Florence visibly relaxed. "Good."

"Then, we can all leave tomorrow," Lina said before striding to the wall of windows and taking a chair.

Her distance from the group sent relief through Bella. Hopefully, arresting her would be quick and easy.

Jax and Amberly appeared in the doorway within a short time. "Lina, we need to speak with you."

She scowled at the two lawmen. "About what? We're all exhausted. The help went to bed. Why can't we?"

Jax reached into his pockets and pulled out the packet of rat poison from Lina's first aid kit. "Would you like to offer some explanation?"

All color ebbed from her face as a low gasp escaped her. "Why were you snooping in my room?"

"How did you know that's where Agent Hastings found the poison?" Amberly asked.

Lina turned bright red when she realized her mistake. "I don't know where he found it."

"I think you do, Lina, and it would be easier for everyone if you admit the truth," Jax said. "It's obvious you went to Syl's room when everyone was at dinner on Friday night. You put this stuff and some glycerin in her hip flask in hopes she'd drown her sorrows after Lauger rejected her earlier. Maybe you even heard their exchange outside."

Lina grasped the chair arms, but said nothing. A look of fear tightened her features.

Bella crossed the room and took the chair next to Lina's. "We all understood why you were angry with Syl, but why take a chance on making her sick?"

A sneer abruptly replaced Lina's anxiety. "I wasn't taking a chance. I wanted her to die."

Although Bella had realized that was a possibility, she was stunned by Lina's ferocity and her admission. "Because she flirted with Kenton?"

Lina's nostrils flared with a sharp intake of breath. "Flirted? She stole him away by seducing him. Bart Lauger was far from her first paramour." Lina's voice was shrill with anger. "She ruined my life. I loved Kenton. We were going to be married, and Syl destroyed everything. Then, days after he left for France, she was out on the town. My cousin lives in Chicago and saw her with other men. While Kenton was in some muddy trench fighting and dying. I don't feel one bit sorry for what I did, either. Syl deserved it."

Her friend's cruel words were hard to absorb. For a seemingly endless time, Bella simply stared at her. So did the others.

"Lina, how could you?" Florence's voice was filled with shock.

Ida put both hands to her face. "I can't believe you would do such a cruel thing."

"It wasn't any crueler than what she did to me," Lina shot back.

"Come with us, Lina," Jax said.

"Sure thing." She crossed the room without a backward glance at her friends, who all stared in silence at the retreating figure.

Chapter Fourteen

♥

Shortly after dawn, the lawmen transported their prisoners to the Cove on the two crafts they'd used to get to the island. The young ladies, with Monica in tow, used the Remingtons' boat. The deputy served as their boatman. During the trip, the college friends said little. From time-to-time, Bella glanced at Florence, who sat at a distance from the others looking grim.

When they were almost to the shore, Ida spoke. "The weekend didn't turn out at all like I hoped. It's still hard to believe Lina poisoned Syl. I wonder if she'll plead guilty?"

Bella shifted to face her friend. "It would save her and everyone else a lot of grief."

"But will that matter to her?" Blanche, who sat on the other side of Ida, asked.

"Maybe not. She hasn't been concerned before now." Bella's gaze went to the other two boats, already docked. Lina was barely visible on one of them.

After their boat docked and they were off, Bella looked for Jax. Within moments, he left the other lawmen and headed toward her. While the others went ahead, Bella stayed back. "Will Constable Amberly keep all the bootleggers and Lina here?"

"He doesn't have enough space, so we need to work that out, among other things. Unfortunately, I'm not finished with either case. We'll question the group about bootlegging before Yankton and Finnagin leave, so I can't take off for a while. Griff will get the Chummy, so you and Ida can put your bags in it." His green gaze searched her face. "If you're willing to wait a couple of hours, I can drive you home. But I'll have to come back."

Even a short time together, without worrying about bootlegging or murder, was welcome. "We can wait," she readily agreed. "What about Monica? She'll be coming to Ballantyne, too."

"Constable Amberly and his wife will put her up overnight. I gave him money for her train fare and said you'd get her at the Moreley station tomorrow. He'll pass the word on to her."

"And Blanche?"

"She just needs to make a statement. Then, she can also stay at Amberly's place and take a train home tomorrow."

"What about Ida and me? Don't we need to make statements?" Bella asked.

"I talked to both of you. So did Amberly, and that's good enough for now. You'll probably need to come for the trials. I'm sorry about that," Jax said.

"We thought Lina might plead guilty."

He shrugged. "She said nothing on the way over here. Amberly will make sure she has a lawyer. After that, who knows? You might have to testify against her."

"I can. What about you? Will you be here for both trials?"

"I will."

Bella beamed. "Then, despite everything, I'll look forward to them." All too soon, he'd be back in Philadelphia for an indeterminate time.

His lips twitched. "I will, too. Just let me tie up a few loose ends. Stanley took Lina and the others to the station house, but they'll need me for a couple of hours. Blanche and Florence will need to come along for now, so they can provide more details."

Mrs. Amberly, a petite brunette in her middle years, welcomed Griff, Ida, and Bella into her home. Since the weather was pleasant, the group sat on the porch and chatted, but Bella's attention wandered again and again. After two hours turned into three, Jax finally arrived. Although their hostess offered him refreshments, he politely refused. "I appreciate your hospitality, especially to Monica and Mrs. Carriger. Your husband will bring them over soon."

After bidding Mrs. Amberly goodbye and heading to the Chummy, which was parked in front of the house, Jax glanced at Griff. "I think you should drive."

"I think so, too," the other man replied. "You look exhausted."

After they all piled into the automobile and were on their way, Ida swiveled to face Bella and Jax, seated in the back. "The weekend didn't turn out anything like I expected. A murder and bootlegging." She rolled her eyes.

"I agree," Bella said. "I knew Lina held a grudge against Syl, but to cold-bloodedly plot to kill her. I would never have thought Lina capable of such hatred."

"It's horrible, and I dread testifying against her. Not that she doesn't deserve punishment." Ida sounded as distraught as Bella felt.

"There's a chance she'll plead guilty." Bella repeated the hope, although it might be a futile one.

"I wish she would, but we'll be needed in the bootlegging trials, won't we?" Ida asked.

"Probably so," Jax replied. "It depends on how the case develops, but the trial won't be right away."

"What about Florence? Is there any possibility she'll be charged?" Bella asked.

"I wouldn't think so. Since she was being blackmailed, she may be in the clear as long as she cooperates. Her father is apt to give her that advice. After all, he is a lawyer." Jax laid one arm on the seat behind Bella. "As far as explaining to her parents and fiancé. That's going to be tough."

"Getting so deeply into debt made her an easy target for blackmail." Ida made the statement.

"She used terrible judgment in gambling and borrowing money," Bella said.

"Sylvia might've continued to ignore the debts, but Darre and Lauger wouldn't. At least they've been charged with bootlegging, so she won't have to pay back the debts. Will she?" Ida looked at Jax.

"Those two are likely to be in jail for a while. Besides, if the games were rigged, they won't collect on illegal gambling debts."

"Good." Ida settled back in her seat.

"That's a relief." Bella rubbed her forehead.

"Tired?" Jax asked.

"Not any more than any of you are," Bella replied.

"I'll sleep better tonight," Griff said from the driver's seat. "The last few have been tough."

"That's for sure," Jax agreed.

When Bella rested her head on his shoulder, Jax brushed his lips against her temple. The light caress ended when Griff snickered.

"No wonder you didn't want to drive, Hastings. We'd be in a ditch."

Ida immediately swiveled to again peer into the back seat. A low laugh left her. "At long last," she said.

A flush rose in Jax's lean cheeks as he sat back, but Bella chuckled, too. "All good comes to those who wait."

Chapter Fifteen

A month later

After leaving the Burnley Cove courtroom, Jax shook hands with Constable Amberly and Deputy Stanley. "Thanks for your help. We wouldn't have nabbed the bootleggers or solved Sylvia Sawyer's death without the two of you."

"If you hadn't gone to Winnabee, I doubt if we would've caught up with Lauger and Darre for a while. Maybe never." Amberly turned to Bella, Ida, and Griff. "Good to meet all of you, although I'm sorry for the circumstances. Have a safe trip home."

The group responded with their good wishes before heading to Jax's Chummy. Jax was about to follow when Amberly spoke again. "Be careful, son."

Jax nodded. "Thank you. I will."

When he got to his vehicle, the others were already inside. Jax glanced at Ida and Griff in the backseat. "Looks like I'm driving home this time."

Griff slipped an arm around Ida's shoulders, and she leaned into him. "You are," the golf pro said.

A chuckle left Jax before he got behind the wheel and headed south.

"I'm glad to have that behind us," Bella said once they were on the main road.

"Me, too," Ida agreed. "I don't know that I added much, but it's good one bootlegging ring is out of commission."

"My boss is happy," Jax said.

"What about their customers?" Griff asked. "The group supplied some information about them to get reduced sentences. Are you investigating those contacts? Or can't you say?"

"We've got plenty to do with our current cases, but the contacts are being monitored. The local bar owner is out of commission, mostly due to Amberly and his deputies." Jax glanced at Bella, who had shifted to watch him.

"You didn't say when you need to leave," she said.

A long breath escaped him. "Tomorrow morning."

"Back to Philadelphia." Bella's voice was well-modulated, but a trace of dismay underscored her words.

"Not right away. The investigation has tentacles beyond that area, but I can't say much about it," Jax replied.

"Of course not." Bella shifted to look straight ahead. "At least you won't have to interrupt your case again by coming back for a murder trial."

Jax wasn't sure how to respond, and Ida found her voice first.

"Lina pleading guilty, and not putting up any defense, surprised me. I hoped she wouldn't, but I'm relieved because I hated to think about testifying against her."

"I'm glad, too, but also surprised she didn't want to get on the stand and berate Syl," Bella said. "Lina was eaten up with resentment."

"This way, she won't be going to the electric chair, which was a possibility." Out of the corner of his eye, Jax saw Bella shudder.

"Ohio was the first state to send a woman to the chair," Griff said. "Pretty grim."

"I'll say, not that spending the rest of her life in prison isn't." Ida groaned. "Let's not talk any more about Lina and Syl. I feel bad for Florence since her fiancé called off their wedding."

Bella nodded. "I do, too. At least her father didn't seem angry with her, and he's pensioning off both Stricket and Mrs. Longley before selling the house on Winnabee. Earlier, I talked privately with Florence. I invited her to come to Ballantyne before the summer is over. She'll think about it."

"It'd be a wonderful change for her," Ida observed. "She feels so guilty about Syl."

"Being the last one to see her alive has to be hard, especially since the two of them were chatting and laughing." They'd finally found out who had been talking with Sylvia, and that Stricket was the one in the hallway. As she and Ida had postulated, the butler had checked to ensure all was well. Bella turned to look at her best friend. "Did Florence tell you Syl was sipping on the flask when she went into her room before the storm?"

"She did, and she said Syl mentioned needing a couple of drinks to sleep. Florence told her that couldn't hurt." Ida paused for a long moment. "But it did."

"Florence couldn't have known Lina slipped toxic booze into the flask. The autopsy showed a high level of strychnine in Syl, so Lina used a lot," Jax put in. "Just as she admitted."

"Lauger said Eyelers cut poison into their supply. Do you know if any of their customers got sick?" Griff asked Jax.

Jax shook his head. "Not that we've heard. A lot of the bottles were tested, and some had a fair amount of toxin. Probably enough to seriously harm people, if not kill them."

"It's good that liquor will never reach the public," Griff added.

The others agreed.

For the rest of the trip, the group chatted about casual matters. When Jax pulled the Chummy to a stop in front of Ballantyne Inn, Ida and Griff exited the vehicle, leaving Bella and Jax alone. She shifted to face him. "I suppose you can't say more about the O'Donnelly case."

Jax turned toward Bella. "Not a lot." He ran a hand over his face. "It's more complicated than we initially figured. Once I got to Philly, I found out there were two gunmen, along with the driver. They all holed up for a few weeks. Now, with the help of the main boss, they've moved."

"Do you know where they are now?" He glanced beyond the Chummy, which further unnerved Bella. What wasn't he saying? How much longer would he be gone?

"We have some ideas."

The brief reply did little to ease Bella's concerns. "I don't expect you to provide details."

His gaze swung back to her. "I'm not sure what the additional details are. Derringer is playing it close to the vest. Right now, I only know where we're meeting, and he wants that kept secret."

"I understand." Bella understood completely, but she hated considering what dangers stood in store for Jax and his fellow agents.

"I hope you do." Jax's voice took on a ragged quality, and his expression grew solemn. "This is turning out to be a lot more complicated than I initially figured. The gunmen and driver have ties to a large bootlegging operation, which complicates the Bureau's job. Derringer's superiors want to take the entire outfit down, or as much of it as we can."

The admission boded ill for Jax coming home to stay soon. "He expects you to remain with the Bureau until that's done?"

"We all want to get whoever sent the gunmen to kill Mick and murdered Jocelyn instead." After a long moment, he spoke again. "I'm sorry, Bella. I thought the case would be over by now."

"But it isn't, and it won't be soon." Bella made the observation with both certainty and dismay.

"I'm afraid not, and I doubt if I'll be able to visit again in the next month, maybe longer."

His disappointment was obvious. Did he think she wouldn't understand? "I wish you could, of course, but you promised to help Mick, and you're a man of your word. That's a good thing." When relief swept over his face, Bella grinned. "But you're here now, and we can make the most of what's left of today. I'll change clothes and fix a picnic basket. Then, we can take one of the boats and have supper on the river. How does that sound?"

A smile chased the doubt from his expression. "Terrific. I brought a bag, so I'll change, too."

"Use Matt's room." When Jax nodded without losing his smile, Bella relaxed. They were making progress. How much progress, only time—maybe a long time—would tell. But they were together now, and she planned to enjoy every moment

Afterword

♥

Thank you for reading <u>A Fatal Reunion</u>. I hope you enjoyed it! I love to get feedback from readers, and I welcome ratings and reviews, which can be posted on the digital storefront where you purchased this book. You can also post reviews on Goodreads and BookBub. You will find my author page at:

https://www.bookbub.com/profile/d-s-lang
For more information on the Arabella Stewart Historical Mystery series, including new releases, please visit my website:

http://www.dslangbooks.com

About the Author

D.S. Lang started making up stories to entertain herself as an only child. She is still creating them, but now she puts the stories into writing.

After obtaining Bachelor's and Master's degrees in Education, D.S. worked as a golf shop manager, teacher (junior high, high school, and college), program manager, tutor, and mentor. She has a lifelong love of history and often gets sidetracked with research when she should be writing.

When she is away from the computer, D.S. enjoys reading, swimming, spending time with friends and family, and walking her dog Izzy

Books in the Arabella Stewart Historical Mystery Series

♥

Book One-<u>A Precarious Homecoming</u>
Book Two-<u>A Lingering Shadow</u>
Book Three-<u>A Lethal Arrogance</u>
Book Four-<u>A Baffling Absence</u>
Book Five-<u>A Fatal Reunion</u>
Book Six-<u>A Surreptitious Undertaking</u>
Book Seven-<u>A Treacherous Accusation</u>
Book Eight-<u>An Uncertain Ceremony</u>

To purchase the above books, please see my website:
https:www.dslangbooks.com

D.S. LANG

www.ingramcontent.com/pod-product-compliance
Lightning Source LLC
Chambersburg PA
CBHW051339020726
47501CB00007B/2171